BY MARISA CRANE

I Keep My Exoskeletons to Myself
A Sharp Endless Need

A SHARP
ENDLESS NEED

A SHARP
ENDLESS NEED

A Novel

MARISA CRANE

THE DIAL PRESS
NEW YORK

Published in the United States by The Dial Press, an imprint of Random House, a division of Penguin Random House LLC, 1745 Broadway, New York, NY 10019.

THE DIAL PRESS is a registered trademark and the colophon is a trademark of Penguin Random House LLC.

LIBRARY OF CONGRESS CATALOGING-IN-PUBLICATION DATA
Names: Crane, Marisa, author.
Title: A sharp endless need : a novel / Marisa Crane.
Description: First edition. | New York, NY : The Dial Press, 2025.
Identifiers: LCCN 2024012596 (print) | LCCN 2024012597 (ebook) |
ISBN 9780593733646 (hardcover ; acid-free paper) | ISBN 9780593733653 (e-book)
Subjects: LCGFT: Bildungsromans. | Queer fiction. | Romance fiction. | Novels.
Classification: LCC PS3603.R3844 S53 2024 (print) | LCC PS3603.R3844 (ebook) |
DDC 813/.6—dc23/eng/20240325
LC record available at https://lccn.loc.gov/2024012596
LC ebook record available at https://lccn.loc.gov/2024012597

Printed in the United States of America on acid-free paper

randomhousebooks.com
penguinrandomhouse.com

2 4 6 8 9 7 5 3 1

First Edition

BOOK TEAM: Production editor: Cara DuBois • Managing editor: Rebecca Berlant •
Production manager: Ali Wagner • Copy editor: Sheryl Rapée-Adams •
Proofreaders: Julie Ehlers, Jennifer Sale, Annette Szlachta-McGinn

Book design by Elizabeth A. D. Eno

The authorized representative in the EU for product safety and compliance is Penguin Random House Ireland, Morrison Chambers, 32 Nassau Street, Dublin D02 YH68, Ireland. https://eu-contact.penguin.ie.

For all the queer jocks who have fallen for a teammate

Here is the repeated image of the lover destroyed.
—Richard Siken

The heart is always being played for.
The heart is always playing itself.
—Hanif Abdurraqib

I wasn't a point guard. I was a killer.
—Allen Iverson

A SHARP
ENDLESS NEED

PREGAME PUMP-UP

We wanted legacy. Liv and I, we wanted our names in bright lights, our names in everyone's mouths. Names people would remember. No *just on the tip of their tongue*s, no *let me get back to you*s; none of that shit.

We wanted fans so loud everything went quiet inside our heads. For a while, we might have had them.

We made canvases of our bodies. We sweat and we cried, rivulets flowing down face and chest and limb. We boasted bruises from hard-earned buckets, birthmarks we gave ourselves.

We moved with animal instinct, smooth like panthers going in for the kill.

We won loose balls, and if we didn't win them, we caused tie-up after tie-up, wet bodies coalescing on the wood floor: rip, rip, roar. When the game was on the line, and when it wasn't on the line, we sacrificed our bodies. Not because we were told to, but because there was no higher honor. We sacrificed our bodies for something not quite holy, not quite mortal. Where does the body end and immortality begin? We wanted to find out.

On offense, our passes were so sharp they could cut through butter, handles so smooth we lulled our defenders to sleep with the rocking. On defense, we had magic hands, fly-quick hands, hands tugging jerseys and pestering shorts, hands that swatted, hands no one could swat. Hips pressed against glutes, bodies that wouldn't budge an inch.

We wanted to live forever. Who could blame us? We wanted to live ball in hand, ball against backboard, ball licking the bottom of the net. We wanted to be in history books. For what? We didn't know. We certainly weren't the first to do anything—not to ball, not to win, not to lose, not to suffer, but that didn't matter. To us, basketball was a historical record of all the ways a body can move with and for another. What could be better than the strange and perverse pleasure of being known?

If we couldn't live forever, we at least wanted pleasure, in big dripping buckets.

More so, we wanted the knowledge that we were still capable of enjoying our pleasure, that pleasure itself hadn't become yet another goal to work toward.

Dizzy with fervor, we knew nothing of moderation, of balance.

We wanted excess. More trash-talking, more chest-thumping, more bumping and grinding. We drove hard, we drew fouls. We stomped our feet and raised our fists in celebration.

We wanted to make sure our opponents could feel us coming. We wanted their student sections to heckle us, tell us we were pieces of shit with no outside game, no heart, no skill. We liked the taunting; it gave us all the more reason to pin our hands behind our backs and raise our middle fingers when the refs weren't looking.

We wanted speed, reckless speed. The white-hot heat of a fast break pecking at our heels. The court opening up before us like a parted sea.

On the court, we were married. The referee whistles like wedding bells ringing inside our chests. Only, we didn't call it a marriage. We called it shared language, tongue-heavy language, locked-and-loaded language, the most reliable form of communication. One bound not by syntax, but by rhythm, by the beat, beat, beat of human music, by the simultaneous seeing and knowing of another.

The game bonded us in a way words could only dream of. And if we had an animal instinct, a panther prowl on the court, then basketball had a hound dog nose. It could sniff out and track our desires before those desires had even arisen in us. That's what we needed, what we counted on.

Some people said basketball was like dancing, you needed rhythm, you needed to feel the ball's desire like you needed your heart to beat right, but we knew, in the deeps of our hips, that basketball was even more erotic than dancing; it was a collaboration, a mutual creation, a way of fucking without touching.

But when we stepped off the court and headed to the locker room, when we ripped off our sticky-with-sweat jerseys, when we untied our laces, when we could no longer hear the bellows of the crowd, when already the game-time focus had become a thing of the past, when already we forgot the heated glory of all eyes on us, the stomp of the fan feet, the clap of the fan hands, the echoing beat of the ball in a last-play quiet—when we did all that, we stripped down to our raw pink skin and wet the game away, our eyes pinched shut under the rushing stream.

We showered next to each other, alone together in our ritual, acutely aware of how space worked differently without the layers of jersey and shorts and crowd and competition between us. In the shower, we were exposed. In those moments, we greeted each other as if meeting for the first time.

Hey, we said.

What's up, we said.

We risked glances at each other, then we shied away. But we always looked back.

When we stepped off the court and took off those jerseys, those jerseys with names and numbers and histories, we wanted anonymity. We wanted a temporary refuge where we could be unknown, anonymous to everyone but each other.

FIRST HALF

1

PEP TALK IN THE HUDDLE

Before I met Liv, before everything changed, my dad took me to a Sixers game. The whole drive into the city we were buzzing, and he kept messing with the radio trying to find a station that reflected our excitement, but there was nothing but commercials and bad pop music and public service announcements about the dangers of marijuana. *There's nothing natural about getting high,* a man scolded us.

There was traffic on the Schuylkill like usual. We were going to be late. In the car next to us two men, boys really, were making out in the back seat, hands gripping the meat of each other's necks. The two boys in the front were a silent film of laughter, heads thrown back, mouths open wide as if to swallow all the light in the city. I tried not to look at the ones kissing, though I liked it, liked what they were doing with each other. Dad didn't notice them, he was too busy driving with his knees while he turned a map every which way, trying to find a detour, although I doubt he would have made some rude comment. I take that back—he might have said something rude like

Nobody wants to see that, but it wouldn't have been because they were gay, it would have been because they were young and happy, and he was old and unhappy.

My junior season had just ended with a loss in the district quarter-finals, not a bad run for a team made up of mostly other-sport athletes. For them, basketball was just a way to stay in shape between soccer and track, field hockey and softball. The only other serious player, serious as in trying to get a scholarship to play in college, had been this senior who never saw a shot she didn't like. Double-teamed, feet not set, didn't matter. All she cared about was how many points she put up, no matter how many shots it took her to get there. No matter how many points *she* gave up. I was glad to be rid of her, I'd be free to make more happen.

The Sixers parking lot was an absolute shit show. Every time my dad pulled over and put on his blinker, some other car would slip right in and steal our spot, and Dad would speed away, pounding the dashboard and cursing up a storm. Eventually, we found a spot by a group of people doing so many poppers it looked like a birthday party. A woman in a tracksuit did a handstand and everyone hugged her legs, pressing their cheeks to the thighs, the knees, the calves of her swishy pants. I thought about mentioning how weirdly touching I found this scene, then I thought again.

"That's what losers look like, Mackenzie," said Dad, though he was smiling, a wistful smile like maybe he missed being a loser, though I couldn't imagine a time when that could have been true.

After all that, we ended up having nosebleed seats. I'm talking outer-space level. My dad double-checked the tickets like fifteen times when we got to our seats, his brows knit tightly as he turned his Sixers hat backward then forward then backward again, his eyes moving from ticket to seat. The game had already started. I watched a tiny Allen Iverson hit three jumpers in a row before Dad finally admitted defeat.

"It's okay, what matters is that we're here," he said, even though I hadn't said a word about it.

He made sure to buy us cotton candy and popcorn and whatever else we could stuff our faces with. And when he whistled and beckoned for the old guy with the hairy forearms to bring him a beer, he bought two, setting one in my cup holder and gesturing at it with a big meaty paw. It was the first time he bought me my own beer, and for some reason, maybe because I missed stealing a few sips of his here and there, missed the brush of our hands as we passed the cup back and forth, it made me want to cry. To keep from crying, I made a joke about how Mom should make note of this milestone in my baby book, but he wasn't listening. He was already sucking down his beer and yelling at Kyle Korver to stop being such a pretty boy and take a fucking charge.

"We get it, you hate him," I said, laughing. He turned to me, mouth twisted in worry.

"Don't tell me you actually like him," he said. "My heart can't take it."

I assured him that I didn't give two shits about Kyle Korver's face or otherwise, but we did need him to win, so he might as well suck it up.

He seemed satisfied by my answer. I drank my beer and made a big stink about how good it was even though it tasted like bitter creek water. I drank all the time with my friends, but he didn't know that; he thought he was giving me a special treat.

Our section was pretty full, with tons of families around, including a dad a few seats away who kept eyeing my beer and then pulling his preteen daughter closer as if, at any moment, I might tie her up and pour it down her throat. I watched her while I drank. She crossed her legs at the knee and kept flipping her hair this way and that. She wore some cute lacy top that could have been from Limited Too or something. It looked a bit young for Wet Seal, though I was sure she'd graduate to those cleavage-y tank tops any day now. Me, I was in baggy sweats and my Jordan 3s. But it wasn't just our clothes that differentiated us. I got the sense that, on an elemental level, she was different from me. She probably had a boyfriend; she probably actually liked her boyfriend. Wanted his lips on hers, his hands up her shirt in the back row of a movie theater. I didn't know what that was like. To desire something so dull, something so easily attainable. I wanted to want that, I really did.

"Careful, there, kid, don't want you getting trashed on my watch," said my dad. His beer had been replaced by a sad, dented cup. "Hey, you don't happen to have any money on you, do you?" he asked.

I gave him a strange look before answering. "No, Coach Puck hasn't paid me yet."

He'd never asked me for money before. I would have thought he was kidding if he didn't look so earnest.

Coach Puck was my high school coach. He paid me twenty dollars an hour to clean his house. It wasn't for the faint of heart, either. None of that dusting or vacuuming shit. He was a hoarder, lived in a house with eight dogs, two kids, and a wife he loved to hate or hated to love, I was never sure which.

"My goddamn cokehead of a wife," he was always saying, running a hand through his greasy, shoulder-length hair.

I wasn't even sure his wife was real. I'd never seen her, and I was over there often enough that my mom started asking me what business a forty-eight-year-old man had with a sixteen-year-old girl. According to Coach, his wife spent all her time in the basement, buying and selling troll dolls on eBay, high off her ass. Anyway, one Saturday I spent all day trying to scrape unidentified dried goo from the inside of his refrigerator. I didn't mind, more money for me. His front yard had some things going on, too. It was a mishmash of whatever the fuck didn't fit in the house or garage, I guess. Two old, ratty couches, a few tires, a bathroom sink, a broken printer, you name it. No matter the time of year, you could count on there being falling-down Christmas lights and a blow-up reindeer. He really was an odd guy. I loved him the same way I loved my dad: with a violence that terrified even me. I would throw a right hook for them. Would stab a motherfucker.

"Well, what about the last payment?" said my dad. "What'd you go and spend that on?"

"Drugs," I said. Then, "Tattoos."

"Strippers."

"Sneakers."

Laughing, he said, "My son. My prodigal son." I smiled, happy to be his son. He leaned closer to me and said, "I was just messing with you, by the way. I got money, don't you worry."

We watched the first half through squinted eyes and clapped when we were supposed to clap, high-fived when we were supposed to high-five, all the while wishing we'd brought binoculars.

"This is great. Isn't it so great?" he kept saying, his voice going up a little at the end.

It wasn't long before he grew restless and had begun attracting nearby listeners with talk about how I was Division I–bound. Everyone wanted to know where I was going and I said I didn't know yet, that it was still early. Truth is, I kept telling myself I had plenty of time, but the NCAA official signing date was creeping up on me. I still had a little over a year, but most players committed well before signing day. Judging by how mixed-up I felt about choosing a school, I guessed that most players just wanted the decision out of the way so they could sit back and relax a little, maybe even enjoy their senior year.

"That's right, she's got so many choices," said my dad. He beamed and threw an arm around my shoulder.

I smiled up at him. This was how he loved me best: through basketball, his pride and joy.

Three little kids climbed over their parents to ask for my autograph, shoving their Sixers programs in my face while my dad dug around in his pocket for a pen. You could always count on him for a pen and paper, though the paper was usually covered in point spreads and money lines.

All at once, the kids started telling me what I needed to do in order to make it to the big leagues.

"Turn into a ghost!" said one of the girls.

"Oh, I know," said the other girl. "Roll onto your back like a turtle."

"How is that going to help?" I asked.

"You could also try complimenting your defender," the turtle girl said.

"Oh," I said, smiling.

"Tell her she's so pretty she deserves to be on the cover of a magazine," said the ghost girl.

"You could learn to dunk," said the little boy, his lollipop covered in lint.

"Shut up," said the ghost girl, shoving him. "You can't even make a layup."

I signed their programs next to Allen Iverson's headshot and they scurried away, back to their caregivers, squealing about how they'd just met a famous person.

I was embarrassed because I was supposed to be, but the truth is, I liked the attention, ate that shit up. On the court, Allen Iverson double-crossed, no triple-crossed someone so hard it made the whole crowd go *Ohhhhhhhh*. My dad nudged me and told me that was going to be me one day. I looked at the players, their muscled bodies, their liquid movements, their power, and their grace. They were artists; they were gods. I hoped that he was right. Nothing else interested me but basketball, nothing else set my nervous system aflame. Was that how it was for everyone? They had their one thing and that was it?

My dad left the game several times to make phone calls. I was old enough then to know he was calling his bookie, but when I was younger, he told me all sorts of fairy tales about long-distance calls to witches and warlocks, to shape-shifters and time travelers. When I asked him why they never called Mom, he said they used to, long ago, before I was born, but then she changed her number.

The first time he got up to leave, Derrick Coleman dunked over Jermaine O'Neal, and the crowd went wild, hands, foam and real, punched to the sky.

When he came back, he asked what he missed and I smiled and said, "Nothing, don't worry."

The second time he got up to leave, Iverson crossed someone so hard it made my teeth hurt. The announcer asked us if there was anything this man couldn't do.

When my dad came back, he asked what he missed and I said, "Nothing."

The third time he got up, Eric Snow drove past Reggie Miller for an and-one. The little kids who'd asked for my autograph high-fived everyone in our section. I went to take a sip of my beer but found that it was all gone. I chewed on my gold 12 necklace for something to do with my mouth.

When dad came back, he jogged down the stairs, slapping fans' hands as he passed. Like an overgrown child running for mayor.

He asked what he missed, and I shook my head and pushed the plastic seat down so he could sit.

I said, "Look at the score, it's crunch time."

"Our favorite time," he said, before getting up to leave again.

His habit of repeatedly leaving and returning made me think of an outdoor cat, how no matter how long or far they strayed, they always came home. Sometimes they were fine, sometimes they were licking a wound from a back-alley fight. I wondered if he'd always been a big dumb idiot who didn't seem to know what he wanted out of life, forever straddling two worlds, not fully in either one.

Tied with twelve seconds left, Sixers' ball, it would all come down to Iverson. Snow inbounded the ball and Iverson dribbled at the top of the key, lulling Eddie Gill to sleep, between the legs, between the legs again, cross. Suspended in time. People held each other's elbows. No one blinked, no one breathed. We waited in devoted silence. A family brought together by hope.

Everything outside of that stadium, our problems, our anxieties, our fears, could wait; nothing else mattered but this last play.

I thought about what my dad always said about how NBA bench players had the best jobs in the world. They got to travel all over the country, they made a disgusting amount of money, and they were never under any pressure. Essentially, they were glorified practice players with fat bank accounts.

"But what if I like pressure?" I always countered.

"Nobody likes pressure," he'd say. "They just say they do."

"I do."

"You don't like pressure, you like the high you get when you conquer that pressure."

I didn't know what to say, probably because he was right and I didn't want to admit it.

"Like when my band would get a standing ovation after a killer set."

He would nudge me when he said this, wanting me to be proud of his old music-playing days, but I hadn't been alive back when he was playing shows and now all he did was jam in private in the garage, sometimes for hours, until the light came back to his eyes.

The seconds on the court clock peeled away. Another between the legs, another cross, his defender low and disciplined before him, and with just enough space to get the shot off, Iverson rose, fading, kicking his feet forward—a bullet of a shot, hardly any arc on the thing, but it clanked against the back of the rim and fell straight through the net. We all leapt to our feet with a collective roar that could have blown the roof right off.

Everyone around me hugged each other in celebration. The little kids with my autograph. The dad and his preteen daughter. I hugged myself, hard; I rubbed the tension from my shoulders.

A drunk woman two rows down turned around and waved at me. I smiled stupidly at her.

"No, look," she said, pointing to the jumbotron above the center of the court.

My enlarged face glared back at me. The words KISS CAM appeared in red on the bottom of the screen. I sat there awkwardly, wishing I could will myself out of existence. The cameraman kept the camera on me. I remember thinking that he might never leave, that I might live the rest of my life with my sadness on display for all of

Philadelphia to see. Finally, the turtle girl ran over and kissed me on the hand, her legs curtsying behind her. Some people said, "Aww." Her pity felt worse than being alone.

When I found my dad, he was sulking by the water fountain. His hands were clean, unbloodied, so he must not have lost too much money, but it was still enough to put him in one of his moods.

"What did I miss?" I said, feeling I deserved to be a little bit cruel.

"Don't be an ass," he said.

Then he said, "He really fucking screwed me," as if Iverson had it out for him.

It occurred to me that most spectators only like athletes for what they can give them: money, pride, excitement, and entertainment. Otherwise, they'll write them off faster than the time it takes AI to shake a defender.

That game was the last real thing we did together before he died. Now, when I picture my dad, I see the back of him jogging up the stadium stairs, the wallet bulge in the pocket of his jeans, the sweat stains under his pits, the Sixers logo on his backward hat. His arms pumping at his sides, willing his big body to take him where the odds made sense, at least to him.

At home, my mom asked how the game went and my dad gave her a kiss on the cheek and said it was incredible, she should have seen it. She looked at me to see if this wasn't another one of his lies. I shrugged and went outside to practice my passing accuracy even though it was past midnight. I made an X on the garage door with some masking tape and practiced different passes—chest pass, bounce pass, right-hand step-around, left-hand step-around, behind-the-back. I passed the ball so hard I made a dent in the garage and had to clean at Coach Puck's house every day for a week to pay for the repairs.

2

TIP-OFF

A few weeks later, my dad died of a heart attack on the tread-mill. We'd finally convinced him to give a fuck about his health, so he'd gone out and bought all of these brand-name workout clothes and a membership to one of those fancy gyms that has a sauna and an endless supply of warm towels.

I was at practice when it happened, which meant that I, too, was running because someone else wanted me to. By then, I was driving myself to and from Philly twice a week to play on a premiere AAU team that promised me exposure. AAU was how you got recruited. You played in huge gyms with dozens of courts, the sidelines so close to each other you could accidentally wind up in the wrong game if you weren't paying close attention. Hundreds of scouts looking on, wearing their dorky college polos, and carrying their dorky college briefcases. I loved the shit out of those tournaments; nothing compared to the rush of playing in front of a gym packed full of college coaches. Maybe you'd even catch them smiling when you shook a defender so hard they tripped, or when you pick-pocketed a lazy ball handler. I could ride that high for hours, sometimes even days.

That was also the practice when Alex, my closest friend on the team, dumped me. She told me our friendship was inappropriate and that it would be best if we parted ways. That was the word she used: inappropriate. Like she was someone's grandmother. I guessed she was referring to the cuddling, but I hadn't been the one to initiate that. When she ended things, in the parking lot walking to our cars, an incredulous laugh erupted from somewhere deep inside me where the pain was so sharp and pointed that it had no choice but to morph into something lighter, more tolerable. I didn't love Alex, at least not like that, but still, the rejection hurt. And I hadn't seen it coming.

"Stop it," she said, her calm façade slowly giving way to a turbulence. "Stop laughing."

That only made me laugh harder, the type of deep belly laugh that hurts so good it makes you wish all pain was this uncomplicated. I allowed myself to wonder about the rest of the team, what exactly she would tell them. I didn't want to lose them, too.

When I climbed into the driver's seat and yanked on my seatbelt, I finally checked my phone, which was really my mom's phone, and I had fifteen missed calls from our landline and a text from Alex that said *You're insane, you know that? You're a lunatic.*

We didn't have a mass or a service. Dad hated religion, any formalities really, the way some people hate slow walkers or thinking about others. He'd kept a final-wishes document in our home office, and it said he would be open to a celebration of life—a deathday party, he called it—after we unceremoniously put him in the ground. His instructions had also included a playlist of all his favorite shit— Warren Zevon, Chuck Berry, Bob Dylan, Jimi Hendrix, and the like—we were under no circumstances to play the radio or a NOW CD. The high school let us host the celebration one Sunday in the gym since my dad had coached the JV team and all.

He'd also requested a giant bowl of Skippys, which was apparently a drink from his college days: part beer, part vodka, and lemonade powder to mask the taste. I'd never seen him drink anything but beer or whiskey, but then again, I wasn't surprised by his request. Unfortunately for him and my mother, he was a nostalgic guy— I suspected he only knew how to love something once it was already gone. It seemed like a wretched way to live, but what did I know?

At 3 P.M., the start of the party, I was standing by the bowl of Skippys, occasionally stirring it, when I saw a lump of lemonade powder surface. I was wearing my dad's XXL Eagles sweatshirt with some jeans and navy Chucks. The sweatshirt, which damn near went down to my knees, smelled like him: notes of cedarwood and toasted almonds from his cigars mixed with his sweaty, pungent musk.

Beside me, Katrina, who I'd known since our Fisher-Price hoop days, making her my best friend by default, was drinking a Yuengling and quietly celebrating the end of my friendship with Alex. She hadn't understood it in the first place, and by hadn't understood it, I mean she didn't like me having a close friend who wasn't her. A bit hypocritical, considering she also had a friendship that could certainly be deemed *inappropriate* by some.

I was annoyed with her, so I poured a shot of Skippys in a red Solo cup and threw it back. It tasted like what I imagined the floor of a college bar might taste like.

"Blackout city, here we come," I said.

People were trickling into the gym, which my mom and I had decorated with huge blown-up pictures of my dad from birth to death and half-assed streamers at the entrance that dipped so low some people had to limbo just to get through the door. People in flannels and trucker hats, Eagles and Phillies gear, Chevy shirts and Fuck Chevy shirts. I spotted Dad's work buddies, a bunch of financial advisers looking out of place in their sleek suits. Grayson, my dealer and buddy, was making the rounds, shaking hands, slapping shoulders, and slipping drugs into people's pockets. So far, there was no sign of my AAU teammates, so I guessed Alex must have sold them on quite the story. I was afraid to message any of them, in case they were done with me.

"All I'm saying is, fuck Alex," said Katrina, adjusting her gold

KATRINA necklace, her name falling just above the ABERCROMBIE on her off-the-shoulder sweatshirt.

"Kat, it's my dad's funeral."

"I know, and I'm sad about that part," she said.

"How sweet of you."

She sniffled a little. "He practically raised me."

This was fundamentally untrue; it was just something young people liked to say when someone older than them died, and I told her as much.

She finished off her beer. "Shut up," she said, pointing with the neck of her bottle. "What is this, gym class?"

On the other side of the gym, my mom and Katrina's mom were trying to corral everyone who wanted to participate in a three-point version of Knockout—just one of many more of my father's demands. He'd had a better chance at hitting the lottery than he did a shot from behind the arc, though he thought he was a sharpshooter, a real Reggie Miller. Even if he went one for eighty, on that one he made, he'd run around the gym or driveway waving his shirt over his head, his hairy belly hanging over his waistband. My dad's real talent had been music—he was one of those people who could listen to a song then pick up his guitar and play it damn near perfectly.

"I could have been better than Hendrix" was a common refrain around our house. I got sick of hearing about what he could have done if he'd really tried, sick of living in the wake of his regret, especially when his regret had to do with me and the fact of my existence. Not that he ever said that, but it was easy enough to guess that he blamed his lack of fame on family life. But now, of course, I would have done anything for him to slap me on the shoulder and tell me not to let anything get in my way.

"Go on, there might be cute guys," I said.

I thought that might encourage her to join the game and leave me alone with my grief—she wasn't ever one to say no to attention—but she stayed rooted beside me.

I turned my attention to the herd of aspiring three-point champions. And that's when I noticed Liv. She was first in line, palming the ball with her left hand, dressed in a sweaterdress that looked distinctly unloved, like it had been retrieved from storage. I felt my pulse quicken, all the heat in my body rush to my face, my groin, the base of my skull.

She was solid, muscular around the shoulders and thighs, strong brow, chiseled face; I could see her jaw muscle flexing from sixty feet away. I wanted to bite it, feel how it pushed against my teeth. When she shot her first three, her arms moved through the air like swans, smooth and silky, ending in an elegant follow-through. Nothing but net. When she moved, she moved like water. Even in her chunky wedges, I could see her quiet tranquility; I knew the ball was a part of her body. I'd be lying if I said I wasn't threatened by her talent—it was easy to see she had something special—and it was because of that intimidation, which bordered on aggression, that I permitted myself to also want her. I couldn't explain my desire to myself, let alone anyone else, but I wanted to be next to her, I wanted to crawl inside her so I could get to know her heart, her lungs, the curl of her ribs from the inside out. I was in trouble.

"Remind me who that is?" I said to Katrina, careful not to give anything away.

I knew I'd seen Liv before, but I couldn't quite place her. Katrina, who would tell you she had her finger on the pulse of the who's who of high school basketball, said her name was Liv Cooper and she played for St. Patrick's, a small Catholic school that wasn't in our conference.

"I heard she's got like a million D-I offers," she said.

I nodded, spilling Skippys down my front, my eyes still stuck to Liv, who had made her way to the back of the long line. Katrina must have mistaken my preoccupation for wariness because she seized the opportunity to talk some shit.

"I heard she picked a fight with a teammate last year," she said. "Over a stupid turnover."

I didn't say anything. Liv was now looking at me with a stoic curiosity. In all my nervousness, I'd forgotten I wasn't behind a veil, that she could notice me back. I patted my shirt with a napkin and when I lifted my head, her gaze had returned to the hoop.

"Or maybe it was a charge?"

"She's got a hell of a shot," I said.

"And?" she said.

"And I think you spend too much time on PennLive."

PennLive was the forum for all things Pennsylvania sports. A place where adults with impulse-control problems gossiped about high school players like we were NBA first-round draft picks. Imagine a middle-aged man finishing up dinner and then making his way to the home office; he sits down and logs in with his anonymous username then writes an impassioned post about how so-and-so on such and such team is overrated and the refs are always favoring her. It's enough to make you want to die.

"Speaking of which," said Katrina, "I saw someone post that Cooper was the best player in the area."

"Okay," I said, searching for somewhere to look that wasn't at Liv. I settled on the bridge of Katrina's nose.

"Doesn't that piss you off?"

"What do I care what some internet person thinks?"

"The person challenged everyone to name one player better than her."

"And?" I said.

"One of the replies named you."

"What do you want me to do, challenge her to a duel?"

I'd intended for my voice to have a sarcastic edge, but I could hear it shaking on account of my nerves. I felt Liv studying me. Suddenly, I was acutely aware of my body in space, my too-long arms, my lazy posture, my fidgety hands, which I tried and failed to stuff into my front pockets—they were tight jeans from the girls' department, the pockets were mostly for show. As an athlete, I was used to people watching me, but this wasn't the same as the attention I received on the court—it was a much closer reading.

"Why is she here?" I asked, pushing my luck with Katrina's omniscience.

"She must be stalking you," she said, making her eyes all spooky.

I shoved her and she fell a few feet backward. Once she recovered, she held her hands up and shadowboxed me a few times before picking up her beer.

"Her parents probably knew him or something."

I accepted this explanation. Everyone knew my dad. When I was young, I thought everyone liked him because he was funny, a good time at parties, but then as I got older, I realized it was because he made them feel better about their own vices.

Just then, my mom came stomping over to our table, her eyes big and wild.

"Katrina, thank you so much for coming," my mom said in a voice that meant Katrina ought to find somewhere else to be. And just like that, I no longer wanted Katrina to leave. I felt desperate. Rubbed raw.

"I think I saw Aaliyah and them come in," said Katrina.

I watched her join some of our teammates, who were paying their respects in front of a photo of my dad carrying a one-year-old me on his shoulders.

My mom pulled me aside and stared me down.

"What?" I said. I watched Liv make a three and knock out the person in front of her. The line was dwindling. My palms were wet.

"We're fucked," she said in that loud whisper of hers.

"I miss him, too," I said.

"No," she said, shaking her head like an animal trying to finish off its prey. "That fucker left us with a mountain of debt."

"I thought you said that got erased with his death."

She fidgeted with her earrings. "*His* did."

"What?"

"Your father opened a bunch of credit cards in both our names."

"Can he do that?" I asked.

"Dead people can do anything they want, Mackenzie."

She adjusted her long blond hair that nearly went down to her ass. A remnant of her pseudo-hippie-dippie days, which she'd agreed to give up when I was six and she'd refused to take me to the emergency room despite my 104-degree fever and inability to keep a sip of water down. Mother Earth would heal me, she said. Medicine was mind control. We can manifest wellness. It took me vomiting up bile for four days before she would listen to my father. To this day, I still don't know where all that came from, but I suspected that summer she spent with her aunt out in Sedona when she was sixteen had something to do with it. Our town's idea of a spiritual journey was drunk-driving from the bar to the Wawa to a ditch somewhere. Anyway, since my father's death, I could sense her slowly slipping back into all that nonsense.

"What a piece of shit. A worthless piece of shit," she said. I suppose she hadn't completed the transformation yet.

"Guess he thought he'd live forever."

She huffed. "Do you know what a dental assistant's salary is, Mack?"

"Can I go now?" I asked.

I didn't feel any more broke than I had five minutes earlier, and I really didn't want to hear about how my dad was a bad person. I didn't understand how credit cards worked. For all I knew, it was fake money. Invisible. Just floating around out there. Still, I decided I'd start cleaning Coach's house every day to put some extra cash in my pocket.

"You're accepting one of those scholarship offers ASAP," she said, grabbing me by both shoulders. Quicker than it takes to swat a ball away from a lazy dribbler, my desire to get a basketball scholarship had gone from status, a mark of achievement and pride, to a need.

I heard my dad's voice: *You don't like pressure.*

"Yeah, I hear you," I said. "You are heard."

I had several offers but the thought of choosing a school gave me vertigo. Already, I was sick of the games, of the deceit and politics. UNC had been my number-one choice ever since I was a kid. I wrote them letter after letter. When I was a freshman, they sent me a letter saying they'd recently watched me at a Blue Chip tournament and had been impressed by my ball handling, speed, and command on the court. Last year, they invited me to visit campus, so my dad and I took a nine-hour road trip, living off Slim Jims and Monster energy drinks. I toured the campus, the gym, and the locker room. I met the team, ate lunch with the coaches. They told me I was their number-one point guard recruit, they wanted me real badly, what could they do to get me there? After I got home, they stopped returning my calls. I felt like I was on *The Bachelor* or some other obnoxious dating show—where were the cameras? Had the ending already been decided for me?

My mom spoke up again. "You never really know anyone."

I watched her open a beer and chug it down. When she was done, she wiped her mouth with the back of her wrist. She asked if I had anything to say to that. I said I didn't. She looked at me with out-of-focus eyes and said my silence would serve me well moving forward. That the best thing I could ever do for myself was to know when to leave someone alone with their words. Then she turned and left me alone with mine.

I snuck a glance at Liv. It was just her and one person left in the contest, Andrew from our boys' team. They raced in circles. Made three after three. Finally, he missed. The ball hit the front of the rim and bounced high into the air. Before it had a chance to come down, Liv's ball was already through the net. They shook hands, then, to my horror, Liv started walking toward me, ball tucked under her arm, sweat dripping down the side of her face in delicious streams. I busied myself with another cup of Skippys, but my hand was shaky; I could hardly ladle any into my cup. I heard her grab a beer from the cooler a few feet away and felt the air change when she arrived at my side.

"I'm sorry about your loss," she said, taking a sip of beer.

"Thanks."

"You're welcome."

"Thanks," I said again. My brain was malfunctioning.

"You said that already."

"Cool, yeah," I said. "Nice three ball, by the way."

She nodded, pleased with herself. I noticed she had a funnel-shaped birthmark on her chin. It reminded me of a tornado on its way to destroy a town. All that anticipatory energy.

"I'm here with my mom," she said.

She pointed to a slender woman with Liv's same frizzy brown hair and big eyes. She had the stiffest posture I've ever seen; when she turned her head, her body went with her. She was nodding politely while a few people talked in her general direction.

"Want to know a secret?" she asked.

"I—"

"I'm transferring to Ekron in the fall," she said.

She told me it was a fresh start, although she didn't say from what. Ekron was my school. We'd be playing together in a few short months.

"Guess that makes me your new point guard," I said, trying to assert some sort of dominance, like a dog pissing on a tree. I worried if I didn't, I might ask her to run away with me.

Liv's lips curled into a slight smile then she took a step toward me and grabbed my hand, not to shake it but to turn it over and examine it, palm facing up.

"Well, you've got the perfect hands for the job," she said, my hand resting in hers, the bright gym lights dancing across her face, which was focused on our hands, how they seemed to have fused into one. Electricity surged through my arm and down my spine. I felt a deep ache in the back of my skull. At the time, I was certain I was reading into the gesture, but now I'm not so sure; how could she not have known the erotic charge of her words?

I looked around the gym, half expecting to find everyone still and silent, bearing witness to whatever was happening between us, but no one was looking; no one saw.

I studied Liv's face, which gave away nothing. The golden-brown bigness of her eyes and the freckle like a star against the white of her right eye. Behind her hung the school's green-and-gold championship banners. My eyes flickered to the women's basketball record board detailing every statistic imaginable, records set by players who had come before us, many of whom, having moved on to husbands and children and careers, probably never thought about the rush of scoring a buzzer-beater in front of an overcrowded gym, the fans' roars and claps temporarily eclipsing the fear that this would all go away one day. Or, they thought about it every day, couldn't seem to shake the haunting feeling that nothing in life would ever measure up.

For just a moment, sweating under the gym's fluorescent lights, my hand in hers, I forgot how badly I wanted my name in big white letters on that board, how badly I wanted to leave a trail of accomplishments behind. But even then, my fingers curled upward toward my palm as if my body were resisting hers, as if it were saying, *No, I still belong to me.*

"What I mean is, let's take home a championship," she said, finally dropping my hand.

I felt we'd gotten away with something, although I couldn't say what.

We drank in silence, watching all the people. Some cried and hugged my mom, said Winston was a good guy, they couldn't believe he was gone. Others shotgunned beers, spraying foam everywhere. Some people told stories about my dad, laughing so hard they couldn't breathe.

My mother blew a whistle. It was time for the finale. As a stand-in for my father, I was to throw a Nerf football, in order to "see who would be next."

"That's not funny," Liv said, laughing into her drink. I liked her laugh. It was full-bodied, rich with life. I smiled, happy that my dad could make this person laugh from beyond the grave.

I stood on one end of the court while everyone jockeyed for position on the other. I was surprised by how many people wanted to participate. I guess a lot of people wanted to die. Liv stood on the side, leaning against the folded-up bleachers. My mom closed her eyes and recited something to herself.

"Everyone ready?" I shouted. The gym erupted with drunken glee.

I wound up and threw the Nerf football as high as it could go. People shoved each other left and right. Three bodies hit the deck. An old man wielded his cane. Two men jumped for the football, their arms reaching for the sky. They both got a hand on it before batting it to the ground, where they pounced on it like street dogs tearing at remains. A man came in and tried to break it up but that wasn't happening. Another dude suggested they take the fight outside, and the fighters stumbled to their feet, brushing off their shirts and gathering themselves. Then they were on the move.

"Let's go watch," said Liv, nodding toward the door. We followed them outside, where we were greeted with the sting of a cold spring evening. The sky looked like a fading bruise above us, the yellows pressed up against the blues. We watched the men roll around like assholes, calling each other faggots and limp dicks. I think I only counted two or three good punches the whole time. We heckled the shit out of them. It kind of felt like we were on a date.

My mom appeared and started throwing crumpled-up dollar bills at the guys.

"Mom, I thought we were broke," I said.

"What difference is a few dollars going to make?" She whistled like she was at a strip club.

I didn't say anything, but she caught the look I shot her.

"It's what he would have wanted," she said, dabbing her eyes with a dirty bill.

After the fight dissolved, Katrina told me the team was going to Applebee's, I had to come. She looked Liv up and down, slowly, apparently deciding whether she was good enough for half-off appetizers, then said she could come, like, if she wanted. Her boyfriend of the week, Micah, pulled around in his truck and Katrina hopped in, greeting him with a tongue down his throat.

"Are you going to go?" Liv asked me. For the first time that day, she seemed nervous.

"I don't know," I said. "Are you going to go?"

"I don't know," she said.

"Well, fuck," I said.

"Are you going to go?" she asked again.

"I don't know, I don't know."

It went like that until she told me to follow her, she had a better idea. We hopped into her Jeep Wrangler, and she turned the music—some hip-hop song I didn't recognize—up to a deafening decibel and smiled real big, the tip of her tongue poking out between her teeth. I thought she was taking me to a spot in her town but then she didn't get on the highway, instead driving toward my house.

The whole drive, she left her right arm draped casually across the back of my seat as if that was something we did, as if that's the way we'd always done things. I stuck my right arm out the window and watched it swim through the air against the backdrop of American and Confederate flags hung proudly in front of homes, whipping in the wind like a bad idea.

"I watched film on you," she said.

"Oh yeah?"

"Yeah."

"Okay," I said.

"Just wanted to get a feel for who I'll be playing with."

"Okay," I said.

"You want to know what I think, don't you?" she said.

"No," I said, resisting my urge to ask.

Truth is, I was feeling on edge from the whole Alex thing. Normally, I would have engaged, would have taken the bait. I would have jabbed and played, would have pushed our new friendship into that probing space where hundreds of questions live but no singular answers. But I was feeling fragile, humiliated, angry, and self-conscious.

Liv tried again.

"You know, you could have gone. You didn't have to ditch your friend for me," she said, her eyes drinking me in.

"I didn't ditch her." I didn't understand what Liv wanted from me. I felt touchy, on edge, as if she'd planted booby traps in my muscles and now I couldn't even trust my own body. "And it wasn't for you," I added.

She laughed. "Who was it for then?"

"I don't know," I said.

Searching for a distraction, any distraction, I dug around in my backpack and pulled out an envelope. It had Kansas State's purple letterhead on the upper-right-hand corner. I held it in my lap, suspecting that if I didn't hand it over, she'd feel compelled to take it. I was right.

"Oh, shit. Look at you," she said, pressing the letter against the steering wheel.

I told her it was the first recruiting letter I ever received, that I'd gotten it in eighth grade.

"I like carrying it around with me," I said. "As a reminder, or something."

"Of what?"

"I don't know," I said. "I guess that I'm wanted and have been for a long time."

My voice faltered a bit. I hadn't meant to admit that. All my life I'd wanted to get a full scholarship to play D-I basketball. I wanted to be a champion, I wanted to be loved; I assumed they were the same thing.

Liv knit her eyebrows together but didn't comment. Instead, she said she couldn't believe we were going to be seniors come fall, that we'd have to commit to a school soon.

"No pressure," she said, laughing.

"Everyone wants to know where I'm going to go," I said.

"And they expect the biggest and the best," said Liv, finishing my thought.

I told her how Gonzaga had called and offered me the other day, that my dad and I had visited their campus the year before and I'd stayed with a junior on the team, Keisha, who snuck me into a bar using her friend's French passport. I said it like I was commenting on the Slurpee flavors at 7-Eleven, but I was showing off big-time.

"They offered me, too," she said, tossing the Kansas State letter back at me. I couldn't believe it.

What I wanted to say: We should go there together.

What I said: "The weather's depressing in Washington."

Liv laughed, shaking her head. Then, more to herself than to me, she said, "This asshole can come back from an ACL tear in three months but can't handle a little rain."

That got my attention. She hadn't just watched film on me. The only way she'd have known about the timeline was if she'd read my write-up in the newspaper last year. Everyone loves a good comeback story, especially when the doctor sings your praises, says he's never seen anything like your recovery. Despite every burning muscle in my neck and back telling me to turn toward Liv and make her say it to my face, make her admit that I fascinated her in the same way she fascinated me, I didn't turn. I continued looking forward, pretending to be interested in the cars, the trees, the curious rhythm of life moving fast in every direction.

"Bet I can make this," she said, flooring it through an orange-squeezed light.

That day I know I must have felt sad, but I can't remember the sadness with any type of clarity, only other, more shameful feelings, like I remember sitting there, in the passenger seat, my body hot with the charged potential between us, and feeling—I don't know how else to say it—grateful that my dad dying had brought me and Liv together the way that it did.

We drove by a horse and buggy, which seemed to be going impossibly slow next to Liv's Jeep. The Amish world, though a constant, was always a shock when it intermingled with ours. When I was a kid, we used to go on field trips to visit the Amish, as if that were a normal thing to do, take a trip to go stare at fellow human beings. We weren't allowed to take pictures of them, I remember that much. They said it went against their religion. Something about vanity.

Eventually, I asked where we were going—we had just passed the Sunoco and Rita's, by my house—and Liv said she was taking me to the outdoor courts where she liked to clear her head. It was called Sycamore Beach even though there were no sycamores, only cedars, and there was no beach, she said. I knew the spot and didn't get what was so special about it. Plus, the hoops were double rimmed and unforgiving—anything but a perfect swish was bound to rim out.

After a few more miles, she pulled into the parking lot of a municipal building then turned onto a tiny-ass dirt path, more pothole than dirt. We were surrounded by a thicket of red cedars.

"What's there to do around here anyway?" she asked, driving right over a pothole.

"Probably the same shit you're used to," I said.

She laughed. "That bad, huh?"

"The good news is, there's no shortage of parking lots to hang out in," I said.

"We're almost out of this shithole," she said, slamming on the brakes when we reached a clearing where the court emerged like an oasis in the desert. "Just hold on a little while longer."

She looked at me with those eyes usually reserved for religious zealots, believers in a place so much better than here that they'd risk their lives for it.

The sun was setting, and with it rose the moon, barely visible except for a small sliver of gold that could have been the sky's secret smile. I got out of the car while Liv changed out of her sweaterdress and into basketball clothes in the front seat. I could hear her cursing the stupid thing while she wrestled with the sleeves. Once she looked more like I imagined the real Liv looked, she grabbed two balls, tossing me one, and a six-pack of Lionshead from behind the driver's seat. I was disappointed they were cans instead of bottles because the Lionshead bottle caps had word puzzles on the bottom to give you something to do while you drank.

I examined the ball she'd given me. It was worn out in a way that made me feel romantic. I spun it in my hands, marveling at how this dumb thing made of leather and rubber and fingerprints and whatever the fuck else could mean so much to her, to me, and so little to someone else.

Empty cans of PBR and Yuengling lined the courts, which had once been painted, decades earlier by the looks of it, and now held the faded memory of paint. The backboards were covered in graffiti:

FUCK YOU BITCH ASS
SUCK MY COCK
FEAR = DEATH

Although I'd never thought much of this court, knowing it was Liv's place and that she wanted to take me there made me reconsider. I found myself storing it away in the part of my mind reserved for the courts I admired, the ones that made me feel changed when I stepped onto them. I was a collector of courts; they were my places of worship.

Some tattooed men were finishing up a game of two vs. two. They wore cutoff tees, the holes for their arms so big you could slip your whole body through them. One man threw an alley-oop for his taller teammate, who, way past his prime, jumped to dunk it but couldn't even get the ball over the rim. He didn't curse like I had expected him to—instead, he stood under the basket, deflated, hands on his hips, eyes on the blood-red horizon.

I knew, intellectually, that one day I'd become a has-been just like this man, the intoxication of college ball having dissolved into the barely detectable buzz of pickup games, the euphoria of being able to jump so high having receded into talking about having been able to jump so high—and yet, as I watched the man indulge in a moment of self-pity, I felt a wave of repulsion wash through me.

We nodded to the men then headed to the opposite end of the court. Liv cracked open a can of beer. It had been shaken by the car ride, so it sprayed all over her. Like satisfaction made manifest. I remember thinking that, aside from a ball falling through a chain net, there was no better sound in the world. Liv took a deep drink and then handed the can to me. We passed it back and forth until it was gone. We did the same with two more. It went down good and easy, not like the Skippys, warming me from the inside out. I took off my dad's sweatshirt and shot around in jeans and a T-shirt.

Liv's first shot was intended to show off—a little between the legs, reverse layup action. I pretended not to be impressed by her hops. She nodded toward me to let me know it was my turn. I drove hard toward the paint, shoulder down, and pushed off of my front foot, exploding backward into a perfect step-back jumper.

"Okay, I see you," said Liv. I shot her an arrogant smile.

"And I don't even have home-court advantage," I said.

"Oh, whatever," she said, dribbling between her legs. "My dad used to bring me here when I was a kid."

We began taking turns shooting around while Liv told me how her dad had up and left two years ago but it had taken two stupid, agonizing years for the divorce to be finalized. She said she was glad to have him out of the picture, he'd been nothing but a loudmouth up in the stands, heckling Liv so bad she forbade him from attending games anymore. Her mom would throw a fit if he showed up.

"I doubt anyone could have impressed him," she said. "Anyway, I'm over it."

At this, Liv bricked a three-pointer, missing the rim entirely. She looked down at her hands as if they were to blame for her miss. I listened, not saying much of anything, just listening to the pleasant rhythm of our dribbling balls—one, two, one, two, one, two—an intimate melody I couldn't make alone. I got the sense there was more to the dad story than Liv was giving away, but I didn't want to press.

"What about you?" she said.

The dark was starting to settle in around us. I half waited for the lights that weren't there to come on. The men, having finished their last game, slapped one another's hands, and then they were off, into the night, back to their problems.

Eyes burning, I cleared my throat, wondering what exactly there was to say. "Well, you know."

"I mean, were you close?"

I bent down and began to dribble the ball between my legs, low and fast, just how my dad had taught me. He used to swear up and down that, if I were disciplined enough, there shouldn't be a single move I couldn't perform right in front of a defender. All I needed was quicker hands, superior control. Liv stood still, ball tucked under her arm, watching me.

"I guess transferring for your senior year wasn't in your plan," I said.

Liv looked at me, surprised, like I knew something she didn't, then quickly rearranged her face into indifference, shrugging.

"What about your mom?" Liv asked.

I told her about her whole hippie relapse, that I was almost certain she was bringing the moonstones and crystals out of storage as we spoke. Her meditation pillows, too.

"She's always telling me to trust the moon," I said. "You know."

"No, I really don't know," laughed Liv.

"It's nice. She's nice," I said.

With that, I rolled my ball off to the side and began guarding Liv at the top of the key, initiating a casual game of one-on-one, if there were such a thing. My hands pestered the waistband of Liv's shorts while Liv, body positioned sideways to protect the ball, swatted at me. Liv dribbled around, crossover here, behind-the-back there, trying to shake me.

"My mom's very traditional," she said. "Devoted Catholic and all that."

Ball fake, ball fake, but I didn't bite.

"What about you?" I asked.

Liv paused before answering, perhaps deciding whether to answer my question or defend her mother.

She tried a quick cross, then between the legs, but I kept my eyes locked on Liv's belly, disciplined.

"I'm all she has," said Liv.

Frustrated that she couldn't shake me, Liv turned around so her back was facing me. She started backing me down in the post, her ass pressed against my pelvis. I ground my hips in response to the contact, determined not to give Liv an inch. Typical defense, but this bumping and grinding, it made me feel like my blood was pumping in reverse. Waves of blood colliding at their peaks.

The next step of the dance was for Liv to hunker down and push backward, forcing me to straighten long enough to knock me off-balance, but just as Liv lowered herself into a deeper squat, two kids, maybe eleven or twelve, stepped out of the dark with a flashlight, its beam illuminating the intimacy of this dance. Liv, as if struck by lightning, leapt a few feet away from me. She was breathing hard. I stood there, amused but also curious. What did she think we'd been caught doing?

"Sorry, we just came out here to smoke," said the one, holding up a homemade bowl made out of tinfoil. They left us alone.

"I should be getting home anyway," I said. I headed over to the grass where my backpack was, my flip phone sitting on top of it.

Liv recovered quickly from the incident, and her typical confidence was restored. She followed me and grabbed my phone, saving her number in it before reaching around me and sliding it into the back pocket of my jeans. I didn't know how to tell her it was the phone I shared with my mother.

"I have a boyfriend," said Liv, as if that cleared up the confusion. "James, he's on St. Patrick's boys' team."

"I'll text you so you have my number," I said.

She asked if I wanted a ride home and I said I'd walk, it wasn't too far. She smiled with her eyes and tapped my sternum where my number 12 necklace dangled.

"Night, number twelve," she said.

"Night."

"Number one," said Liv.

"Like . . ."

"T-Mac," she said.

"Tracy McGrady is your favorite player?"

Liv confirmed this with a smile and one last tap of my chest. She walked to her Jeep, turning to give me a small nod before climbing in.

I returned the nod, knowing that if given the chance, I would follow her anywhere.

On my walk home, in the dark cloak of night, I thought about my favorite player, Iverson, and why fans called him the Answer. There were the obvious theories, like if the other team scored, he always had a response, a three ball or a floater or a falling layup, and the Sixers had had something of a losing problem before he arrived. These explanations made sense, but they didn't satisfy me. I had the sense that AI had some type of wisdom that went beyond acrobatic shots and splitting double teams. Some Yoda-type shit. I had so many questions for him, like How badly do you have to want something in order to get it? What about someone? Is there a limit to desire? And what happens when you reach it?

3

HARD-EARNED BUCKETS

My dad's celebration of life was in March, and every day for the rest of the school year, Liv and I would meet up at Sycamore Beach and run drills together. She brought her Jumpsoles, and we'd take turns strapping them to our sneakers and pretending we were men on the moon, not having to answer to gravity. I'd bring cones and pads, a broom to turn me into a seven-foot defender. When she drove to the basket, I hit her hard with the pads, let her know there was something behind that hit. And she did the same for me, sometimes rattling me so hard my neck would crack.

When Liv ran through a drill, I studied her every micromovement, from her hand placement on the ball to when she lifted her foot on a jab to where her eyes focused when she did a spin move. When it was my turn, she watched me with the intense concentration of a scientist examining a new microbe under a microscope.

Her pull-up got smoother, my three ball improved. Her cross got quicker, my step-back got crisper. We marveled at the influence we had over each other. We were little gods playing with fate. But we didn't idolize each other. In retrospect, it might have been better if we had—that way, both parties would have been primed for disappointment from the start.

Those afternoons, practicing together, it felt like we were collaborating on something that predated language. Something so primitive you could only revert to that wild state by pushing your body to ill-advised limits. By pushing so hard that you eventually found what was on the other side of fear. Of loneliness. What we found in each other was a recognition so potent, so concentrated, we could hardly stomach it.

The season couldn't come soon enough.

Once we were done practicing, we'd sit on the grass and smoke a bowl. My buddy Grayson always hooked me up, gave me the *I'm in love with you but only know how to say it with discount drugs* deal. And thanks to his discount and my commitment to living off the McDonald's dollar menu, I could afford middies. With Liv, I felt tense; the weed helped. She didn't need to know how I felt about her. If basketball taught me anything, it taught me how to deceive people with my body. I made sure there was always at least a foot of space between us. Except for one day when she asked me about my knee.

I'd been slathering handfuls of Icy Hot on it, the menthol burning our nostrils and eyes. I told her most days it was sore as hell, that I'd worn my ACL brace for all of two months after I was cleared to return to play. It was clunky, it slowed me down.

"That doesn't sound smart."

I shrugged. I didn't care how much damage I did to my body. I was trading the future for the present at a remarkable pace.

"Although I'm sure I would have done the same thing," she said.

"Only place it doesn't hurt is around the scars," I said. "They're pretty much numb."

As if by invitation, she scooted closer to me and ran a finger along my scar, just below my kneecap. My breathing quickened.

"Can you feel that?" she asked. She looked at me with big, beautiful, bloodshot eyes.

"Nope."

She tried just below the scar.

"What about there?"

"Nope."

Then beside it, closer to the inside of my knee. I felt it in my hips, my stomach.

"Yeah, a little. I have to focus on feeling it, though," I said.

Her finger still on my knee, she furrowed her brow, eyes tracing my leg. She didn't look up at me when she spoke.

"That must be weird, having to focus on feeling something."

"I guess."

She looked at me.

"Usually, it's the opposite," I said, immediately embarrassed by my admission.

"Yeah?"

I swallowed hard, focused on the wind bothering the cedars. I thought the trees looked unhappy, although I couldn't say why.

"Yeah," she said, answering her own question.

We got to talking about college, as we inevitably did. She didn't know where she wanted to go either. And her mom wasn't much help, she just wanted her to go as close to home as possible. I asked her about James, if they were trying to go to schools near each other. I'd never seen him play and was secretly hoping she'd tell me there was no way in hell he was good enough to play in college. Instead, she put her face in her hands and rubbed her eyes. When she lowered her hands, I noticed the vein snaking down the middle of her forehead was pulsating.

"Sorry, we can talk about something else," I said.

When Liv spoke, her voice was higher and more mature, a sort of mid-Atlantic housewife feel to it.

"It's such a beautiful day, let's not wreck it with talk of our stupid husbands." She held up her hand, holding an invisible drink. With her other hand, she removed an invisible olive from what I now realized was a martini and pretended to eat it.

"Oh, uh, how silly of me," I said, trying to imagine what my stupid husband must look like. I saw a lot of khaki in this alternate life.

"Check out the pool boy," she said, nodding at the hoop, its rusted pole.

I didn't know what she was doing exactly, beyond introducing me to an alter ego, but it was clear she didn't want to talk about James. On the rare occasions that I asked her how her night with him was, she'd tell me to fuck off like she knew I really didn't want to know. The only reason I ever knew they were hanging out was because of her away messages on AIM.

With James, hit up the cell ;)

I thought that meant they were watching a movie in his basement while he made her touch his abs. Or they were drinking Gatorade and vodka in a parking lot while one of his friends blew something up. Once, I made the mistake of hitting her up while she was with him. I don't know what she told him about me, but he wound up stealing her phone and texting me to go find something else to do with my Friday night. She'd apologized profusely for that one. Tossed me a quick wink when she said he was just jealous of all the time we spent together.

"Tight cheeks," I said in appreciation of the imaginary pool boy.

Liv laughed, breaking character. She glanced at her phone.

"Let me guess, it's time to head home?" I asked.

Her mom was very strict; Liv wasn't allowed to miss dinner. Her mom said it was about respect, I think because she didn't know how to say it was about loneliness—hers, specifically. I didn't blame her. Nobody likes to say the words *I'm lonely.* They'd rather say things like *I'm pissed off* or *I need you to fix something* or *Would you bring me that beer?*

"Nah, she has some church fundraiser tonight," she said. "So, I'm free."

I told her I'd been planning on going to Coach Puck's to clean like I so often did on weeknights.

"I know it's not exactly the most exciting way to spend your freedom . . ." I trailed off, leaving the implied invitation hovering between us like a lightning bug in the golden-blue dusky light.

"Well, I have been saving up for some weighted balls for us," she said. She leaned back on her hands and lifted her leg to kick me.

"For us," I said.

"Yeah, who else?" she said, laughing.

I didn't understand. It was like we were speaking two different languages.

"Just don't be surprised when he's, like, not what you'd expect."

"What do you mean?"

"You'll see."

She dug around in her bag for some eye drops. We both used them and then got in our cars, with me leading the way.

When we got there, Coach Puck was out front, digging a hole for a reason that wasn't immediately obvious to me. Around the side of the house, I could see a bunch of dog noses through the slats in the fence, a symphony of whines and yelps blending in with Coach's grunts. Several Labs, a pair of pugs, and a monster he claimed was part wolf.

I got out of the car while Liv parked then reparked then reparked her Jeep, trying to maneuver it in beside my car without running into some trees.

"You're high," said Coach by way of a greeting.

"No, I'm not," I said. My car was still running.

"You fucking punk," he said. "You think I don't know a high person when I see one."

I mumbled something about how mirrors don't lie. He held up his hand, signaling for me to stop right there, I had it all wrong. He didn't fuck with weed; acid had always been his drug of choice, but it had given him a bunch of tiny holes in his brain.

"That's why I sometimes mistake you for a superstar," he said.

He stopped digging and scrunched up his face at me, waiting for my reaction. I slid into the driver's seat, pretending to look for something, then took the keys out of the ignition.

"Guess I'll be transferring to Cathedral Catholic after all," I said when I emerged.

It was no secret the Cathedral Catholic coach, Coach McKeegan, had been illegally recruiting me. After games, he'd shake my hand for a beat too long in line and whisper something about how my talents weren't being utilized at Ekron.

Coach laughed a barking laugh like a sea lion but didn't take the bait. He shouted to Liv that she could park in the front yard, he didn't give a shit, just be wary of the hole. I went over and knocked on her window and repeated what he said.

"I swear I know how to park," she said.

"Your secret's safe with me," I said.

She rolled up the window and backed out into the street so she could get a better angle to pull into the yard.

"So, which of your idiot friends is at my house now?" Coach asked.

My body stiffened, my cheeks warmed with blood. He nodded.

"Oh, that one," he said, scratching his scruff.

I'd told him how she was transferring to our school in the fall. Of course, he already knew who she was, had heard all about her, and I could see after I gave him the news that he was already practicing his postgame speech for when we won the state championship.

"I will kill you," I said.

Liv climbed out of the driver's seat and approached Coach and me. I fumbled my way through an introduction. Coach was acting a little starstruck, repeatedly complimenting her outside stroke. I told him to chill out, and he did, though I could tell Liv liked the attention.

"What can I do?" Liv asked, smiling.

"You know you really don't have to clean," I said. "You can just hang out."

"I want to," she said. She looked pretty high, like she was made of melting clay. I wondered if I looked that way, too.

Coach poked at the earth with the blade of the shovel a few times, thinking. Much to my dismay, he returned to the drug conversation.

"You know, in college, the athletes were always the ones who did the most drugs."

I didn't say anything, unsure as to where this was going. Liv shifted her weight from foot to foot, probably wondering what type of authority figure this man was, though I'd told her not to expect professionalism. The dog noses switched positions at the fence so fast they reminded me of the moving cups in that cups-and-ball magic trick. Follow the sniffer.

"It makes sense," he said, looking from me to Liv. "How else do you silence something as loud as perfectionism?"

"I never really thought of it like that," said Liv.

Coach nodded at me, raising his eyebrows.

"Must be loud in there."

"Yeah, yeah," I said.

"Yeah, yeah," he said in that voice adults use to mock teenagers.

"Guessing in there, too," he said, pointing to Liv's head. "Mack is what you might call selective."

Liv tilted her head, not understanding.

"Only takes to her own kind," he said.

"About that cleaning," I said.

"Oh, I think I can find plenty for the both of you."

He guided Liv inside the house. She glanced over her shoulder and smiled with the tip of her tongue poking out how she did. The floodlights came on, illuminating the front yard like a stage.

I considered sitting on his outdoor couch then saw some green gunk and thought better of it. He came back out, pointed to a long rectangular box, and told me to put together the basketball hoop, said there were some tools in the garage, if I could find them. Assembly wasn't necessarily one of my strengths, which is what I told him. He laughed and told me then I ought to make it one of my strengths. I opened the box and dumped the parts out. Coach's kids, Codi and Bryan, spilled out of the front door and into the yard. They had long, tangled hair and dirty faces. They didn't listen worth a damn. Coach always said they were free, whatever that meant.

They hovered around me, commenting on my work.

"That's the wrong screwdriver," said Bryan.

"That's not a wrench," said Codi.

"Have you ever *seen* a basketball hoop?" said Bryan.

They giggled and cartwheeled away from me. They tackled each other to the ground, wolf pups rolling around in the dark. I read the assembly directions for the twelfth time, the words indecipherable. Then Coach wheeled out one of those rolling TVs they have in classrooms, a tangled mess of wires trailing behind it into the garage.

"I got the film you asked for," he said, shoving a VHS into its mouth.

"Not while she's here," I said.

"She's in the basement," he said. "Trust me, she'll be a while."

I looked at him.

"The wife's territory." He shuddered.

"I didn't know she let anyone down there."

"She's at her mother's for the week," he said. He lowered his voice. "We needed some time apart."

The kids had stopped wrestling and were watching us. He told them to get a life, and they stuck their tongues out at him. He returned the gesture. They told him his tongue was long and gross like a snake. He hissed at them, moving his body in a slithering motion. They ran away, giggling. I liked watching him parent because I knew he gave a shit. It's why he couldn't find it in himself to retire from coaching. Every four years, he found a new player to hang on for. I was coming up on my last year. He claimed once I left, he'd finally retire, but everyone knew he'd pick a freshman favorite and another four years would go by, followed by four more.

He removed a cigarette from his pack and let it dangle on his lower lip, then gestured toward the kids, who were standing at the base of a tree, discussing the best way to climb it. "My life's work right there, man," he said, shaking his head in what I thought must be disbelief. "My two favorite idiots in the world."

I tried to imagine my dad talking that way about me, to his friends, co-workers, anyone who would listen, and I felt the tears burning my sinuses before I felt them roll down my cheeks. I hadn't cried since my dad died. I had tried thinking about puppies and kittens getting run over by a car. I thought about stillbirths and child cancer. But the tears wouldn't come. Now I needed them to go back in. I turned and wiped my face on my forearm and gathered myself. *I was his son, his prodigal son,* I thought. *But I didn't leave, Dad. You did.*

Either Coach didn't notice or didn't want to admit he noticed, because he gave me the dignity of not being perceived, instead pressing play on the VCR, and there was Liv, hair up in a bun, high black socks with black sneakers, light-blue jersey tucked into her long shorts. Ever since our first meeting, when she told me she'd watched film on me, I'd felt like I needed to level the playing field. But not a few seconds into the video, there was Liv running cross-court to shake hands with the referee, and already I found myself grieving all the time I'd missed out on, the time before we knew each other. What was I doing while this was filmed? Playing a game of my own? Practicing in the driveway with my dad? Riding along on a bake ride with Grayson?

Coach Puck said it was St. Patrick's league championship game from the year prior. They were playing Chester, who was undefeated. We watched a few possessions together while Coach smoked a cigarette and bitched that he needed to quit these nasty things.

"She's a special player, isn't she?" he said. She'd just jumped a passing lane and taken it coast-to-coast for an easy two. The announcer boomed Liv's name, parents cheered, and the camera shook with the cameraperson's excitement.

"That's what you say about me," I said. He did a hybrid laugh-cough and put the cigarette out with his boot.

"I know all your buttons, Morris," he said. "Every single one."

I shook my head and examined my work in progress, the pathetic hoop on the ground before me. I thought about Liv in the basement, cleaning when she could be anywhere else.

"You really like her, huh?" he said.

"She's a great addition to the team," I said.

"That's not what I said."

"I don't like anyone," I said.

"Yeah," he said, nodding. "I've used that line before, too."

He ran his hand through his hair, blinking into the distance. The dogs played and fought, a symphony of barks and yips. He dug around in his jacket pocket and pulled out his pack, removing another cigarette and lighting it. We watched the film in silence while I worked on the hoop. I would get up to stop the video and rewind it whenever a play caught my attention. Liv proved to be just as good as I'd suspected. She was methodical, both playful and controlled; she didn't force anything, she let the game come to her. Watching her made me feel like anything was possible, like there was an absence in me only she could fill. The very thought made me quiver. No one should have that much power.

Her go-to move was a hesitation followed by a deadly crossover. Usually, she crossed right to left so she could drive to the basket with her left hand, her dominant hand. I noticed that the hesitation before the cross didn't look the same as her regular hesitation move—it was a bit higher, more drawn out. An observant defender might note that tendency and pick-pocket her when she went to change directions. I wondered if the Chester coach had picked up on it and put it in the scouting report, noting her telltale hesitation before the cross. Judging by Liv's success in the first half—she had at least seventeen points and her team was up by five—I assumed he hadn't.

Either way, I relished learning this small but vital Liv detail. It made me feel close to her, in a one-sided voyeuristic way that was admittedly pleasurable.

I read and reread the hoop instructions, eventually figured out which screw needed to go where. Coach returned to his hole, moving some dirt around for a while. Eventually, Bryan jumped in it and said that it was a grave. He lay on his back and crossed his arms over his chest while Codi shouted at him to get his stupid butt out of there, she needed his help defeating the couch monster.

"How do I know you aren't the couch monster?" he shouted from his position in the hole.

"Guess you'll never know," she said, giggling.

Bryan clawed his way out of the hole.

"You know the backboard's on backward?" he said, pointing to my work.

I told him to mind his own business and he filed a complaint with his father. When I looked back up at the screen, I noticed it was the last few seconds of the game, and I stopped what I was doing and got to my feet for a better view. The camera zoomed in on the scoreboard. Chester 62, St. Patrick's 60, 3.4 seconds on the clock. 3.4 seconds separating either team from a league championship. More than enough time for St. Patrick's to get a good look at the basket. When the camera returned to the court, you could see Liv's coach drawing up a play in the center of the huddle, the team fanning out around him like panting flower petals.

The stands were packed. I thought I could just make out Liv's mom in the second row, directly behind St. Patrick's bench, though I couldn't know for sure, the film was grainy and dark. Whoever she was, her steepled hands were pressed over her mouth in silent fear. You could hear people sitting near the camera talking. From what I could tell, a bunch of douchebags were fighting over nachos. I could practically smell the gym. Cigarettes and winter and too much cologne over BO.

I think everyone in that gym knew the ball was going to Liv for the last-second shot. And thanks to our workouts together, I knew the prime conditions needed for Liv to sink it: a hard chest pass to her left breast, the bottom of the ball positioned just below her shoulder, and she'd want it early, a second before she came off the screen. That way, she could attack the ball like a caged tiger set free for as long as it took to sink its teeth into its next meal. Trigger quick, the shot would be up and in, the bottom of the net smoldering while the team ran onto the court to lift her into the air.

The ref blew the whistle and the teams spilled back onto the court. A mess of red-and-white and light-blue bodies. Liv stomped on a sticky pad by the center table then she slicked back the stray curls that stuck to her cheeks. Her coach paced the sideline, both hands on his hips, eyes darting back and forth.

Liv's defender face-guarded her, eyes at chest level, one hand pinned to Liv's waist, the other stretched out to the side, ready to deflect a pass. I watched her hands grip the sides of her shorts, her veins branching from the trunk of her wrist. Her jaw, unlike mine, was relaxed, her lips slightly parted.

She looked as if she'd always been there, in the middle of expectation, seconds away from victory.

Liv didn't pay her defender any mind. Didn't swat her hand away, didn't stiffen at the closeness. Her lips parted into a mean smile, and in that moment, I loved her. She was like an assassin, milliseconds before the kill, when the bullet has left the barrel, and all has gone silent.

When everyone was in position, the ref blew the whistle, and Liv darted to the three-point line, her defender hot on the chase. She held her hands up, framing her left breast, ready to receive the ball. St. Patrick's point guard picked up the ball, pass-faked high then stepped low around her defender, firing the ball to Liv's right hand. Liv, likely expecting the pass to her left hand, her shooting hand, fumbled it, just slightly. Not enough that the average onlooker would turn to their friend and say, Damn, what the fuck was that? But it was there, nevertheless.

Recovering, she swept the ball from right to left then released her shot, fading a little to avoid her defender's outstretched arm. It was a high arching shot, a little higher than is typical of her threes, a slow shot that moved in the realm of time and space reserved solely for last-second shots, the ball floating at the peak like it wanted a taste of space before coming back down to earth.

The ball, falling, falling, falling, looked like it might be good, looked like it might get St. Patrick's the win, but it was a few inches too short, hitting the front of the rim and landing in the arms of a Chester player. Liv's hands dropped to her sides, her shoulders slumped. The Chester players ran onto the court in celebration, hugging and high-fiving, expressions distorted into a happiness that somehow seemed cruel in the face of Liv's devastation.

I found myself irritated at St. Patrick's point guard, the foolishness of her passing it to Liv's right hand. It was her job to set her teammates up for success, and she'd failed. And the worst part was, I don't think she had any idea. I watched her walk up to Liv and put her arm around her shoulder, comforting her. People would remember that Liv missed that shot, but everyone else would be off the hook. No one would remember the bad pass, the subpar screens, every play prior to the last one that had put St. Patrick's in that position in the first place.

Liv came outside just as the game dissolved into static waves. She looked like a gorilla who had just emerged from her nest at the zoo, except instead of twigs and leaves, she was covered in feathers and cobwebs.

"I watched film on you," I said. I could feel Coach's eyes on us.

"Is that so?" she said, glancing at the screen.

"Don't you want to know what I think?"

She squinted at me, pressing her lips together in thought.

"You know what," she said. "I do."

I wasn't expecting that. I looked at Coach for help. He put his hands up in surrender, gave me a look as if to say, *you're the one that put yourself in this position.*

Nearby was a box of broken, sorry-looking crayons and a pad of construction paper. I grabbed half of a blue crayon, ripped a piece of paper off, and bent down to use my thigh as a writing surface. I wrote up a scouting report on Liv Cooper, number one, lefty shooting guard.

First, her strengths: Lights-out three-point shooter, always needs a hand in her face, even several feet beyond the arc. Killer one-dribble pull-up. Can attack the basket with either hand. Takes contact and finishes around the rim. Smart, decisive, great hustle player.

Under weaknesses, I wrote *She telegraphs when she's going to change direction.*

Flooded with hubris, I handed the paper to her. She read it over then looked at me curiously, a smile tugging at the corners of her lips. She folded up the paper and stuffed it into her sweatpants pocket, her hand pushing it down as far as it could go.

4

TIME-OUT #1

It was a humid summer night, the air so thick it stuck to you for days, and Liv wanted to know everyone's secrets. We were sitting on a bench outside 7-Eleven drinking Coke Slurpees we spiked with rum. It felt like I was cheating on Wawa, but Wawa's one flaw was that it didn't have slushies. Liv fanned herself with a neon flyer for a local punk concert. People were out and about, walking dogs, smacking mosquitos on their arms, smoking cigarettes and covert blunts, going and coming from places.

She pointed to a bald, tattooed guy climbing off his motorcycle and heading into the store, helmet tucked under his arm. He looked weathered, maybe a little sad around the mouth where his lips were framed by deep wrinkles.

"What do you think he's hiding?" she said.

I said the first thing that came to my head. "Masturbation problems."

"Can't do it, or does it too much?"

"Too much," I said.

"I bet he even does it while he's riding," she said. "Poor guy."

I thought of that morning, lying in bed, my hand moving beneath the sheets. I had, for the first time, pictured Liv in a sports bra and underwear, her hair loose across her shoulders and chest, one arm tucked behind her head so you could see the definition in her bicep and shoulder. Her sports bra pulled low, revealing her sternum, the delicious canal between her small breasts. It felt so fucking good, I almost couldn't move my fingers fast enough, as if I were chasing down my own runaway feelings, forever a few steps behind. If there'd been a thirty-second shot clock, I'd have sunk my shot just moments before the horn blew.

Prior to that, masturbating had never really worked the way I knew it was supposed to work. It helped me fall asleep sometimes when my brain was alive with worry, but I knew there was something more you were supposed to gain from touching yourself, something beyond surface-level pleasure. Thinking about Liv made me understand why some people got addicted. If you had a good enough imagination, you could almost believe that person was there with you.

"Maybe masturbation isn't the problem," I said.

"You're right. I think it's something deeper."

I looked at his bike. It wasn't the sleekest thing around, but it had character; it reminded me of an old, loyal horse.

"He's romantically involved with his motorcycle," I said.

Liv smiled, her eyes widening. This was the juice she wanted. She craned her neck to get eyes on the guy inside 7-Eleven. He was weighing the pros and cons of various potato chip flavors.

"He must have forgotten which flavor was her favorite," said Liv.

"How do you know the bike's a woman?"

Liv stiffened.

"I just do."

"All right," I said, throwing my hands up in defeat.

The man exited the store and ate a jumbo hot dog next to the trash can. He ate it quickly and efficiently, taking big, carnivorous bites. We were maybe ten feet away from him.

"He kept his secret hidden for years," I whispered, leaning closer to her.

"Well, with something like that, you have to," she whispered back.

I thought of my dad and his secrets. Of the fact that my mom was always sitting at the kitchen table with a bottle of wine, balancing the checkbook, massaging her temples. The cupboards full of family-size cans of beans and whatever pasta was on sale that week. I decided maybe keeping secrets was what you did when you wanted to keep the people you loved most.

"But one day," I said, "he finally worked up the courage to tell his best friend."

"No," she said, shaking her head. "I see where this is going, and I don't like it."

"That was years ago, and they haven't spoken since," I said, nodding sagely.

Liv shook her head again. The man swung one leg over the bike and put on his helmet. The bike growled a few times, and he was off.

"Why do you always have to take it there?" she said.

"Where?"

"To tragedy," she said.

I opened a bottle of water and squirted some of it down the back of my neck, but it didn't do much, it was already so warm. Liv reached behind her head and pulled her cutoff T-shirt away from her neck so I could do the same for her. I watched the water trickle down her vertebrae and disappear under her shirt, wetting it down to her ass. We finished off our Slurpees, which had melted into watered-down mixed drinks. Liv waved her flask at me then folded a ten into my hand. I wondered if she'd heard about my newfound debt or if she was just being nice. I hoped it was the latter because the alternative made me want to die; what was worse than being pitied?

I headed inside to get us two more Slurpees. The store smelled like booze and sweat and tangerine. I heard someone throwing up in the bathroom. A cop, a slender, pink salmon of a man, kept opening and closing refrigerator doors, unsatisfied by whatever he found behind them. His presence made me nervous for all the obvious reasons, so I sent mental messages to Liv, telling her to hide the flask. I smiled and gave the cop an enthusiastic nod then made my way to check out. The cashier, this dude who graduated a few years ago, was playing on his Game Boy. I paid for the Slurpees and looked up at myself in the security camera. Was this the same face I'd woken up with? I didn't understand who I was, what anyone wanted with me. Without looking up, the cashier handed me some grease-slicked ones. I stuffed them into my pocket then picked up the Slurpees.

"Thanks," I said.

He looked up and brushed the hair out of his eyes.

"Oh, it's the basketball star," he said.

"Sure," I said.

"Sorry to hear about your dad. That dude was a fucking riot."

"How—"

He waved me off, quieting me. "My parents own The Barn. You could hear him leading the Eagles chant from two blocks down, I swear."

"Cool," I said. The weird thing about my dad's drinking was that it went in catastrophic waves. He'd go a month or two without a single drink and then decide, for one reason or another, to go on a bender for two weeks straight, then stop again. When he wasn't drinking, he'd volunteer on weekend mornings to drive old ladies to pick up their medications, stopping to get them pastries even though he wasn't supposed to take them anywhere but the pharmacy.

When I came back outside, Liv stopped typing on her phone and stuffed it into her pocket. She smiled at me and patted the spot on the bench beside her as if we'd just happened to run into each other in public and she was inviting me to stay awhile. She pulled out her flask and poured some rum into her Slurpee and then mine. When she stopped, I motioned for her to top me off. We slurped, we smacked our lips, we thanked the 7-Eleven gods. My brain felt at once fuzzy and clear. I could see into everyone's minds, and it wasn't pretty.

I watched an olive-skinned woman with a pixie cut, maybe forty-five or so, dressed in a pencil skirt and blouse, pump gas. She held the pump as far away from herself as possible, nose scrunched up. She looked familiar but it wasn't until she turned to face us while she cleaned the windshield that I recognized her as my eighth-grade science teacher, Mrs. Williams.

"What about her?" said Liv, following my gaze.

I told her who she was, that she'd been having an affair with the math teacher.

"You can do better," she said.

"No, it really happened," I said. "I'm not making this one up."

"How did you know they were having an affair?"

"I just knew."

Mrs. Williams put the squeegee back where she got it, adjusted her skirt, wiggling her hips as if fighting with the fabric, then climbed into the driver's seat. She fiddled with the radio for a few seconds. I thought about waving at her; I don't know why; she'd hated me and my smart mouth.

"Okay, but how did you know?" said Liv, drinking her Slurpee.

"They used to call each other during our tests," I said. "She was always flirty as fuck."

"Nope," she said. "Won't hold up in court."

"Come on, you know when two people are fucking," I said. "It's obvious."

"What about when two people are in love?" she said.

"I don't know shit about that."

"Weren't your parents in love?"

"About as much as yours."

She knit her eyebrows together and looked down at her lap, nibbling on the inside of her cheek like she kept her thoughts squirreled away in there. My intention had been to relate to her, but I knew I'd succeeded at pushing her away instead. There was so much pain, everywhere you looked—what were you supposed to do with it all?

"Okay, so what *do* you know shit about?" said Liv, her eyes meeting mine.

"What's it matter? An affair's an affair," I said.

Liv put her head back and blinked at the sky, at all the stars watching us and wondering how all this was going to go down.

"I don't want to talk about affairs anymore," she said.

"Okay."

Liv squinted at me then put her head on my shoulder and left it there, as if I had just said the sweetest thing in the world. Something that had brought us closer. I thought about Alex. How many times had she done this very thing to me? How many times had she tiptoed toward the flames of intimacy, some nights daring to wave her hand over it, only to retreat when she felt the intensity of the heat, when the fire spit out a spark or two?

I checked the time. She would be fast asleep in the hotel by now, exhausted from a day of AAU games. The coaches had been calling me: *Where you gonna be this summer? What's your schedule? I see your team, where you at?* I told them I wasn't playing AAU that summer, didn't say anything about the money or the ex–best friend. Some of them seemed confused, a few were concerned. Most didn't actually need to see me play again, they were just trying to win me over, get me to choose their school over all the others. It was a business, after all, and I was, at the end of the day, a commodity. A few coaches agreed to come to one of my high school games when they got the chance. Others said I knew where they stood, they'd love for me to come there next year.

Liv, though, was still playing AAU. The next weekend, she would go away to a tournament in Hershey. She would come home on Monday with huge bars of chocolate and stories about this team and that team, how many coaches she'd counted at each game. But I didn't want to think about college coaches anymore. The more my mom and everyone else pressured me, the more I wanted to scrap the whole thing, maybe move to Europe after graduation and develop a cigarette-and-absinthe habit. Not that I could ever actually quit basketball—I loved it too much, or perhaps I loved what it could do for me. The attention, the validation, all that shit I never would have admitted needing back then. I guess it's hard to tease the two apart, the love and the need.

"And her?" I said. "What's her big secret?"

I pointed to a bird-thin woman in jean shorts and a halter top who had just emerged from the store and begun dancing. There was no music except for the bass bumping out of passing cars. Her dance was slow and loose, a dreamy quality to it, as if she were channeling some type of entity. As if she were trying to communicate with all of us, if only we would listen. Her body didn't seem to have rules. She could twist it every which way.

"Oh, you mean Loose-Limbed Linda?" said Liv.

Liv lifted her head to look at me. I tried to hide a smile.

"You mean to tell me you don't know triple L?" she said. "Everyone knows her."

"Is that so?"

"She's lived through six wars."

"That's a lot of wars."

"She's seen things you could only dream of."

"I don't doubt that."

Liv laid her head back down on my shoulder.

"Legend has it she comes here every night and dances for her long-lost love," said Liv. "Her dancing sends out a signal. You know, like echolocation."

"So why won't he," I said, pausing for a second, "or she, receive it?" I was suddenly frustrated for Loose-Limbed Linda.

I felt Liv's jaw flex against my shoulder. I watched her hands wrestle in her lap. Linda danced all over the parking lot but stayed away from the light, like a moth that didn't know how to be a moth. Liv started to tell me why she'd hung up on me the previous night, how there was nowhere she could be truly alone in her house.

We'd been talking on AIM all night long, typing as fast as our fingers would allow, then we moved to a phone call when her mom told her it was lights-out. The whole time, Liv's voice was low and hushed, sometimes barely louder than a breath. We'd talked about Katrina, how she didn't like the idea of Liv one bit.

"It's nothing personal," I'd said. "She just doesn't want me to have more than one friend."

"Is that all it is?" Liv said.

I shrugged, knowing Liv wouldn't be able to see me.

"Lucky for her, you and I aren't actually friends," I said. "I just feel bad for you."

I said this because I hoped it would get a reaction out of Liv. A live one. Untamed and bloodthirsty. What I wasn't expecting was a timid sweetness. When she spoke, her voice had a forced steadiness to it.

"I hate that I can't hide from you," she whispered. I got the sense Liv was a secret she kept even from herself.

"I know."

"Asshole," she said. "Fall asleep with me."

"Okay."

"Okay."

"Now?"

"Sure."

"Good night, number one."

"Good night, number twelve."

We sat there in silence for a while, listening to each other's breathing, muffled by the static and ambient noise. It was the most at peace I'd ever felt.

Liv stirred her Slurpee with her straw, told me how she'd heard sounds of feet hitting the floor, the squeak of movement. The footsteps moved closer to her and once they were outside her room, she stuffed the phone under the covers, snapping it shut just as her mom entered the room.

"No boundaries," said Liv. "She said she heard whispers, wanted to know what was so urgent that I couldn't wait until tomorrow."

I wanted to remind her that we'd agreed not to talk about all the things that ripped and clawed at us on a daily basis—our moms and dads, our indecision about college. But my ego got the best of me; I wanted to know what she said about me when I wasn't around.

"What did you say?" I asked.

Liv put her hand on my thigh and left it there. She had never done that before. Although I'd studied her hand hundreds of times, it looked different on my leg. A strange alien of a hand. I forgot what we were talking about. I tried to calm the erratic thump, thump, thumping below my waist, emanating out through my legs like hot wires. I wished that everyone in the world would disappear—the cashier, the drivers, Loose-Limbed Linda, my mom, Liv's mom, Katrina, our team, everyone. Although I wasn't sure what I would do with all that freedom.

"Well, I couldn't very well say you, now could I?" said Liv. And just like that, she removed her hand from my burning thigh.

Her mouth was curled into a hesitant smile. I forced a laugh a few beats too late. She flipped open her phone and snapped it shut without reading her messages, though I swore I caught the contact name "Dad."

I wanted to say something, but I didn't know what to say. All these words were available to me, and not one made any sense. A drunk guy walked by and catcalled us. I felt cheated; unlike me, he knew where to find words, the words *you* and *two* and *sexy* and *things* and *need* and *a* and *ride?* I gave him the middle finger, and Liv threw her near-empty cup at him. It was late and I was drunk. I needed to go home and cry.

5

FULL-COURT PRESS

Around November, this dude Lars started coming around the house. Like most other men, he liked lecturing me about basketball. Since he'd been staying over, our fridge and pantry had gotten fuller with whatever diet-trend shit my mom wanted: everything whole grain and low-fat and low calorie, no red meat. My mom spent less time with the checkbook and more time fawning over this man. One evening, I found an old jar of Marshmallow Fluff on the floor of the pantry and made myself a fluffernutter sandwich at the kitchen island while he monologued about my assist-to-turnover ratio, punching his Budweiser bottle toward the ceiling like a torch.

"Every turnover is a chance you don't get at the basket," he said.

He took a slug of beer, swishing it around in his mouth before swallowing it. I folded the Fluff half onto the peanut butter half and bit into it. With my free hand, I sifted through a stack of old recruiting letters my mom must have pulled out of the filing cabinet.

"Think about it," he said, tapping his stupid head with his beer. "If you turn it over and the other team scores a three-pointer, you're actually down six points. Since you missed out on a potential three points for your team."

My mom appeared at his side, rosy-cheeked and chemical-happy. I assumed she'd come to save me from my misery, but I was wrong—she immediately started telling me how she'd spent many a night manifesting Lars and could I believe that now here he was, in the flesh? I wondered how much of this man she'd wished for: Had she manifested the filthy John Deere hat? What about his small, pinched mouth? The way his eyebrows disappeared halfway across his eyes? I knew my mother was hurting, which is why I continued to let this man feel important. She got on her tippy-toes and kissed his scruffy cheek while he took another drink. I noticed my mother was wearing a new necklace, one that looked fancy and expensive, the type of necklace my dad would have bought her when she was pissed at him for staying out too late or breaking the railing on the basement staircase. He never provided excuses for his blunders; there was a certain nobility in him standing there and absorbing her insults with the serenity of a monk.

My mom grabbed a stack of letters. "Did you hear Kyle Murphy committed to Lehigh?"

"Good for him," I said. I didn't give a shit about all the people who could sit back and relax now that they'd made a decision. My mom looked at the letters like they were one-hundred-dollar bills. I wouldn't have been surprised if she'd pressed her nose to them, taking that fresh money scent in.

She held up a letter for Lafayette. "Keep or toss?"

I shook my head. "Too close to home."

"Rude," she said, forming a discard pile. She held up Mount St. Mary's next.

"Too small."

"Snob."

Lars snorted, covering his mouth and nose with his fist. He finished off his beer and made his way past me to the refrigerator. He smelled like pollen and old milk.

"What about West Virginia?" said my mom, accepting a beer from Lars.

"The coach gives me the creeps."

"Okay, fair," she said. "Didn't he marry one of his players?"

I nodded.

"UCLA looks promising."

I told her I watched one of their games on TV and that the head coach, Coach Russo, seemed like a control freak—she didn't let the point guard make any calls herself. I didn't want to go anywhere where the coach was more of a puppet master than a collaborator.

She flipped through a few more, sorting them into her own system. Methodical as a dealer at a casino. Lars said something but I wasn't listening. I watched her deal the cards, mesmerized. The deck was stacked in my favor. But still, I was immobilized, staring down my April commitment deadline, not wanting to choose. I guess I was afraid of what was on the other side of that choice. What happened when the coach no longer needed to woo me, and I was just another player on the team fighting for playing time? For recognition? For the smallest scrap of praise?

Once my mom was done sorting, she looked up from her work to ask if I was sleeping over at Katrina's tonight. Lars poked her in the back, and she giggled, reversing a few feet to slip her arm around his waist. I tried not to imagine what they would do with a night to themselves, but still, I heard the distant saxophone notes of smooth jazz.

I took another bite of my sandwich and nodded. It was a beginning-of-the-season party that doubled as my birthday celebration.

"That'll be fun," she said, wobbling a bit. "Tomorrow we can have cake. Lars is picking it up in the morning."

"I don't need cake," I said.

"Of course you do," said Lars. "What kind of birthday would it be without cake?"

"The kind where I hate cake," I said. Truth is, I didn't want to celebrate my birthday without my dad around. I planned to spend the entire evening drinking his whiskey and smoking his cigars, his Sixers hat, stained around the inside, adjusted to fit my head. I might even venture into the garage to mess around with one of his precious guitars, though I figured lightning would probably strike me dead the second I threw the strap over my head.

"Mack," said my mom, head down, looking at me out of the tops of her eyes like she did when she'd had enough of my shit. "Do you have to ruin every good thing that comes your way?"

"I love you, too," I said.

I slung my duffle bag over my shoulder and grabbed the keys to my dad's junker that ran just well enough to get me to Katrina's house. The radiator was just about shot, and it tended to overheat if you drove it more than a few miles. I didn't want to spend one more second with the drunken lovebirds.

"You and that car," my mom said as I was halfway out the door. "You're just begging for your father to come back and haunt us all."

I smiled at the thought. My father had been very private about his car. No one had been allowed to touch it, let alone drive it. He'd saved up to buy it in high school, was very sentimental about the whole thing. My mom had tasked me with cleaning it out so we could sell it for some spare cash, but I hadn't gotten around to it yet. Plus, we'd have a better chance of paying someone to take it off our hands than selling it. Either way, I liked being among his things. His stupid air freshener in the shape of butt cheeks. His Warren Zevon cassette tapes. A high school championship trophy. He never even drove the thing, just used to sit in the car out in the driveway, smoking his cigars and listening to his tapes.

With just a little trouble, I started the car up and backed out of the driveway. Liv and her mom had moved to a neighborhood over from us, just on the edge of the school district line. Close enough that we no longer had to settle for midnight phone calls; we could meet up in person. We'd lie on the grass in my yard and look at the sky and pretend to give a shit about the stars and which constellations looked like which animal or piece of cookware. We sometimes stole George W. Bush signs off of people's lawns. Don't get me wrong, we weren't political by any means, but we knew enough to know he was one of the bad ones.

I pulled up to Liv's house, which I realized I'd never seen from the inside, and saw her waiting in the window of her bedroom. She disappeared from view and a few painfully long seconds later, she spilled out of the front door. Standing on the porch, her eyes locked with mine then she broke into a jog. She ran through the lawn, kicking her mother's Bush sign down, both of us knowing she didn't have the guts to actually take it. Her eyes looked like asteroids in the night, coming right for me. I didn't care if that made me a dinosaur destined for extinction; I welcomed the devastation.

She opened the back door and tossed a duffle bag into the back seat, bottles clanking against each other like wind chimes. In the front seat, she slipped off her white-and-blue Jordan 4 Retros before putting her feet up on the dashboard. I did the same with my left foot.

"Time to get fucked-up," we said at the same time.

"Same brain." We smiled, our voices blending into one.

We didn't say much on the drive to Katrina's. We bobbed our heads to the radio, we sang when we knew the words. We wiggled our toes, we cracked our ankles, we examined our legs, the hairy spots we'd missed while shaving. We punched the ceiling when we squeezed the orange through a light. We signaled for a truck driver to honk his horn once, twice, three times. We smoked a Black & Mild, filled the car with milky smoke. We felt young and old, both new and used.

About a mile from Katrina's house, my (and my mom's) phone rang. It was a number I didn't know, a Washington area code. I answered, and a woman's deep, throaty voice introduced herself as Coach Harris, the assistant coach of Gonzaga. I'd never spoken to her before; the head coach, Coach Adams, had been the one who'd called to offer me a scholarship. My breath froze in my chest, my ears grew hot; I got nervous talking to coaches. I wanted them to find me charming and interesting, more delightful to talk to than the other teenagers they were fated to call. Liv mouthed, *Who is it?* and I waved her off. She shrugged and started tossing her phone back and forth between her hands, though I noticed her forehead vein was throbbing like it did when she was trying to stifle her feelings.

"Sorry, I couldn't hear you. What did you say?" I asked. Already, the steering wheel was slick with sweat. On the sidewalk, a man and woman walked hand in hand, looking miserable.

"I was just calling to wish you a happy early birthday." It sounded like she was driving in the rain.

"Oh," I said. "Thanks."

"And well, just wanted to remind you that we'd love to have you join our team next fall."

I didn't say anything; my heart bucked inside my chest.

"No pressure, just something to think about," she said, clearing her throat. "Doing anything fun to celebrate this weekend?"

I figured it wasn't really cool for me to say I was going to a party, so I told her I was going to my teammate's house for a sleepover.

"Well, that sounds like a nice time."

"Yeah," I said.

Sweat dripped down my sides, wetting my T-shirt. I wasn't sure what else to say.

"Well, I don't want to keep you. I'm sure you have better things to be doing with your time," I said. I wasn't being self-deprecating; I thought this must be the worst part of the job: pretending to care about a teenager's life—birthdays, proms, high school games, what movies we've seen, what our favorite classes are.

"To be honest, my life is pretty boring," she said. Her windshield wipers squeaked in the background.

"Boring enough to call a seventeen-year-old on a Friday night?"

She laughed. "Well, when you say it like that."

Her laugh, which was warm and sounded genuine, immediately endeared her to me, made me feel like she might be the type of coach I could rely on. I glanced at Liv, who had unbuckled her seatbelt to retrieve a bottle from her bag and was now taking big swigs out of the Bacardi Razz bottle.

"Mine's pretty dull, too," I offered.

"Maybe I'll get some houseplants," said Coach Harris.

"Make sure to talk to them a lot," I said. "I read that affection helps them grow."

Coach Harris laughed again. "I got you, Morris. I got you."

Liv looked at me like I was insane then signaled for me to wrap up, we had places to be. Coach Harris told me she'd let me go, but she would make sure to keep my advice in mind. She sounded like she really meant it, like she was going to go out first thing tomorrow to buy the most pathetic-looking plant she could find in order to talk it back to life. I hung up the phone and pulled onto Katrina's street, which was lined with the biggest houses I'd ever seen in real life. I told Liv who had called. She stiffened a little before responding that they hadn't called her since offering her.

"They probably just don't want to be up your ass," I said.

"Yeah, probably," she said.

Not wanting to deal with any more calls, I stuffed my phone into the glove compartment and we headed toward Katrina's house. Liv said she could never get away with leaving her phone anywhere, that sometimes she felt like her mom's husband.

"That's me, husband Liv, reporting for duty," she said, saluting me before entering through the front door.

We followed the music through the foyer and down the stairs to the basement, the bass filling up our bodies. I thought about how badly I wished my mom would call me. I wanted her to worry. To ask me how I was doing. She never did that. Instead, she left me little notes around the house. Things like *Depression is merely a symptom of spiritual imbalance,* or *When you're feeling alone, look within.* Sometimes she included a crystal. Turquoise for this, quartz for that. The depression note, along with its siblings, the anxiety and anger notes, annoyed me more than the rest—they told me that my mom suspected I was going through it but wasn't going to do shit about it.

It was clear everyone at the party was already a few drinks in. Katrina's freckled face was flushed, and she wore a goofy, uninhibited smile. Aaliyah, our center and only teammate with an ounce of melanin, yelled my name and told me to play catch-up. Bree, who looked like a bull with braces, all muscle and nostril flare, announced that the birthday bitch had arrived. Liv smiled at me, happy, I thought, to be by my side.

A handful of pathetic balloons bobbed in the corner of the basement. From the mantel, a half-fallen HAPPY BIRTHDAY sign dangled by the *H.* The TV in the background played a rerun of *The Real World,* a bunch of drunk people arguing in the kitchen of their house over sex, and laundry, and rumors. Our team sat in a circle on the carpet, ready to start a game of King's Cup. Through the speakers, a rapper bragged about his fat-ass hoes and cash flow while our white-ass team bobbed their heads. Katrina leapt to her feet and hugged me, her breath warm and spicy. Ignoring Liv, she told me the good stuff was behind the bar. Liv handed me her Bacardi Razz and joined the circle, knowing I'd make her a drink.

"My parents said they don't care what we take as long as we don't water it down after," Katrina explained. "That would be a cardinal sin."

Her parents were on a weeklong trip in the Catskills, where they had a cabin. They were both lawyers, not the good kind but the kind that made good money. They had the biggest house of anyone I knew, the nicest cars, the most extravagant vacations. Before my dad died, I never thought too much about money. We had food and clothes and a home, and we could afford for me to play AAU. Of course, I knew Katrina's family had more than most, but what that meant for me was that I got invited down the shore with them and didn't have to pay for anything, not even our seafood dinner. Now I understood how much power money held, that it could turn my mother into the type of person who falls for a man like Lars if it meant not having to change her spending habits.

I grabbed two red Solo cups and crouched behind the bar, examining the bottles as if it mattered one way or another whether I drank the good stuff or the waste at the bottom of the barrel. I decided to go with bourbon. Something about the golden caramel color was inviting. I filled my cup to the halfway mark then topped it off with some Cherry Coke. I sniffed it, gagged, then took several large, burning gulps before making Liv's Bacardi Razz and Sprite. I joined the circle, which looked suspiciously like an Abercrombie & Fitch advertisement. I was in my usual sweats and T-shirt and hoodie, hair rolled up in a bun—same with Liv. Baggy clothes made me feel most comfortable.

I sat down between Katrina and Liv, passing Liv her red cup. She thanked me with her eyes. I felt as if we'd been together for several lifetimes already, that this was just what we did, make each other drinks. Cards were spread in a circle before us, face down, with a red Solo cup in the center. After several chugged drinks, the gossip began: who was pregnant, who'd been to the abortion clinic, who was sleeping with their best friend's boyfriend. Then Katrina brought up Cathedral Catholic, our longtime rival.

"You know," she said, smiling around the circle, "I heard some stuff about Dani."

"What stuff?" I asked. Dani was their point guard. She had short curly hair that flopped when she ran and a face like Peter Pan.

"I heard she's dating that Kelsey girl on her team."

I glanced at Liv. She sipped her drink, seemingly uninterested. I felt lightheaded and my face started to go numb, the tingling starting at my neck and working its way up to the crown of my head. All the things in the world to talk about and we'd landed on this.

"The one with the perfect ponytail?" asked Bree.

"Yeah, that one," said Katrina.

"I don't know these people," said Liv.

"But I thought Kelsey was fucking Marcus?" said Aaliyah.

"Oh, yeah, she totally was," said Katrina. "But I'm just saying what I heard."

"What's it matter who she's into?" I asked. Katrina tilted her head at me as if it were the first time she'd laid eyes on me.

"Well, I think it's gross," said Bree, staring right at me.

A tense, stormy energy swirled around the circle. Everybody drank their drinks. I looked around at all these people I'd known most of my life. It occurred to me that I didn't even really like them. They were selfish and shallow. And yet, I felt attached to them. Maybe it was nostalgia. I'd known all of them since we were kids and I wanted to hold on to that. Strangely, I felt a softness toward these people, even the mean ones. I knew their struggles, their aches. I knew Bree wasn't comfortable dribbling even though she was a guard. She could rebound like hell but once she pulled it down, she panicked, looking around for an outlet, and I liked to be that for her, able to quell the panic.

There wasn't anything like being a part of a team. Moving through life as one big amoeba. The sacredness of it. They were just around. In classrooms, cafeterias, hallways, at practices, spaghetti dinners before games, games, postgame dinners at Applebee's. There was always someone to laugh with, someone to make fun of for being a dumb fuck. The way I saw it, at least as far as I can remember, was that fucked-up community was better than no community.

Bree's twin, Sam, broke the silence and said she'd thought Dani was checking her out last season. On defense, she said, Dani had a tendency to press her hand against Sam's hip for a bit longer than she was comfortable with. Katrina agreed that that had happened to her, too—she was sure of it.

"What can I say? Boys *and* girls like me," said Katrina.

I rolled my eyes and shoved Katrina's shoulder, toppling her into Aaliyah, who shoved her back toward me like a pinball.

"In all seriousness, though," said Bree, "I don't really want someone like her touching me."

Most everyone nodded along, though Aaliyah did tell Bree to chill out. When Katrina glanced at me to check if I agreed with the room, I granted her the smallest of nods, hoping Liv wouldn't see. I watched Liv get up to make a new drink, grabbing my empty cup on her way over to the bar. It seemed like the moment had passed but then Bree pushed on the tension like it was a new bruise.

"What about you, Liv? What do you think?" she called across the room.

Liv took her time pouring our drinks. Once her cup was full, she took a few sips then leaned her elbows on the bar and drank. There was that vein again.

"Yeah, you've been quiet," said Sam.

"Ignore them," I said.

Katrina snapped her head in my direction and asked what got up my ass, they were just having some fun. Maybe it was the look of betrayal on her face or maybe it was my fear of giving myself away, but I whispered, "You already know I think Dani's disgusting." She raised her eyebrows and smiled, satisfied. I don't know why I'd felt the need to please her so badly. I felt dirty for having said it, cloaked with a film of shame. I nearly forgot Liv was there until she spoke up at last.

"I think I'd be more concerned with getting my ass off the bench if I were you."

It wasn't clear if she was talking to Bree or Sam, but it didn't matter, neither one played very much, and Liv knew that because I'd told her so when I gave her a rundown of the team. The room stopped its chatter, everyone wide-eyed and waiting. I concealed my laughter with my fist. Katrina grinned like a crazed puppet master. Aaliyah shook her head, eyes in her cup. Bree cleared her throat, took a long sip of her drink, and gave Liv a venomous glare. Sam was beside her, arms folded across her chest, acting all tough.

"Didn't know you were such a fucking dyke, Cooper," said Bree.

"We should have known, though," said Sam. She glanced around the circle. "I mean, have you seen her walk?"

Liv rolled her tongue around in her mouth, fighting a wicked smile. She came out from behind the bar, and I stood up to meet her. She handed me my drink, our hands briefly brushing over each other.

"You can tell that to my boyfriend when he gets here," said Liv, raising her eyebrows.

Splitting the world in two, Liv opened the sliding glass door and headed outside to the back patio. I couldn't help but follow her; I wanted to soak up every second with her before the guys showed up. I pulled up the hood of my sweatshirt, which tented over my face, then plopped down on a patio chair and dug a dime bag and bowl out of my pocket and started packing it. Liv sat down and watched me, not saying a word.

"You okay?" I asked.

"You going to smoke that whole thing yourself?" she said, gesturing to my bowl.

"It's okay to be upset," I said.

She shrugged, looking anywhere but at me, her eyes blinking real fast. I decided to give it up. Once I was done packing the bowl, I took a hit, the sizzle of the blue-orange flame tickling my brain just right. I tried to forget about what had happened inside: the targeted cruelty, my shame on top of shame, my guilt at having said what I said to Katrina. But it was no use; all the bad feelings, they stuck to my ribs like mashed potatoes on Thanksgiving.

"Pass it here," said Liv, holding out her open hand. I looked at her, slow to decide on which snarky remark to make. "Or," she said, "we could just cut out the middleman and shotgun."

She left the comment there for my taking but I didn't bite. I still didn't trust that my eagerness wouldn't later be used against me if she decided to pull an Alex and end our friendship. My mom had told me my silence would serve me well, and although I'd thought it was just one of her stupid throwaway phrases at the time, now I thought maybe she was onto something, that she knew more about me than she let on. Silence was only good, I decided that night, as long as it helped you keep the lie going, even just a little while longer.

"I hear you get higher that way," Liv said to the towering syca-mores lining the yard. I imagined her backpedaling to get back on defense after a missed jumper.

I drank my drink and pressed the weed down in the bowl with the end of my lighter, focusing all of my energy on arranging my face into the kind of face that wouldn't betray me.

"Okay, fine," I said, eyeing Liv.

I took a slow hit from the bowl then leaned in closely. Liv met me halfway, pushing my hoodie back off my head as she did. Our lips were mere inches from each other. Our eyes a dreamy half-closed. I blew the smoke into Liv's mouth, and she inhaled, lips slightly parted, eyes still half-shut, allowing the smoke to fill her. We opened our eyes and stayed perfectly still, each of us daring the other to go the extra inch. Tight-chested, I watched the wind hassle the hair around Liv's face. I thought about pressing a thumb to the birthmark on her chin, and what it might mean to smother a tornado. I wanted to know what Liv wanted, where she thought this could go, if any-where. But Liv broke the moment in two like a wishbone.

"I stole something for you," she said, grabbing my forearm, hard. It hurt a little, but I wanted more of it, forever. When Liv released me, I rubbed the spots where her fingers had gripped me. "Jericho should know better than to leave them lying around their gym un-attended," she said, smiling. When Liv was proud of herself, she couldn't hide it.

Out of her pocket, she pulled a piece of paper, which had been folded several times so it was no larger than her palm, and handed it to me. Her eyes were bloodshot and droopy.

"Is this what I think it is?" I said.

"Happy birthday," she said.

I unfolded the paper and saw that it was Jericho's scouting report on our team, which they would use to prepare for our upcoming game against them, the season opener. It detailed every play, every defense, and every player's stats, tendencies, strengths, and weak-nesses. Under normal circumstances, I could never really know what the other team's coach had written about me, what they were instructing their players to do. As a player, you could get an idea come game time, that is, if your opponent actually stuck to the coach's plan, but still, it was only an idea. I don't know about anyone else, but for me, there was a perverse pleasure in being handed a scouting report and being told *This is how someone else sees you.* Maybe that was because I was suspicious of compliments given directly to me; I never trusted that people actually meant what they said, that they didn't have some ulterior motive. But a scouting report, well, it was unfiltered; it was never meant to get into my hands. That's how I knew I could believe it.

I looked up at Liv, smiling. She'd given me an irreplicable gift.

"I know you like to be one step ahead," she said.

I read over the scout, absorbed the nice shit about me, my speed and craft, my spectacular court vision, my leadership and intellect. I took another hit while I read, was slow to blow the smoke out. I was so high my limbs felt loose, like someone had taken a wrench to my joints. The last line on the scout was an instruction for whoever was guarding me to stay a few steps off of me, to force me to beat them from the outside.

"According to this guy, my three-pointer is inconsistent?" I said, laughing, the weed a soothing balm.

"That's a load of horseshit," said Liv.

"Either it's all true or none of it is," I said. "Can't pick and choose which parts to believe."

Liv thought on this. She held her hands out in front of her, maybe nine or ten inches apart. At first I didn't understand what she was doing, but then I realized her fingers were gently curled around an invisible basketball. She bounced it a few times next to her chair then shot it into the night sky, which swallowed the ball. Now, an invisible sniper gun in her hand. She aimed at the tops of the trees and pulled the trigger.

"Not everyone can be a sniper like me, though," she teased.

"Wow, humility looks really good on you," I said.

"I'm not sure it has to be all-or-nothing," said Liv.

I waited for her to continue but she messed around with the lighter, flicking it on and off. We were silent for a while, the night sky our distraction. The stars hung there like gold medals around the necks of champions. Hues of reds and yellows and browns covered the lawn, the leaves not yet shriveled memories of themselves. I got this crazy idea in my head, just for a second, that this yard belonged to Liv and me. I really believed it. Thought how nice it might be to rake with Liv and then ruin the piles, disappearing beneath the leaves.

We drank our drinks. I took a hit then passed the bowl to Liv. She breathed in deeply, holding the smoke in her lungs for a few seconds before releasing it. Even high, her jaw was wound tight like a spring. She asked if I wanted to know something, something no one else knows. I said sure, immediately thrilled by the intimacy of a secret. Inside the house, our teammates drank and laughed and talked about boys. ("See, I knew you gave him head that day in the locker room.") The sliding glass door a divider between two worlds.

"I'll never forget the last thing my dad said to me before he left for good," she said.

Then she told me how he'd been sitting on the living room floor, flipping through a box of videotapes, each game labeled by opponent and date. She thought he was going to try to sneak out with some, something to tether him to his old life, she guessed. Late at night, she'd often found him watching her old games, on his third or fourth whiskey. But he didn't take any with him. Instead, still fingering the videotapes, he asked if she remembered some game where the other team, thinking she couldn't use her right hand, had forced her right and how pissed off she'd been. Didn't matter that she'd proven them wrong with a few hard drives—she was mad on principle. ("You get it," she said to me.) Of course she remembered, she told him. He laughed and got to his feet, squinting at her like he was trying to find the right setting for his eyes.

"Then he said, 'Liv, if you had to scout yourself, how honest would you be?'" She paused. "Who says shit like that?"

I wondered what he had been getting into that brought about this pathological self-awareness—even in observing himself, he knew he would omit vital information. I hated that I knew exactly what he meant, how he must have felt when he lied to himself.

"He was ashamed of something," I whispered.

"You could say that," said Liv, flicking on the lighter and running a finger through the flame. "He broke my mom's heart. Now it's in three pieces: one for me, one for school, and one for God."

"And none for her," I whispered.

We made eye contact. I wondered if she, too, was recalling our almost kiss. And if she was, what feelings it was stirring in her.

"Hey," said Liv. "What did you say to Katrina in there?" She nodded toward the house.

"I don't remember," I said.

Liv squinted at me. "Sure you don't," she said.

Just then, Katrina opened the sliding glass door, dissolving the two worlds into one.

"Boys are here," she announced. "Liv, I had no idea your boyfriend was so—" And then she brought her pointer finger to her tongue and made a sizzling sound as she pretended to put out a fire. Liv offered Katrina a Michael Jordan shrug then apologized to me with her eyes. I deliberated for a second before finishing my drink and following Liv inside.

A herd of drunk basketball boys from Ekron, St. Patrick's, and Nazareth galloped down the stairs and joined the party, each finding a mate. I watched Liv collide with James, handsome James, who had somehow escaped any teen awkwardness, giving him a long, hard kiss on the mouth. I grew dizzy and hot all over, a numbness speeding down my face and neck. I felt as if I had left my body and was now watching myself from a distance, floating just a few feet over my right shoulder. At one point, I even turned around to check if I hadn't actually evacuated my body, free of earthly limitations like gravity and pathetic yearning.

Liv was performing, I told myself. She was putting on the performance of a lifetime, for the team, for James, for her mother, who was not there but might as well have been.

A player I only vaguely recognized greeted me several times before I heard him. He had disturbingly straight teeth and thin, chapped lips that didn't cover his gums when he smiled. He looked me up and down, making me feel self-conscious about my baggy sweats. I didn't necessarily care about attracting boys, but I did want to feel attractive to anyone who happened to be looking at me.

"Trevor," he said, giving me a nod. There was something about his mannerisms that was practiced, something cultivated, like he was performing the only idea of masculinity that he knew, but something told me if he quit the act, he'd be softer, with a feminine feel to him. I didn't believe he was hitting on me because he wanted to but because of some ideal he'd bought into.

"I'm on my way out," I said. I dipped under his arm and stormed out of the party and up the stairs, leaving him to only guess what he could have done wrong.

I couldn't wait to get home and feel bad for myself in peace, but I couldn't get the car to start. There I was, twisting the key as far as it would go and fucking with the steering wheel, trying, desperately, to put some space between me and the version of Liv that I never wanted to see again.

I opened the glove compartment to grab my phone and out fell a photo I'd never seen before. In it, my father was a much younger, trimmer man with a full head of curly hair. He was wearing bell-bottoms, a blue tie-dye T-shirt, and a matching headband to hold his hair back, his Fender hanging across his waist, cigarette between his lips, and each arm around a beautiful woman, one kissing his cheek and the other gazing at him with some combination of lust and admiration. In the background were two dudes sticking their tongues out, one giving my dad bunny ears. An artifact of his before times, the ones without the white picket fence and a disposed-of dream, without a kid and a wife who demanded his attention, demanded he let go of the past, as a favor, as an act of love. The ones before he was straddling two lives, never fully in either one. I wondered why he kept this picture, of all pictures. Though he looked drunk and happy, it was the sort of compromised, complicated happiness that accompanied an emptiness you could sense but never quite name. I folded the photo once and slid it into my pocket before ditching the car at Katrina's and walking home.

6

TIE-UP AFTER TIE-UP

"**U**rgency, urgency, urgency," I said, giving Liv a shove with every word.

It was our first game of the season and we were waiting in the hallway for the JV game to finish up. Jericho had always had a good, tough squad; I already knew it would be a physical game. Behind us, our team was lined up, ready to burst through the double doors onto the court, where the humming crowd waited for us.

"Patience," said Liv.

She absorbed the blows but didn't throw any back. Everyone gets hyped-up differently. Liv's pump-up was internal; mine needed to live in the physical world. I needed to feel muscles popping, hands punching, feet dancing. Liv closed her eyes, and I knew she was picturing the ball going in the hoop, the score for the home team climbing with every bucket. It was something Coach Puck said to do: visualize ourselves performing exactly how we want to perform. That shit didn't work for me—every time I closed my eyes, I saw my dad in the ground, banging on his coffin; my mom cuddling up to Lars like all was right in the world; Liv and James colliding in a feral, teeth-first kiss.

"Patience is necessary, yeah, but urgency is what separates the good from the great," I said.

I moved on from shoving Liv and started bouncing my fist off the wall. Liv opened her eyes. She watched my hand generate kinetic energy. My face, I knew, was already red; my ears burned. I pressed them one at a time against the cool tiled wall.

"What the hell are you doing?" Liv laughed.

"My ears get hot when I'm nervous."

I looked away, down the hall, and focused my eyes on the Hornet mascot doing cartwheels by the water fountains. I couldn't stop thinking about how good Liv looked in her uniform, how the cut of the jersey accentuated her shoulder muscles.

"Aw, someone still gets nervous?"

"Fuck off. Don't pretend you don't."

"You know, urgency can quickly turn into carelessness," said Liv. She shifted the ball from under her right arm to under her left.

"No, no," I said, pulling away from the wall. "That's not urgency. Urgency is control, you know. Determination."

"Is it, though?"

Liv was smiling now, studying me. She loved to probe, and I welcomed the investigation. The night before, she'd called me an exposed nerve of a person, all frayed edges and jumping sparks. I grabbed the ball from under her arm and shot it into the air to myself.

"Just have one look in Jordan's eyes," I said. "They're absolutely deranged."

"And that's a good thing?"

I gave her a look; she knew it was more complicated than good or bad, the dying for the game, the dying without the game.

"Look at McGrady," she said, snatching the ball out of midair. "He's laid-back and patient, lets the game come to him."

"You're kidding. He's so laid-back he literally falls asleep before game time."

She shrugged. "And he still gets the job done."

"He's never made it past the first round of playoffs," I said.

She shrugged again. "He's still my boy."

It was easy to forget there were other people in the hallway: the rest of the team, including Katrina, who stared straight ahead, both hands on her hips, every blond hair on her head perfectly hair-sprayed in place; Coach Puck, chewing his gum so hard he was bound to crack a molar; and our stat guy, Barry, a bald, heavily moled man wearing the uncomplicated smile of someone who simply appreciates being around the sport.

Coach Puck had already given his pregame speech, harping on communication, teamwork, and a will to win he didn't have any fucking idea how to teach (his words). His speech, I assumed, was what had prompted Liv to ask me which intangible quality I thought all the greats shared.

I bounced on my toes and cracked my neck side to side while Liv nodded along to the music playing in the gym, the warm-up CD of Nelly, Eminem, and Ja Rule that Bree had provided. I was nervous, but not for the usual reasons. For all of preseason, Liv and I had spent every practice memorizing each other's game-time tendencies: If Liv drove baseline, she was most likely going to kick it to the opposite corner; if I was guarded tightly by someone taller, I'd usually shoot a step-back jumper to create some space. We'd relished these moments of discovery, the split-second transition from not knowing to knowing. I was nervous, I suppose, to have the spell broken, or to find out there never was a spell to begin with, that it was nothing more than a delusion I'd conjured up.

"Patience tells you when to strike," said Liv. I loved that she refused to drop the subject; I could have argued with her well into the next life.

The gym doors opened, and we moved out of the way to make room for the JV team to pass by. We extended our hands so they could slap them on their way to the locker room, sweaty hair stuck to their necks and cheeks. I was okay until the new JV coach, this churchy guy with a dark brown toupee, trailed behind the team looking self-important with his clipboard and briefcase, not seeming to give a shit that he'd taken my dad's place. My stomach lurched and some vomit splashed up my throat. I swallowed hard to force it back down, then returned my attention to Liv.

"Like a rattlesnake?" I said. I shoved Liv a few more times, my hands landing just above her breasts each time.

"Yeah, sure," she said. "Like a rattlesnake."

"The two aren't mutually exclusive," I said. "The best players have both."

"Oh, how diplomatic of you," said Liv, smiling.

I shook my head no, my lips pressed together.

"But urgency always wins out," I said. "If you're too patient, you'll let an opportunity pass you by."

I let my words hang there like the prophetic bombs that they were, simultaneously knowing and not knowing just what those words could mean for us, that I was, in my own way, threatening her.

I held my hand out low, palm up, waiting for Liv to slap it. She studied it for a second before folding her hand into mine, not so much a slap as a slow-motion handhold, a question on the move. We looked at each other. I thought she must know; she must know my feelings—how could she not?

"Hey," she said, grabbing my wrist where my black hair tie was creating an indentation. "Aren't they going to make you take this off?"

"Nah."

"Plan on doing your hair a lot this game?"

She laughed and I rolled my eyes, not wanting to disclose how I used the hair tie to punish myself for my errors. Whenever I turned the ball over, missed a foul shot, or let someone score on me, I would pull the elastic band and release it, allowing it to snap against the thin skin of my wrist. I was on a quest for perfection. I would stop at nothing. Have fun, my mother always said. But what's fun about basketball? This is life-or-death, I wanted to say, a belief so juicy you can't help but sink your teeth into it, this is painful, disturbing admiration, it is blood on fire, body under fire. The game is a promise, a pact, a mouthwatering vow. It's no more fun than agreeing to be buried alive.

Over the loudspeaker, we heard the announcer introduce our team. With that, we pushed open the double doors and burst out of the tunnel and onto the court, met by a roar of applause and white-yellow lights so bright we felt like we'd just been born. The stands were packed. There was never much to get excited about in our town and now we had not one but two D-I prospects on the same team, even if we were girls and this was girls' basketball. It was reason enough to muster up even the smallest morsel of pride.

We ran the perimeter of the court, past the announcer's table, past Jericho's bench, and under their basket, where we pretended not to notice the smear of orange jerseys whipping through a passing drill, past the stands, past the shivering people stamping snow off their boots as they entered the gym. Once we returned to our side of the court, we split into two lines—a layup line and a rebounding line—and began a layup drill, an easy warm-up to get the blood pumping, the ball moving.

Standing in the back of the layup line, Liv and I scanned the stands, trying to spot college coaches. It was always nice to know where they were sitting. And not just them, either—everyone who said they'd be there. It was a pregame ritual, taking inventory of the stands and storing the coordinates of every notable person's location. A basketball game was, and always will be, part playing the game before us and part making sure we have someone to bear witness. It was, I realized, the first game I'd ever played without my dad in the stands. Wherever he was, I hoped he was at least betting on me.

Liv dribbled lazily between her legs a few times before going in for a layup, her hand smacking the backboard after the release. She jogged to the back of the rebounding line and scoured the stands. I knew she couldn't be looking for James; he had a game that night, too. Then I watched her gaze settle on her mom, one row behind our bench. A conspicuous silver cross necklace dressing up her Ekron zip-up. Posture like she had a rod through her spine. Liv gave her mom a small wave and her mom received it with a soft, grateful smile. Littered throughout the stands were various college coaches: Illinois State, James Madison University, Arizona State, Lafayette, UCLA, and Duquesne. No Gonzaga.

After warm-ups were through, the ref blew her whistle, and we jogged over to our bench, where we formed a tight huddle. The announcer boomed over the microphone, introducing both teams and the starting lineups. When my name was called, I leapt off the bench into a low crouch and made my way through the tunnel of my teammates, arms extended on either side to rapid-fire slap their hands. Once I emerged, Liv stepped forward and met me in the open court, where we jumped, turning our bodies sideways, our shoulders colliding in midair. We bounced off of each other, grinning. I made my way over to the referees to shake their hands then returned to the line of starters.

More whistles and it was tip-off time. We billowed out onto the court. Liv's face, still scanning the stands, was twisted up with worry.

"You good?" I asked, giving her a small slap on her upper butt cheek.

"You know it," said Liv.

Everyone got into position around center court, hip to hip, shoulder to shoulder, knees bent, eyes on the ball between the two centers, held up by the ref like a serving platter. Then the ball was up in the air, and for a second, it seemed to float at the top of its path before coming back down, Aaliyah tipping it sideways to Liv, who immediately passed it to me, and we were off.

The first play down, I drove to the basket and spotted an opening on the block. No teammate there yet, but I threw a bounce pass into the empty space and Liv ran onto it for an easy two.

In a two-on-one fast break, Liv gave me a quick pass at half-court. I took two dribbles then returned it to Liv at the three, know-ing the defender would chase Liv out to the arc even if it meant giving up a layup. Liv knew this was what I was banking on, having watched Jericho's film with me, and I was right. The defender over-committed on Liv and Liv dumped it to me for a quick bucket.

Liv approached my defender and planted her feet, arms crossed over her chest, setting an on-the-ball screen, and her defender cheated out on me. Before I committed to using the screen, we made eye contact and Liv slipped to the basket. I fired a pass so hard it could have burned her hands on the catch. She took a power dribble then kicked to an open teammate, who hit a mid-range jumper.

Another on-the-ball screen from Liv, only this time I used the pick, having forced the defense to play honest. My defender went under the screen, leaving me some room to shoot, and remembering what the scouting report had said about my outside shot, I rose up and released the ball, knocking down the three.

I noticed a mismatch; a shorter defender had switched onto Liv, so I signaled for her to post up on the block. She got into position, ass in pelvis, and asked for the ball with her hands. I faked a high pass and stepped around my defender to make a solid bounce pass away from swatting hands. She faked one way then spun the other, finishing at the basket and absorbing the foul: and-one.

It was as if we'd been playing together our entire lives. We didn't even have to say anything; we knew when the other's blood was hot with fury. We were alone together; we were a crowd all our own. We were ethereal; we were of the world. We were untouchable; we were touching each other all the time, with every pass, every play, every time-out, every steal.

I still remember how I felt throughout that first game, when all of my suspicions about us and our chemistry were confirmed. That first game was a beautiful, transcendent dream, full of private conversa-tions no one else could intrude on. That's all it took: one game and I never wanted to play without Liv ever again. I just wished my dad were there to witness the magic.

By halftime, we were up by eleven points, too close for comfort. Jericho was aggressive and scrappy. Not overly talented but they made up for it with their physicality, with their willingness to run through screens and take charges. They fouled and they fouled hard. They had an endless bench of fast, aggressive players, and the coach was more than willing to use it. I shifted around on the locker room floor, my tailbone sore from an awkward landing. Liv smoothed Icy Hot onto her banged-up knees, the cool smell of menthol searing everyone's nose hairs.

"This was their plan," said Coach Puck, wiping the sweat off his forehead with a handkerchief. "Hit you so hard, you'll think twice about going in the lane next time."

We sat there, listening.

"Don't think twice," he said. "Fight that urge."

"Don't insult us," I said.

Coach Puck laughed his throaty smoker's laugh.

"I wouldn't dream of it. Now get the fuck back out there," he barked.

The second half was fucked-up. It was more or less no blood, no foul, the way playground basketball used to be played, only there was no jagged fence surrounding the court, no corner only the courageous players chased loose balls into. We continued to play a clean game, focusing on what we could control: execution and communication. Jericho pressed us all half, but we split the traps easily, baiting them into a false sense of security before attacking the seams. One time, I got too cocky and tried to split three defenders, one of whom picked me off. I chased her down the court and not wanting to send her to the line, ran under her, hoping to distract her. She made the layup, though, and before grabbing the ball out of the basket, I snapped my hair tie to remind myself to do better next time, to protect the ball like it was my baby. Liv caught me in the act, and at first she frowned, but then she brought her pointer finger and thumb to her own wrist, encircling it, rubbing the inside of her wrist with her thumb, as if feeling what I'd felt, as if to redistribute some of the pain to herself. I grabbed the ball and inbounded it and got it right back, coming down the other end, an imperfect general leading my team into battle.

I typically didn't pay much attention to the announcers during the game—they weren't important, they were mere connections between the game and the audience—but I couldn't block out their booming voices when they both screamed into the microphone, "And it's good! Count 'em both, baby." "Just a two-point game now, Ekron's lead, with just under three to go!"

I'd called forty-two, a play intended to get Liv an open three, then passed the ball to the left wing, cutting through the key to the other side, where I set a flare screen for Liv. Liv walked her defender toward the paint then backpedaled to the three-point line, going shoulder to shoulder with my screen. I was small, but I set solid screens, never shuffled my feet or leaned away from contact. People will say basketball isn't a contact sport, but that's because they think all contact must be brutal, insincere, and separate from sexual charge. Anyway, Liv's defender, instead of going around me, bulldozed straight through me, knocking me to my back, and the referee blew her whistle to call a foul just as the ball rolled off Liv's fingertips. When the net spit the ball out, we all looked to the ref, who signaled that the basket was good. I rose to a sitting position and threw my fists in the air. The crowd erupted, hundreds of voices in a chorus of "Yes, girls!" and "Let's gooooooooo!"

Jericho was in the double bonus, so I got two foul shots. I lined my right foot up with the basket and waited for the ref to bounce the ball to me. I shook the tension out of my arms, tried to relax my shoulders, take deep breaths. The first free throw was good, and without turning around to check if she was standing there, I reached my left arm backward, palm up, just as Liv stepped forward to slap my hand. She put a little something behind that slap, a little sting, and I wanted to turn around to check that everything was okay, but I knew I couldn't.

I missed the second free throw, my tired legs causing it to fall short. I snapped my hair tie to remind myself to do better next time. When we ran back down the court on defense, I got caught in Liv's searing gaze. I turned around to find what had upset her: the back of her mother's head as she stormed out of the gym, her handbag flapping wildly at her side, spilling its contents as it banged against her hip. She didn't stop, not even to grab her lipsticks, her mascaras, her compact mirror. Coach Puck glanced at her, then back at the game. I kept one eye on my player, one eye on Liv. I wasn't sure what had happened, but from what Liv had told me, it seemed there was only one person who could inspire such a reaction out of her mother, although I thought he'd stopped coming to games when they split.

We got a defensive stop, forcing Jericho to take a rushed shot. We came down with the ball and I signaled for a motion offense to burn some time off the clock, my hand raised above my head, moving in a circular motion. We moved the ball around the court with crisp, sharp passes, each of us cutting through the paint after the ball left our hands. After about thirty seconds, I passed the ball to Liv on the baseline then cut toward the basket, arms in the air asking for the ball, a decoy to distract the defense. I cleared out to the other side of the court to isolate Liv and her defender, who Liv could easily outstep any game. Liv jabbed left then stepped right, driving baseline to the basket, her drive strong and solid, prepared for contact, but when she took off, her feet springs beneath her, a second defender ran over and swept her legs out from under her, her body made horizontal in the air. No whistle, play on.

The defender who'd leveled Liv scooped up the ball and charged down the court on a fast break, one-on-one with Katrina. Liv popped up from the floor and took off, hot on her heels, hobbling just a bit from the fall. For some reason, my feet were stuck to the floor. I watched it all go down in a matter of seconds. The Jericho player shook Katrina just beyond the three-point line, then it was just her and the basket. Until a steamrolling Liv caught up to her at the last second, her long arm coming down on the player's shoulders in a swift downward chop. The skin-on-skin smack made the foul seem worse than it was; the sound stilled the stands. A few boys yelled "Ohhhh," and a woman, most likely that player's mother, screamed that Liv should be ejected from the game. The referee blew her whistle and grabbed her forearm, signaling a flagrant foul.

Liv hovered over the player rolling around on the gym floor. It was a challenge, anyone could see that. Try me, said Liv's face from above. The Jericho player sat up and got her feet under her, rising slowly to meet Liv's eyes. I could see the white-hot anger swelling inside Liv's chest. Her hands clenched into fists, which were practically vibrating with want, and I silently begged her not to go there, not to take a swing. I made my way over to her, breaking out into a fast jog, and just before she could use those fists, I wrapped my arms around her waist, pulling her several feet backward. Hugging her felt like hugging a speaker at a club, the bass of her body rattling my bones. I'd never seen her like this before: ripped apart from the inside out. She spun around to face me, and my hands were now spread across her midback, thumbs digging into her spine. Tears bubbled in the corners of her eyes. She tried to blink them away.

I didn't think about who was watching us, not then, not on the court, where intimate touch was not only permitted but encouraged: men spanked each other, held each other, even kissed each other on the cheek in the name of winning. Me, I wanted that touch to last forever, to leak into every other part of our lives. I wanted to leave my fingerprints on every moment of her body.

She looked at me with these *what now?* eyes. I pressed my lips to her ear and whispered, "Patience, Liv."

Her jaw flexed against my cheek.

"Patience, patience, patience," I said.

7

PICK AND ROLL

After the Jericho game, we waited in the McDonald's drive-through at Liv's insistence. A Big Mac was her favorite post-game meal. All carbs and fat and protein, she said. I didn't argue. Of all the fast-food spots, this was my favorite—I could fill up on dollar-menu McDoubles.

Once we got our food, Liv looked down at her sandwich then gave me a side-eye.

"Big Mack, that's my new nickname for you," she said, smiling.

"Yeah, I like that."

"What? Not Mack Daddy?" I asked. She punched me and I pretended not to be delighted.

We stuffed our faces, then went back to my house, where we played *NBA Street* and mixed some drinks. Allen Iverson broke ankles, Michael Jordan jumped twelve feet into the air, Shaq caught alley-oop after alley-oop. When it was Liv's turn, I urged her not to pick Kobe since he was a rapist.

"Okay, but you can't play with Jordan then."

"What's wrong with Mike?"

She made a dollar-bills movement with her hands, acting as if she were throwing ones at a strip club, though I assumed she'd rather become a nun than set foot somewhere with naked women who could smell the desire on you.

"It's just some gambling," I mumbled. "That's different."

"He pushed off, anyway."

"In '98? Oh my god, are we really doing this?" I said.

She raised her eyebrows, loving to antagonize me. What I didn't say: I want you to tell me MJ didn't push off, then knock me on my ass. Make me feel it everywhere.

I chugged down my drink then poured another. I thought I heard movement upstairs and realized I couldn't remember whether my mom was home or not. Then I figured it didn't matter one way or another. Thankfully, Liv dropped the conversation and made little "ooh" sounds for herself every time she made her little grainy player cross someone. Once we were good and drunk, I brought up the nickname she'd given me.

"So, what you're saying is, you like to eat me after a game," I said, like some kind of idiot. I didn't want to see her reaction, so I stood up to grab more sodas from the downstairs fridge.

"Gobble, gobble, gobble," Liv said, jumping up from the couch and pouncing on me from behind, her legs wrapped around my waist in an uncoordinated piggyback ride. She pretended to devour my neck, my cheeks, my earlobes. Why, I wondered, couldn't it always be this way? Just the two of us, simultaneously discovering and destroying the limits of intimacy as we knew them?

Less than twenty-four hours later, I sat on the toilet of her mom's downstairs bathroom and looked through a Bible I'd found in a basket beside the toilet, waiting for Liv to return with ice. I'd never even held one, let alone read it. I flipped through it until I found a passage marked with a sticky note: Luke 4:1–13. The gist of it was that Satan followed Jesus around the desert for forty nights tempting him with various things like turning stone into bread and hurling his body off the top of a temple. The last sentence was highlighted in green: *And when the devil had ended every temptation, he departed from him until an opportune time.* I closed the book, wondering what would be considered an opportune time to tempt someone.

This was my first time inside Liv's house. It felt weird, clinical. Everything in the bathroom was white and clean. It even smelled like a manufactured citrus scent. And the rest of the house was just as pristine, complete with countless photos of Liv looking nothing like Liv. Hair straightened, worn down around her shoulders, make-upped face and eyes, skinny jeans, and sparkly camisoles. A framed photo of Liv and James at what must have been junior prom, her dress so puffy it kept James at a distance. Liv's mom was absent from all of the photos, which gave the house a spooky feeling, like it was more shrine than home. Thankfully, her mom wasn't going to be back for some time, so I didn't have to become someone I wasn't in order to impress her.

Soon enough, a grunting Liv rammed into the half-closed bathroom door, the bucket of ice in her arms so heavy it nearly toppled her. She set it down next to the running bath.

"Were you planning on wearing your clothes?" said Liv.

I looked down at my Ekron basketball T-shirt and sweats and shrugged, rubbing my sore-ass knee. I wasn't going to get undressed until she did. Though normally I didn't give two shits about undressing in front of people, with her I felt shy.

"Strip," she said, sticking the tip of her tongue out between her teeth how she did.

I raised my eyebrows at her, indicating that she needed to follow her own demands. She nodded and slipped out of her sweatshirt. I pretended to make a study of the Bible while watching her out of the top of my eyes. ("Put that trash down, would you?") Off came her T-shirt and then her shorts. On her side was a California-shaped bruise, stretching from breast to hip bone, deep purple with a black border. Probably from when that Jericho player had taken her legs out.

"Happy?" she said, snatching the book out of my hands. "Your turn."

I stood and did as I was told, careful not to let my dad's groupie photo fall out of my sweats pocket, while Liv turned off the faucet and dumped the bucket into the tub, the ice cubes fizzling in the cold water. I'd taken to carrying his picture around wherever I went. Not out of any simple reason like comfort or love or even grief, but something more complex—a desire to understand how someone could bear to live their life with regrets. Why he would sabotage his dream career, his one passion, for the white picket fence he thought he was supposed to want.

"You were supposed to put the ice in first, so you would know how high to fill the water," I said.

Liv ignored me, instead investigating her body for more bruises. Through her sports bra, I could tell her nipples were already hard, I supposed in anticipation of the freezing water.

"Look, a new one," she said.

She pulled up the left leg of her spandex to reveal a gnarly bruise on her thigh. Looked like she'd taken a knee straight to the femur.

"I like it," I said, pressing on the bruise on my bicep to break up the blood beneath the surface. It felt good to initiate the pain myself. I glanced at Liv, who bent down and pawed at a floating ice cube.

"Remind me why we're doing this again," I said.

"Health and healing," said Liv.

"That's us, the beacons of health."

"Don't look at me like that," she said. "We'll probably do this every day in college."

Maybe it was the strangeness of the situation: the bright white tiles in the shower, the close quarters, the exposed skin, the prisms of sunlight shining in through the window, giving the ice cubes their golden tint, but I felt like nothing counted in here. That I could say or do anything.

"You mean when we go to Gonzaga together," I ventured.

Liv laughed but didn't say anything that would indicate she was leaning one way or another. I kneeled and stuck my hand in the water, quickly retracting it. A shiver traveled up my arm and down my spine, all the way to my toes. I examined my wet hand. It was suddenly the most interesting thing I'd ever seen. Where had it come from? Had I always had that tooth-shaped scar near my wrist? Were my wrists too skinny? Was my heart line too deep? I clenched then unclenched my hand several times, spreading my fingers out as far as they would go. They were big for my height and strong enough to palm an indoor ball for at least ten seconds. Stupid thing to be proud of, but I was anyway. When we first met, Liv said I had the hands for the job. As if she were my keeper. As if she had the power to take this opportunity away whenever she wanted. But I'd already had the job, would continue to have the job without her. I needed to remember that.

"Good old blue-and-white?" said Liv. "Thought the weather was too much for you over there."

"That's not what I said."

I'd been thinking more and more about Gonzaga lately, how it was 2,500 miles from everything I knew, everything Liv knew. I wanted us to go that distance together.

"Rain, rain, go away, come again when it's not game day," sang Liv.

"Good thing we play an indoor sport."

"People look for any excuse to not leave the house."

"The best one-two duo in program history might draw them out," I said.

I glanced up at Liv, who was looking off into space, a soft smile on her face.

"You're right, Big," said Liv.

I leaned on the edge of the tub and rose from my knees, examining the ice water once more. Ask me to take a charge or dive onto the floor for a loose ball, and I'm good, I got you, I'm the first one there, but this was some other shit.

"Both of us aren't going to fit," I said.

Liv rolled her eyes at me. When she spoke, her voice was higher, more maternal.

"This is our first vacation in twenty years," she said. "Don't you think you could at least pretend to enjoy yourself? I mean, did you ever think you'd live to see the Great Barrier Reef?"

I pursed my lips, determined not to reveal the pleasure I derived from Liv's spontaneous role-play. It was nice to pretend we were an old married couple trying to enjoy a miserable, overpriced resort.

"I suppose you're right," I said. "I can be a bit crabby sometimes, huh?"

"A bit!" said Liv. "Get your bony ass in the bath. I'll pour us some wine."

"If you insist."

"Is red okay?"

"Whatever you're having, my love," I said.

Liv furrowed her brow at the mention of love then scampered into the kitchen to retrieve some real or make-believe wine, I never knew what to expect with her. She returned with two wineglasses full of Coke and set them on the floor beside the tub.

"My mom doesn't keep alcohol in the house," she said, breaking character. "Thinks I'll steal it or something."

"Don't know what ever gave her that idea," I said.

"On the count of three, we go in together," said Liv.

We counted slow, drawn-out numbers then stepped into the freezing cold water, my whimpering drowning out Liv's low groan. Liv slowly lowered her ass into the water, speaking only to say, "Oh my god, oh my god, oh my god." In any other situation, she might have been having very good sex. Finally, she sat all the way down, her back pressed against the white wall of the tub, legs spread as wide as they could go to make room for me to stand between her knees.

My breathing quickened; I could feel every molecule in my body vibrating. It was stimulating, this freakish feeling of embodiment.

"Go on, sit," said Liv.

My feet had already gone numb, but it wasn't a pleasant lack of feeling, it was the type of numb that bites at you with its mad dog fangs. It burned like hell.

Liv reached up and grabbed both of my hands to stabilize me while I lowered myself into the water, inhaling sharply when ice hit belly. I squeezed my body between Liv's calves, my legs resting on top of Liv's, my feet tucked underneath her armpits. The water was an inch from overflowing and wetting Liv's mom's perfect rugs. I hunched forward so the faucet wouldn't poke me in the back, and I crossed my arms over my chest. I liked how my arms could disappear my boobs, flatten my chest until it was a boy chest, with boy pecs and boy contouring. I could pretend I was a boy who liked Liv, that all was normal and natural between us.

Liv leaned forward, curling both hands around my ankles as if I might float away otherwise. I tried not to stare at her body, but it was hard not to. Never had we been this unclothed together. It was all cutoffs and baggy shorts. High socks and high-tops. Now that she wore just a sports bra and spandex, I saw the shadowy V her cleavage formed, the deep indentation of her upper abs, which looked as if they were sitting on top of the water, the delicious place where shoulder met trap muscle, the crook of her neck I sometimes rested my head in, only when no one else was around to name what we were doing. We were so close, our body parts slipping and sliding over each other. I couldn't tell where she ended and I began. Maybe that's why I felt comfortable enough to bring up what I'd been neglecting to ask: if that had been her dad at the game the other night.

"Is that why your mom left all upset?" I continued.

Liv ran her finger along the tile beside her, her movements slow and deliberate, as if she were trying to coax something out of the wall. I immediately regretted asking the question, but it was already out there, and admittedly, my desire to hear the truth, at least in that moment, was stronger than my desire to placate Liv. She met my eyes and blinked slowly, confirming that yes, it had been her father.

"I thought you hadn't seen him in years," I said. Then quieter: "You know I saw him texting you, right?"

"You don't understand," whispered Liv, releasing my ankles.

"Make me understand."

She didn't say anything. I was pissed off; I didn't like being lied to.

"I bet he never even heckled you, did he? I bet he was the most supportive, sweet-hearted dad and you couldn't stand it. You couldn't take his kindness. I bet he never went on a bender or ditched you for a gambling spree."

She was calm when she said, "You don't know when to stop pressing, do you, Mack?"

I stirred the water with my hands, looked at my red legs. At least my knee was no longer killing me. No matter what I did, what I said, I could never figure out how to get things out of Liv. She was like a vault. Maybe that's why I loved basketball so much, because it was my way of getting people to do what I wanted them to do—I could poke holes in their defense, make them go right, make them collapse in the paint. I was in charge.

"More, more, more," said Liv. "You always want more."

I shrugged, not sure how to respond. Most people I was happy to never know. But.

Liv blinked her eyes rapidly, her eyelashes a wet blur. She reached over the edge of the tub and picked up her wineglass, bringing it to her lips. She handed the other to me.

"Cheers," she said.

We drank the soda, sipping it like wine. I told her I couldn't feel below my waist. Shifting back into character, she said that better not mean I wouldn't be able to *perform* later. She raised her eyebrows suggestively. I half choked on my Coke, not expecting her to mention my fake cock. Had I had any feeling in my body, I'd have surely felt a new pulse pick up in my groin.

Liv scooped an ice cube into her palm and brought it to my neck.

She asked me how that felt, if I liked the sting. My response was a reflexive moan, a craning of my neck, as if to say, *All over, touch me all over.* And my friend, my friend, my friend ran the ice from behind my ear down to my clavicle, following the lines my anatomy had drawn for her. Across my chest, to the other side, up to my jaw, where she settled into small circles, the ice melting under the heat of her hand. All the while, my friend's eyebrows knit together in concentration. This was art, this was creation. The same innovative play that results in the discovery of a new move on the court.

With the ice still pressed to my jaw, she leaned in and kissed me, her lips buttery and soft and dizzying. It was a slow, glacial kiss, our lips barely moving. We tasted the sweetness of the soda on each other. We stayed very still; we didn't dare break apart. We were married, would stay married for all of eternity, would die together, would have our ashes mixed together. We were afraid.

Liv pulled back, lowering the ice, and with a manic smile said, "Happy fortieth anniversary."

I said it back, the words sticky in my throat. My entire body had become one large palpitation. Liv's chest filled and emptied, filled and emptied; I could tell she was trying, and failing, to control her breathing. Her face looked clownish. I wanted to know if it was just Mr. and Mrs. Thompson who had kissed, or if we had, too.

Then we heard the front door slam. Liv looked toward the closed bathroom door, frozen. Footsteps traveled across the kitchen and through the living room, coming closer until they were just outside the bathroom, the shadow of feet creeping under the door. We held our breath. I knew, instinctually, that what we were doing was not going to be received well. Suddenly, I felt dirty all over. Like the piles of snow pushed to the side of the street by the morning snowplow.

"Liv, are you in there?" said her mom.

"Yes, Mom."

"I saw a car outside. Who's here?"

"Hold on."

I had never seen Liv panic this way; her face was drained of color, her eyes frozen, locked on the white tile of the wall. Refusing to wait another second, Liv's mom burst through the door. I hugged my knees to my chest, my chin resting in the crease between them.

"What is going on here?" her mom asked. She pulled her hair off her neck. Her mouth was twisted up in disgust.

"You look tired, Mom," said Liv, reaching for a towel. "Let me make dinner tonight."

"I said, what is going on in here?"

She looked from her daughter back to me, her eyes crazed, hands pressed together as if in prayer.

"Hi, Mrs. Cooper," I offered.

"Hello, Mackenzie," she said, her lips pursed, wrinkles framing her mouth like rays of a sun. "Can someone please tell me what it is I'm looking at?"

She looked from Liv to me once more. Liv hugged her knees, mirroring me.

"We're just recovering," I said. "Last night was a really physical game."

"Get out," she said, gesturing to Liv. "Now."

Liv stood, her body red like she'd been out in the sun too long, water dribbling off her thighs and stomach. Her nipples hard. Her mother handed her a towel to wrap around herself. She stepped out of the bath over the top of the wineglasses, drawing her mother's attention to them.

"What is this? A date?" her mom asked.

When no one answered, she turned to me. "Mackenzie, I think you should go home," she said.

"Yes, ma'am."

Her mom picked up the wineglasses and dumped the soda down the drain. The drain gurgling it up. She left the bathroom without another word, careful not to shut the door behind her. We heard her banging around in the kitchen. Pots and pans, the soundtrack of fighting.

"I'll have room service bring up another bottle," said Liv, gesturing to the empty wineglasses. Her voice was weak and shaky.

"Are you okay?" I asked. Liv looked at the ceiling and sighed, her body deflating.

"Please," said Liv. "Won't you just pretend for me?"

I took the towel and scrubbed myself down, the pink of my skin deepening into a dark red. But I couldn't shake the shame of being discovered. Her mom's intrusion reminded me that we were never really alone, that any privacy we had was a myth. Liv's mom kept at it with the pots and pans. Blood sloshed around in my ears. Liv stood a few feet away, dripping all over the floor, tiny puddles forming around her, her eyes on me. I don't know how long I stayed there, drying myself, running over the same areas two, three, four times. I needed to remove the filth before it sunk in for good. I tried thinking about college, all that I hoped it would be. Postgame interviews, games on ESPN. Teammates with girlfriends, maybe even teammates dating teammates. It didn't help; nothing did. I felt I was the only person in the world to ever feel this helpless. Eventually, Liv wrestled the towel away from me. My hands twitched; I wanted to reach out and slap her.

8

TIME-OUT #2

It was warm for a winter morning, the piles of snow in the parking lot shrinking like lovers under pressure, and Liv wanted to know why I didn't have a boyfriend. We were sitting on our bench outside 7-Eleven drinking coffee and smoking clove cigarettes, the bottoms of our sweatpants wet from dragging on the ground. I don't know who we thought we were. Old men in a movie, maybe. Liv even grabbed a newspaper and opened it over her crossed legs, flapping the stubborn pages several times before she got them under control. In the sports section, there was an action photo of her going in for a layup against Nazareth. It wasn't a flattering photo. Her mouth looked like a basset hound's flapping in the wind outside a moving car. Still, I wanted that mouth to bite and suck and mark me up.

"Guess it's better than no picture?" I said, blinking at the sky. It was this luscious, almost unbearable white. Normally, I wasn't much for actual seasons, fall, winter, all that, weather's weather—I was either in basketball season or not-basketball season—but lately, I'd been viewing the dying trees and icy roads differently; they meant time was running out. Four months and counting before my future was closed off forever; I had to make a choice, had to commit to a school and not worry so much about whether it was the wrong one or not.

She closed the newspaper and looked at me. "Answer the question," she said. She was moodier than usual, surly even, and not so much avoidant as absent. In her place was whatever sick, sad mess this town spit out.

"I don't know why," I said.

Her question struck me as inane, deliberately obtuse. It made me feel crazy. Had I imagined our kiss last week? Only an hour before, we'd been working side by side at Coach Puck's house, settling into the intimate silence of two people who have become enmeshed, whose boundaries had dissolved. And now I was trying to stifle this awful, gut-twisting suspicion that I couldn't trust myself or my version of reality, that my experiences existed in a vacuum I could never claw my way out of.

"But you're so pretty," she said, examining my face as if the winter light were playing tricks on her mind. Her voice trembled when she said it. I felt like I was talking to Liv's mom instead of Liv.

"Okay," I said.

I stuffed my hand into my pocket to feel around for the dime bag I'd brought along. Folded around it was the photo of my dad. I'd considered showing it to my mom, but I didn't want to hurt her even more than she was already hurting, didn't want to give her even more reason to wipe her hands clean of her late husband.

"I'm annoying you," said Liv, with a proud, stupid smile.

"Nah," I said.

"I am. You fidget whenever you're irritated but don't want anyone to know," she said. "Like you're trying to redirect the energy or something."

I didn't say anything, just fucked around with the photo in my pocket. Just like that, I'd forgiven her for her ignorance. I felt exposed. There was, and still is, a divine pleasure in having someone peel back all the layers and scoop out all the muck in order to get a good look at you. As egotistical as it is, I admit, I wanted to hear about myself, from someone who was always watching, always studying, always storing that information. Tell me more about me, I wanted to say. Go on.

"It's okay, I'm okay with annoying you," she said.

"Why?"

"Just am," she said, smiling, more softly this time. Then, "Do you not want a boyfriend?"

Now she was picking at the calluses on her palm, thick, rough bulges that had developed from lifting. Somehow, she seemed like the most fragile person I'd ever seen.

"No, I do," I heard my voice say.

I don't know why I lied, what good I thought would come from that. In retrospect, I think I felt that the more I lied, the closer I would inevitably come to getting at the truth, the truth that hovered between us like a half-court shot trapped in flight.

"Well, let's get you one then," she said. "Oh, I know. How about Trevor on James's team?"

"The guy from Katrina's?" Though I didn't like him, he seemed, at the very least, nonthreatening.

"Yeah, he likes you."

"He doesn't know me."

Liv waved her hand how she did. "You know what I mean. He wants to get to know you."

My phone vibrated and I welcomed the disruption. It was Katrina, wanting to know what I was up to, I should come over and watch MTV. I told her I was cleaning at Coach's.

She texted me back right away: *Are you sure?*

Yeah, why?

I just drove by you at 7-Eleven with Liv, but okay, she said.

I snapped my phone shut, knowing enough to know that nothing I said could pacify her. She was frustrated, and justifiably so; I'd been avoiding her more and more lately. Truth is, I just didn't have the energy to perform for her, to try to fit into her ecosystem and all that it entailed. Pretending to want to suck dick, pretending to be happy every time she invited guys to come crash our sleepovers. Not that Liv was much better company right about now.

I grabbed the pack of cloves on the bench between Liv and me and flipped it in my hand.

"Did you know we're smoking microscopic pieces of glass?" I said.

"Good," said Liv. Her voice was a little snappy, sharp around the edges.

"What good would a boyfriend do me?" I asked.

"I don't know," she said. "It's nice to be loved."

"What about loving?"

"What about it?"

"Is that part good, too?"

She lit a new clove and sucked on it hard. It made the satisfying sizzling sound that I was fond of. She craned her neck back and blew the smoke into the sky, then she adjusted the cigarette so she was pinching it between her pointer finger and thumb, holding it up in front of my face.

"Who knew little pieces of glass could feel so good?" she said.

Across the street, people spilled out of the mouth of the church and onto the lawn, squinting into the winter sun. I watched the churchgoers between hurried cars on the wet, salted road. Women clutched the arms of men, children ran in circles around each other, babies cried in their strollers and carriers. A little boy bent down and salvaged a snowball from the melting snow. He threw it at his mother, who pretended to be mad. Sergio, a guy I knew from typing class, shadowboxed with his little brother. No one seemed alone; everyone was paired off in one way or another. Even so, they all looked miserable, even the people holding hands, even the people kissing. I knew this wasn't unique to our town, I knew there were miserable people everywhere. It wasn't that I thought the rest of the world was happy,

I just thought the rest of the world might grant me opportunities for new types of misery. Things like going through my first real breakup with a girl, one who would kiss me in public and call me her girlfriend—I would have welcomed that novel pain.

I felt a sort of preemptive grief. Liv was going to leave me and there was nothing I could do about it. Not then, not there. I pulled the weed out of my pocket, packed my one-hitter, and took a quick puff. I offered it to Liv.

"You're going to get us arrested," she said, but she was already grabbing it out of my hand. Now I realize doing drugs in public was the whitest thing we could have possibly done, behaving as if we were untouchable, or rather, assuming we were, hardly giving it any thought. Guess it wasn't the only thing we were doing in plain sight assuming no one would catch on.

As soon as the smoke hit my lungs, I felt better. I wouldn't go so far as to say weed made me feel happy to be alive, but it made me happy despite being alive. I got rid of my cottonmouth with coffee. I glanced at Liv. She was jittering her knee and rubbing her hands together like she was trying to start a fire.

"You look like you're full of bees," I said, sticking my hand in my pocket.

She laughed and made a buzzing sound, pestering my face with her fingers. I thought about what parents might think if they knew Liv Cooper and Mack Morris, Division I–bound basketball stars, couldn't get enough of drugs. From what I understood, parents always thought athletes were straight edge, that we had too much to lose to risk it all for a few hours of escape. It was the only reason my mom didn't question Grayson wearing his drug rugs—he was on the basketball team and that was enough for her.

"What else you got in there?" she asked, nodding toward my concealed hand.

I made a big show of secrecy and after a few *come on, come on*s, I pulled the photo out of my pocket and placed it on my lap. She leaned over and examined it, only half-interested at first, but then she swiped it from my lap as if I'd shown her a picture of us in twenty years. Her hands shook as she looked down at it.

"What is it?" I asked.

She didn't answer right away. I watched her watch the passing cars, the people outside 7-Eleven. A trucker smoked while pumping gas, playing with fate. A leather-faced man pissed against the building. A goth girl, pale as sin, exited the store with an armful of Arnold Palmers. A small, cruel part of me hoped her mom didn't approve of who she chose to be. I wondered what Liv thought of these strangers, if she was hoping Loose-Limbed Linda, our mascot for all that was unselfconscious and unrestrained, would make an appearance again, if maybe this time she'd lead us in a chant about teamwork and then tell us how we were going about it all wrong.

Liv returned her gaze to me. When she spoke, her words came out in doomed little whispers. "That's my dad," she said. "In the background." She tapped the man giving my dad bunny ears.

"What?"

"Yeah."

I looked back at the photo. It was hard to tell what he really looked like, but they did share that same strong brow.

"I didn't know they knew each other," I said.

"Me neither," she said. She looked betrayed; she looked spooked. I didn't know what the hell was going on. Then I remembered Liv's mom had been at my dad's celebration of life, that that was how we'd met.

"Did your dad play an instrument?"

She shrugged. "I don't know much about his past, he and my mom got married really young. He seemed, I don't know, plucked out of a catalog or something."

"He from around here?"

Liv nodded.

"Mine, too."

I tried to make sense of it. Did they play music together? When was this photo taken? Where?

"I wish I knew their story," I said.

She grunted at me, messing with her hands in her lap. "A picture won't bring him back."

"Are you talking to me or yourself?" I said, pissed the hell off.

Her forehead vein throbbed, speaking for her lips, which wouldn't move. A week had passed since her mom found us in the bath, and I regretted it all, the ice bath, the kiss, giving her mother reason to despise me. Her mom had called my mom and told her she caught us drinking, I assumed because that was more straightforward and punishable than what she'd actually caught us doing, which I knew she had no sensible words for; it was more so something she'd sensed between us, something she feared. An inexplicable, unutterable gravity. My mom didn't care about the alleged drinking, though, she was too wrapped up in her new life and new man. But what bothered me most was, I felt I'd lost Liv, even when she was right next to me. I didn't want this version of her. This angry, reactionary version. The enmeshment, it was still there—her moods became my moods.

"Didn't know he could look so happy," she grumbled. "It's not how I remember him."

She stuffed the photo back into my hand. It had transformed; it was now a crumpled, dead thing. I took one last look at the picture, my dad acting like a ladies' man, her dad goofing off in the background, two young men full of reckless sincerity, full of unbridled hope, then tossed it into the trash. That's the thing about magic: it's only as good as it can make you feel.

"And this isn't how I want to remember you," I said before I could unsay it.

Instead of getting mad, she looked at me curiously and asked if she was going somewhere. I said yes, after senior year, weren't we both going somewhere? She peeled a big chunk of skin off a callus and placed it on her thumb.

"Make a wish," she said.

I closed my eyes and blew the piece of skin off her finger. There was hardly any wind that day, so it twirled to the ground like a maple seed pod, landing a few feet in front of us, and all I could think about was the fact that I couldn't even bring myself to wish for Liv, or, more accurately, was afraid to let myself wish for the person I actually wanted. I was, it seemed, afraid she could read my mind. How was it that I was at once feeling like I wanted this, her, too much, and that I was not allowing myself to want her at all?

"How do you want people to remember you?" Liv asked.

"As the best point guard the game's ever seen," I said without hesitation.

"What about when you aren't playing?"

"I'm never not playing."

She made this hmm sound, tipping the clove package upside down and tapping it, but nothing came out; we'd smoked them all.

"Man, we've got lonely lives, Big."

"Maybe so."

That seemed like the end of that, but I was afraid of what would happen if we stopped talking, if we accepted the loneliness of our lives without more of a fight.

"How do you want to be remembered?" I asked.

Liv stared at two men bent over scratch-off tickets, going to town with their coins. They were too far away for us to see their eyes, but I knew that as long as there were still numbers left to reveal, their eyes would be looking straight through those cards and into a future that, for now, didn't seem so out of reach.

"As someone who made people happy."

"You can't make everyone happy, though," I said.

"No," she said. "You can't."

9

SUBS OFF THE BENCH

Trevor drove us through some curvy mountainous roads that I didn't recognize while we waited for the ecstasy to kick in, some weird jam band on the radio, the heat blasting. I drummed my fingers on the back of Trevor's seat and examined his gold chain and long, floppy curls that might have fit in on a soccer team more than basketball. It was the type of hair you could only tolerate if you were already in love with him. Beside him, James was jiggling his legs and turning around to smile at Liv and me every few seconds.

It was my first time officially meeting James, having only briefly crossed paths with him at Katrina's party. I'd been putting off meeting him, and consequently, Trevor, but Liv had an answer for every one of my excuses. I didn't feel well—take some meds; I had plans with a friend—reschedule them; I had to get a lift in—then meet them after; I needed to study film—that is a want, not a need; I had to get two hundred foul shots up—shoot four hundred tomorrow.

I'd had some time to think since she'd asked about my dating life, and I now understood why Liv needed me to meet them both so badly. Liv was, on some level, feeling guilty about our kiss, and she could assuage some of that guilt by closing the gap between James's imagination and mine. Meeting made each other mortal. We could examine each other's weaknesses up close, whittle away at the desirable qualities until they, too, meant nothing. And Trevor, well, setting me up with him was proof she didn't want me. The question was, proof to whom: James and her mom, or herself?

Either way, I had no intention of going into this mess sober. Which is why I'd snagged some ecstasy from the skater kid in my English class the morning before. He was usually good for some E, Adderall, and coke, but acid or shrooms I had to get from Grayson.

"They should start using this shit in therapy," I said.

In the rearview mirror, I watched Trevor half giggle, half scoff, as if he couldn't decide who he wanted to be.

"No way," he said. "That would be crazy, right?"

He looked at James for approval, but James didn't react either way. It had only taken minutes with the two of them for me to realize that this was how their relationship worked. Trevor used his arrogance to cover up the fact that he moved through life with the uncertainty of a newborn deer, and he needed James there to guide him. That's why Trevor would never start at point guard. He'd be delegated to backup point guard for as long as he couldn't make a decision without consulting his boy.

"So," said James, turning around to look at me, "you're the famous Mack I've been hearing so much about."

"Sure, yeah," I said.

Liv leaned forward and punched him on the shoulder. "Stop being weird."

"I'm only talking." He turned to look at his girlfriend. "Can't I talk?"

"Only if you stop talking weird," said Liv.

"Is it so bad that I want to get to know the one who's been stealing you away from me?" he said, laughing nervously.

I couldn't help but feel a little bad for the guy. He was losing her, and he simultaneously knew and didn't know why.

James hadn't been addressing me, but I felt compelled to respond anyway.

I said, "I don't know what you mean."

I felt my jaw muscle tighten, my teeth start grinding. The drugs were kicking in.

"She never shuts up about your pull-up jumper," I lied. My heart was a quivering bird released into the wild for the first time. It didn't want freedom; it wanted to go back in.

James seemed satisfied by this and turned back around in his seat, the streetlights dancing on his face like a projector. In the back seat next to me, Liv lit a wine-flavored Black & Mild. The car filled up with smoke and no one said anything. Through a blur of smoke, I studied Trevor's long eyelashes while he turned to look at his friend. Even though his hair was dark, his eyelashes were light. He looked at James with a fearful sweetness, though James didn't notice—he was too busy reading aloud all the mundane signs we passed: two-for-one hoagies, today only. It seemed even the boys had anticipatory predrug nerves. I tended to like the predrug nerves; they made me feel like I was sitting in the locker room, head between my jittery legs, waiting to transform into a god for an evening.

Finally, Liv rolled down the window to ash her Black & Mild, but she didn't realize how hard you've got to flick downward when you're in a moving vehicle, and the embers flew back inside and bit my cheek.

"You can't take me anywhere," said Liv. She reached over and tried to wipe them off, instead smearing them all over.

When her hand met my skin, she let it linger there for a moment or two, and I thought, or rather, hoped, that Liv was reveling in the freedom the drugs would allow us. Maybe we'd even kiss again.

After ten minutes or two hours, Trevor pulled into a CVS parking lot and chose a space in the corner, under a huge tree that seemed to be reaching out for something. There were a few other cars in the parking lot, one of which, I noticed, had a decal: Calvin from *Calvin and Hobbes,* pants down, naked little cartoon butt showing, was peeing onto the word LIBERALS. He was looking over his shoulder, toward the observer, a mischievous smile on his face. I was rolling by then and I looked at Liv and saw that she was, too, her legs bouncing up and down and her teeth grinding themselves to a pulp. James and Trevor climbed into the back seat, splitting us apart.

James threw his arm around Liv's shoulder. "You feeling good, babe?"

"Yeah," she laughed, looking past his face and meeting my eyes.

It occurred to me that Liv and James, both dressed in baggy sweats and matching Air Force 1s, looked more like brothers than anything else. With her hood up, Liv could be just another basketball guy looking to get into some trouble with his boys.

"This stuff is strong," said Trevor.

"I told you you'd like it," I said.

Trevor looked me up and down like he had at the party—this time I was dressed in jeans and a tight tank top despite the cold—though I didn't feel like I was being appraised, more like he was imitating a male mating ritual, then raised his hand to high-five me.

"See, I told the guys that you were hot when you got done up," he said.

"That's not the compliment you think it is," I said, rolling my eyes.

James laughed and nudged his boy. "Don't even play, you thought she was hot looking like a dude."

As much as I told myself I didn't care one way or another what guys thought, his comment still hurt. Even now, years later, I still think of it sometimes when I don't have time to change after a game and end up going to the bar in sweats, hair pulled back in a bun.

"It was, I swear," he said, leaning toward me.

It was clear to me that this would be a pairing-off situation, that I was intended to hook up with Trevor while James and Liv hooked up beside us. So, we did that for a while, the jam band still playing. Trevor's lips were chapped, and his tongue was long and snaky. He smelled like Hot Cheetos and Axe body spray, and his hands made imprecise movements, sort of fluttering around my thighs and stomach like he wasn't sure what to do with them, if he even wanted to be doing anything with them. Another reason, I thought, that he'd never be a star player: I could tell his ball control wasn't great, like the wires connecting mind to hand were shredded. I hated everything about him, his mouth, his hands, his pointy elbows, his touch, his boring eyes, but I felt indifferent about making out with him.

At one point, I risked opening my eyes to catch a glimpse of James and Liv. James was nibbling at her bottom lip and making these awful little moaning sounds like he was going to cream in his pants. Liv's eyes were squeezed shut. She made no noise at all. I had been sure the boys would want to watch me and Liv make out—that's what boys always wanted girls to do, and yet, when the situation was primed for it, the boys seemed perfectly happy to keep us separate. Could they sense something between us they didn't want to uncover?

Liv looked at the clock and announced that only six minutes had passed since we'd parked.

"Wow, I just had the best time of my life in six minutes," said James.

He laughed with the confidence of a man who assumed he'd invented laughter and didn't care to fact-check. Without asking, he pulled a notebook out of my backpack and flipped to a random page then wrote *10:06* in Sharpie, circling it a few times for emphasis.

I said, "Yeah, we get it. Give it here."

I grabbed my notebook and Sharpie and signed my name in the dark before passing it to the others.

"Let's never forget this night," said Trevor. He gripped both my and James's thighs while he said it, connecting us through false promise.

The moment wasn't revolutionary. It wasn't even interesting. And yet, I would remember the weight of the cool night sitting on my shoulders for years to come. It felt like I was saying a million quiet goodbyes to myself.

It was clear to me that rolling was good fun for these guys. They weren't trying to escape their brains. How nice for them, I thought.

James and Liv gave each other a look and then announced that they were going to walk around CVS for a while.

"Want me to get you a soda or something?" asked Liv.

I shook my head no and said that I wasn't thirsty, though I was, I just didn't have any cash on me, had spent the last of it on the drugs, would need to scrub some more shit off Coach Puck's fridge. And then they were off. He spanked her ass as she climbed out of the car and she forced a laugh, or did I only imagine that it was forced? They walked on gelatinous legs to the store entrance, where two beer-bellied men were smoking cigarettes and glaring at them. James put his arm around Liv and grinned with all the dopamine inside of him. I wanted to be as fake happy as James looked. When I had first started dating guys, I spent a lot of time attempting to mimic that joy, but I knew I wasn't any good. What do you do with a desire that doesn't desire you back? I now know that wanting isn't the end of something. Sometimes you can fill a desire with an alternative—say, a pill instead of that teammate you would run blindfolded into a fire for—and sometimes, if you're lucky enough, you can fill your emptiness with more emptiness, like how air fills a room but no one ever thinks of it that way except for scientists.

Once they were gone, Trevor smiled cheesily at me, his pupils as wide as tunnels, and said he was preparing for Bardo, which he explained as the state between death and rebirth. I guessed this meant he'd recently read exactly one book and wanted everyone to know it.

He said, "I don't know where we're going, any of us."

"Okay," I said.

He tried to kiss my lips and missed, slurping the top of my chin, then giggled and said, "You want to know a secret?"

I stared out the window at the store entrance, waiting for Liv to emerge alone, somehow having lost James in one of the aisles.

"I'm afraid of stickers on fruit," he said. "James has to remove them for me at lunch."

I laughed, assuming that this was a move of Trevor's, his way of disarming me. He wanted to appear vulnerable so that I would choose him as my mate for the night. But upon closer inspection, I realized just how earnest he was: stickers scared him, and the drugs were digging this fear up, bringing it to the surface.

Trevor leaned forward to kiss me, this time landing on my lips. He pushed his weight into me until I was lying on my back across the back seat, the door handle digging into the top of my head. I had never had sex before, but I didn't feel attached to my virginity in any way. I simply hadn't had the energy to make it happen. I still didn't, but hell, I was rolling and the one I wanted might as well have been a thousand miles away. He climbed on top of me and unzipped my jeans, his fingers trembling. The E made everything feel like it was happening in slow motion, to someone else. I lay there for what I could only assume was hours while he pulled my pants off, one leg, then the other. Then he unzipped his pants and slipped them down around his ankles. His dick was soft, which surprised me. It reminded me of a slug.

"Come on, come on," he whispered to his dick, working at it with his hand while I lay there and wondered what Liv thought about James's dick, if she liked it enough to compliment it, to take it in her mouth, even down her throat.

Eventually, he got it up, and even hard, his dick was on the smaller side, which I was glad about. I'd seen a few before, done some hand and mouth stuff, usually drunk. He ripped a condom wrapper with his teeth, which were so impossibly white and straight that I laughed, picturing a toothpaste commercial gone awry.

"What's funny?" He practically whined when he said it.

"Nothing, nothing," I said.

"We doing this or not?" he said.

"Yeah, let's do it," I said.

He closed his eyes when he entered me, carefully at first, then all at once. With his first thrust, he groaned like he'd been punched in the stomach. I sucked my air in quickly, the pain sharp and concentrated, then slowly, it spread and dulled into an ache that felt only slightly better than feeling nothing at all. Up close, I could see every one of Trevor's pores, and it astounded me. All of these little holes. I couldn't believe that we carried around trash from our day inside our faces.

"Holy shit, holy shit," he said, his eyes still squeezed shut.

I stared at him, unblinking, until his face transformed into Liv's, and I took those thrusts, those very few thrusts, fast and hard like a jackhammer, as if Liv were dicking me down, and it was okay.

Afterward, he stayed inside of me for a few long seconds, and I wondered if someone was going to guide me through Bardo now, or if I had to achieve rebirth all on my own. I was immediately repulsed by him, but I tried to hide my disgust with a smile. Slowly, he pulled out. The condom was streaked with blood. He used a sweatshirt to slip it off. I couldn't tell you what came over me in that moment, but before I knew what was happening, I had slapped myself in the face, hard, and Trevor, still hovering over me, looked shocked but also interested. He smirked a little like he was daring me to do it again. So, I did it again. And again. Little else was on my mind but the anticipation and subsequent satisfaction of the slap—I could need and supply, want and fulfill. Once I started, I couldn't stop. It wasn't punishment, exactly—that's what sex with Trevor had been for, among other things. It was the opposite, in fact. The stinging felt like heaven. I was deliciously woozy. I thought if I could just lie there forever, slapping myself, right cheek, left cheek, right cheek, left cheek, then I could somehow escape the cruel confines of reality. A reality in which I was terrified of myself and the things I wanted to do and who I wanted to do them with. I had tried but failed to find a worse fate than having to spend time with myself. In that sense, Trevor was like a gift; the combination of him and the ecstasy made for an adequate escape.

Once I snapped out of it, I pushed Trevor off of me and pulled my underwear and jeans back up. He seemed to snap out of it, too.

"Pfff, therapy," he mumbled, getting dressed.

He looked like he'd rather be crucified than with me. I didn't respond. I ground my teeth and looked out the window at a one-legged pigeon hopping around with a fry in its mouth.

"I'm not going to bother asking how it was for you," he said, looking at the pigeon, looking hurt.

"You're so stupid," I said, feeling stupid.

He gnawed on his fingernails and spit one on the floor.

It worried me how easily Trevor could sense me not wanting to be with him. I felt as if, when it had been time for me to enter this world, I'd been assembled hastily, at the last second, with whatever spare parts had been lying around.

Liv and James came back a short while later with Sour Worms and Robitussin and gel pens and Thinking of You cards.

"For our moms," said Liv, opening and closing the card in her hand.

Trevor climbed into the driver's seat, fixing his hair in the rearview mirror and acting happier than he was, and James got into the passenger seat beside him. Liv slid into the back seat next to me, scooting into the middle seat and pressing her left thigh against my right thigh. Trevor pulled out of the parking lot and turned up the music, bobbing his head.

Liv examined me as if I'd been replaced with an impostor.

"Is it really you in there?" she said, pretending to clean a fogged-up window.

She reached out and touched my face, my hair, my shoulders and arms. I knew she was joking, but it felt nice, this excuse for touch. Once she was satisfied that this was the real me, she retracted her hands and squeezed them between her legs, as if they couldn't be trusted.

I rolled down the window and stuck my head out of it like a dog. The cold air felt good against my cheeks, which were burning all kinds of crazy. I wondered what my mom was doing, if she'd appreciate a Thinking of You card. Or maybe a Thank You card? My guess was that she would—what mother wouldn't? But I wasn't feeling particularly thankful for her at the moment. A few nights before, mind restless with grief, I had slipped on a hoodie and sweats and let my ball do the talking. It never got old, shooting around in the middle of the night. That night, I shot three-pointer after three-pointer from my dad's favorite spot. He'd made sure to measure every spot on our driveway so that we knew for sure we were practicing a real foul shot and real three-pointer. After maybe an hour or so into shooting around, my mom came outside, wrapped in her robe, and asked me what was going on. I said I missed Dad.

"I hate him," she said while looking like she loved him.

"Everybody loved him." I don't know why, but in that moment, I needed to believe that was true. She sighed.

"It's easy from a distance."

"You're shit at this, you know."

"We have no choice but to accept that this was meant to be," she said, clutching the turquoise crystal she wore around her neck. "You just have to trust the universe."

Seeming to believe this was a great source of comfort, she opened her arms, no doubt hoping I would fall into them. But I didn't. I turned toward the hoop, holding the ball with just my fingertips. From the back, I probably looked like I was preparing to shoot a foul shot, slow and thoughtful. But then I wound up, ball in one hand like a pitcher, and threw it as hard as I could against the backboard, releasing a guttural scream that seemed to take on a life of its own outside of my lungs, the residue of sound sticking to the tree branches for days after, just waiting to be shaken out.

When I brought my head into the car, James turned around in his seat and dangled a Sour Worm in front of me. I took it with my mouth then turned and spit it into Liv's lap. Without hesitation, she scooped up the spit-covered worm and ate it, smiling with her eyes as she chewed. I watched Liv take her time with the worm, almost as if she were savoring my saliva. And then, a familiar wetness between my thighs, a new pulse in my pelvis. Is this what I had wanted all along? For Liv to savor me in ways I hadn't even imagined? For Liv to desire even the unsavory parts of me? What could possibly be more erotic than watching someone take what they want and knowing that what they want is to consume you?

"You're fucking nasty." James laughed. "Save some of that for later," he said, winking at Liv.

"It's a gummy worm," she said.

He said, "I'm scared sex on E will ruin sex forever."

This dipshit was marking his territory. I looked to Liv for a reaction—she was all yeah, yeah, whatever, shut up. The night, it seemed, was plateauing. A decision had to be made about which way we were going to go. I knew Liv felt it, too. And it was Liv who went for it, who pushed it over the edge.

"Hey," said Liv, smacking Trevor on the back of the head. "Pull over for a hot second." Trevor looked at James and shrugged then took the first right onto a quiet residential street. He put the car in park then looked at Liv in the rearview mirror.

"You need to blow chunks?" he said.

Ignoring him, Liv said, "You guys ever think about kissing each other?"

I don't know what I'd been expecting, but it wasn't that. I did my best to twist my face into mild disgust, a practiced reaction. Both boys turned around in their seats to deny the accusation with their whole faces.

"Fuck off," said Trevor.

"Babe, not this again," said James.

"Again?" I said, turning to Liv.

"Fuck you ask that for, Cooper?" said Trevor.

"I'm pussy, pussy, pussy all the way," said James. "You know that."

The way he said it made me think there wasn't any way these two hadn't thought about each other's dicks before.

"Stop all your macho shit for a second," I said, "and really think about it."

"There's not shit to think about," said Trevor. But he glanced at James when he said it, as if he wasn't so sure of his own words.

"We aren't fags," said James. He looked at Trevor out of the corner of his eye, though he reached his hand out to Liv. She smacked it away, told him his hands were too sweaty.

"I don't think you can say the word *fag*," I said.

"You can't either then," he said.

I made a face to indicate that he was right, I wasn't a fag.

"It's not gay to be curious," said Liv.

She was really on one at that point. She couldn't be stopped. That's how I knew just how badly she wanted me. I did my best to access the boys' anxieties, their vibrating pleasure, their singular focus on fighting the desire to give in.

"We think it's hot," said Liv, glancing at me. "Don't we?" She looked excited. I know I did, too.

She pressed her thigh into mine then released it, a little nudge.

"What are you talking about?" said James.

"You don't even know any fags," said Trevor. "No one around here is gay."

"They are, you just don't know it," said Liv, her voice going quiet.

I peered at Liv then watched the boys, watched the energy between them begin to spark and flare. James faced forward in his seat and stared straight ahead out the front windshield, but I could see he was licking his lips.

"I'm rolling so hard," he mumbled. "Like I'm out of my mind."

"We all are," I said.

He took a deep breath and held it for a few strained moments before releasing it. It was so quiet that I could hear, for the first time all night, despite the sex, despite the closeness, the unadulterated human noise of everyone in the car. Trevor's teeth chattering, hands rubbing his biceps. James's tempered breathing, how the air floundered in his throat. Liv cracking her knuckles, once, twice, three times. A shiver ran through my body, ending at my fingertips, where it then reproduced, and in its new life-form was dying for somewhere else to go. My saliva was thick and hot on my tongue, my throat mossy.

"Is this some kind of trick?" said Trevor.

He was already leaning across the middle console as he said it, like he didn't care to hear the answer. Or like he knew they temporarily inhabited a world without deception. Liv slipped her arm behind my back and gripped the back of my neck, her thumb digging into the meat of my traps. An ownership. *You are mine,* said Liv's grip.

"Answer us back there," said James, half turning his head to look at us.

We stayed silent, an audience tethered by want.

"I'm rolling so hard," James said again, this time to Trevor.

"Me, too," said Trevor. "Shit."

"I probably won't remember any of this tomorrow."

"I'm on another planet, man."

Then it happened. Trevor grabbed James by the face with a thin, spidery hand and pulled him in for a kiss; lip to lip, they stayed still as surrender.

We watched, we reveled, we lusted after a forever we couldn't yet conceive.

"Why are you crying?" Liv whispered into my ear.

I wondered the same thing, though I didn't bother wiping away my tears. Together we watched the boys' lips pick up speed, grow hot with fever. They moved with a new hunger, their fists swinging at random body parts, as if to beat away a more sinister pain. We loved them softly, in the way one can only love a wounded animal, fresh tire marks seared across its face.

"Why are you crying?" she said again, this time tightening her grip.

10

TRASH-TALKING

Aaliyah, Katrina, and I were drinking in Katrina's basement after we beat Corinth by a cool twenty-two points. I turned on Katrina's TV and flipped through the channels until I found RCN, which was airing the replay of our game that night. Katrina flopped down on the couch next to me, shooting me a measured smile. She flipped aimlessly through an old issue of *Tiger Beat*, which had Justin Timberlake, Avril Lavigne, Nick Carter, and B2K on the cover, noting how she'd gotten the highest score for how good of a kisser you are, then tossed it on the floor. Aaliyah stood to the side of the screen, hands stuffed in her pockets, eyes scrutinizing.

"I look so slow," she said.

"No, you don't," Katrina and I said in unison. And she really didn't. But I understood what it was like to have a brain full of distortions.

"Easy for you fast bitches to say."

On the TV, we were still warming up, moving from a layup drill to a three-man weave to a drive-and-kick drill. Liv and I followed each other from line to line, one of us never too far away from the other. We slapped hands, we exchanged nods, we wiped the dust off our shoes and made them squeak on the shiny wood floor. We grabbed each other by the shoulders and shook the tension loose.

Before the game, my mind had been itchy with anticipation, but I knew once the ref blew her whistle and tossed the ball into the air, every thought and worry would dissolve into a focused blankness, one that allowed me to access the most private cavern of myself, where I stored my bruised-knuckle resolve. My desire to be extraordinary. To do extraordinary things.

I listened to the announcer talk about our rivalry, how Coach Puck and Coach Brighton had competed against each other since high school. My guess was maybe eight or nine people were watching this replay, somewhere out there, including my mom and Lars all snuggled up on the couch, my mom nuzzling her face in his armpit and cheering every time I made a wide-open jumper during warm-ups. I sipped my Smirnoff Ice, which Katrina had refused to let me pay her for, pretending as if she owed me even though we both knew she didn't, and told her how good her braids looked on TV. I was trying to tend to her feeling of neglect. She patted her braids with both hands and said they'd gotten fucked-up when some bitch fouled her under the basket.

"Shut up, it's starting," said Aaliyah, still standing, smiling the small, satisfied smile of someone who can't wait to relive a good memory.

On-screen, she outjumped the Corinth center and won the tap, hitting the ball back to me. I brought it down and drove hard down the right side of the court, kicking it to Liv for a three in the corner. Butter smooth, she rose, released, and drained it. On our way back on defense, she brought three fingers to her lips and kissed the sky. After her celebration, Liv brought her arm back down to her side, and I watched her point to me, a movement so quick, so discreet I hadn't noticed it the first time around. I looked between Katrina and

Aaliyah to see if either of them had picked up on Liv's acknowledgment, but if they did, they showed no signs of it.

Liv wasn't with us because she was off drinking with her old St. Patrick's teammates, at this girl Brittany's place. I'd never met her, but Katrina and she had been friends ever since they worked at summer camp together, chasing kids around by day and getting trashed in the woods at night. Or so they said. Who knew what they really got up to in the woods, but what I do know is Katrina came back from that camp with a lip gloss addiction.

By now, I'd made the connection that Katrina hadn't known about Liv from PennLive, like I'd assumed at my dad's deathday party, but rather from Brittany.

Judging by the way Katrina spoke about Brittany, you'd have thought she was dating her and not Patrick, her new boyfriend. Micah was long gone by then. Had been replaced with Adam then Rex and now Patrick. She had the same complaint about every single one of them: they were way too into her, it was such a turnoff. Brittany this, and Brittany that. I was careful not to speak the same way about Liv. But that didn't stop me from texting her all night long. It was a compulsion. Once you've found that one person you like all the time, even when you want to kill them, everyone else becomes like a right-handed layup or a simple crossover, so common you barely even notice them.

How's Brittany's? I texted Liv.

We're drinking Smirnoff Ice, I said.

Aaliyah calls them little bitch sodas, I said.

Even the mundane shit, I wanted her to know. And she wanted to know it, too.

What do you see right now? she replied. *Like, this very moment. What does your world look like?*

I told her about Aaliyah, in pajama pants and a tank top, standing in front of the TV imitating all of our great plays from the night while we looked on, clapping. Katrina's half up and under on their six-foot, three-inch center. My pull-up in transition—the defender tapped my elbow, but no call. After a few reenactments, Aaliyah stopped for a drink, panting. She threw back half of her Smirnoff Ice.

"You're like her little pet," said Katrina.

I looked up to find her glaring at me. I quickly shoved my phone into my pocket.

"Whose?" I asked.

Aaliyah took this time to finish her drink and help herself to a new one in the basement fridge. On-screen, I turned the ball over and right there, on the couch, I snapped the hair tie against my wrist.

"When she tugs on your leash, you come running."

I imagined Liv walking me around on a leash. I didn't hate the idea. I was sick of myself and my indecision, about college, about everything. It might be kind of nice to put someone else in control for once. Liv, my owner, had just four months to decide where I'd be playing ball for the next four years.

"Knock it off, you're drunk," I said.

"You don't even know the real her. She's fucked-up, like really fucked-up."

"Katrina," warned Aaliyah.

I tried to shake off her comment; I knew why she was being such a dick. It was what Katrina had always done: use misdirection to draw the audience's attention away from herself. But what she didn't realize was the more she pointed, the more people looked at the person attached to the finger. Or maybe that wasn't true; maybe I just wanted it to be true. Either way, she'd become insufferable since I met Liv. Pitying her was the only way I could continue to access our friendship. Our friendship, which, I'd begun to realize, only existed out of habit and convenience.

"When you're good, does she give you ear scratches and belly rubs?" she said, scratching behind her ears, her leg kicking.

On the TV, I made a risky fast-break pass that got picked off. I turned away, furious at my mistake all over again.

"I said fuck off."

"Just thought you'd want to know," said Katrina. She applied some lip gloss. "Everybody's thinking it."

Aaliyah shook her head at me to let me know that she wasn't thinking it, but it didn't matter. All of the heat left my body and gathered in my face and ears. I knew they must have been ten different shades of purple. Katrina stopped there, but I could have kept going for her: whenever my paws were muddy, Liv would ask where I'd been, what I'd gotten into. Like the week before when I'd gone on a bake ride with Grayson and hadn't answered any of her texts.

You'd have thought Katrina and I, having recognized our shared desires, would find refuge in each other, but we didn't. She was defiant, and I was unreachable. Maybe we preferred suffering in silence.

I went to the bathroom and texted Liv from the toilet. When I came back, Aaliyah was filming Katrina trying to put her sweatpants on like a sweatshirt. Katrina's phone, which was charging in the corner, played her ringtone, "My Boo" by Usher and Alicia Keys. She trotted over to it.

"I'll be right back," she said, making sure to leave the room before she answered.

"Must be Patrick," said Aaliyah, but I knew better.

Katrina always answered in front of us when it was a boy, and his ringtone was "Yeah!" With Micah or Adam or Rex or Patrick, she kept the conversation short and sweet, using us as an excuse for having to hang up. I knew who this was, and I knew she would be gone a long time.

"Did you kill her fish or something?" said Aaliyah.

"What? No," I said.

"Did you fuck Patrick? Did you steal her identity? Let me guess, did you scratch her Fall Out Boy CD? Crash her car? Did you tell the teacher she cheated on her math test? Oh, I know, you kissed her dad!"

She paused, twisting her mouth up in mock deliberation and pressing her pointer finger to her cheek.

"Oh, I've got it," she said. "You didn't pass to her when she was open."

"Yes," I said. "All of the above."

Aaliyah laughed and swallowed me into a hug. It was the way a hug from a friend was meant to feel: easy and comforting and unselfconscious. When we hugged, I didn't feel like I was making love in public.

"You'll be okay," she said, releasing me.

"How do you know?"

She laughed and turned off the TV then disappeared beneath the island, riffling around in the cabinet. She surfaced with a bottle of spiced rum and two shot glasses. They were from Ocean City, Maryland, and had neon-green beach sandals on them. She poured two shots, sliding one over to me. We clinked the glasses then threw them back, chasing the burn with a swig of Smirnoff Ice. She talked some about her boyfriend, Arnie, the only guy in the school who was taller than her. They seemed happy together. They talked about getting married and having kids like they weren't sixteen.

We drank and drank. I kept riffling through the freezer just for something to do. After about thirty minutes, Aaliyah grew agitated.

"Where did she go?" she asked, looking at the ceiling.

"She's on the phone with Brittany," I said, the burn of Katrina's comments still lingering.

"What? How do you know?"

I shrugged, not knowing how to explain that I could smell the shame on her, could sniff it out like a bloodhound sent into the woods to search for itself. Not that I would have used that language. Back then, I didn't know shame from guilt from plain old fear.

Aaliyah opened a bag of pretzels, defeated, then flopped onto the couch, digging around in the cushions for the remote. Once she found it, she put on her favorite show, *Mongoose Kingdom,* and told me about Hamlet, the mongoose who had rescued newborns from a rival clan before mysteriously disappearing. He belonged to no one.

It was a touching tale, but I couldn't focus. I said we should make Katrina hang up the fucking phone.

"Why can't we ever just hang out uninterrupted?" said Aaliyah, an edge in her voice. I knew she was most likely including my constant texting in with that complaint, but I feigned ignorance, or rather, denied complicity.

"I know, right?" I said.

She shook her head but didn't say anything. My phone buzzed in my pocket. I fought the urge to check it.

Upstairs, we heard Katrina's muffled laughter. Our eyes met, first asking then permitting, and we nodded at each other. Quietly, we crept up the stairs, making sure to avoid the creaky steps. Aaliyah wanted context for Katrina's secretive behaviors; I wanted the satisfaction of knowing I wasn't alone.

When we got to the top of the stairs, I peered around the corner. Katrina was sitting on the floor in the foyer next to an outlet, phone plugged in, knees tucked under her chin like a little kid. She was whisper-talking in a baby voice, the type I'd heard girls use with their boyfriends. We sat at the top of the stairs and listened.

"No, I'm not drunk," she said, giggling.

Patrick? mouthed Aaliyah, maybe hoping.

I shook my head no, then took out my phone.

Liv: *Have you talked to Trevor at all?*

James has been acting sorta weird

Since that night, I mean.

Of course I hadn't spoken to Trevor, I'd never planned to. I responded with a question of my own: *Are you with Brittany?*

Liv: *Yup she's on the phone though.*

Thought so, I said.

So annoying, said Liv, the text accompanied by a colon and a slash, a slanted mouth.

I was feeling the spiced rum, so I told her I missed her. I held my breath, hiding my screen from Aaliyah, who was still eavesdropping.

Should have come to Brittany's, said Liv.

You didn't invite me, I said, returning the slanted mouth.

Aren't we beyond invites Big?

That pet name made my vision go kaleidoscopic.

"Don't go," Katrina whined into the phone. "Okay, fine." She paused then pressed her lips to the phone. "I love you so much," she whispered.

When she hung up, Aaliyah and I tiptoed down the stairs, but Katrina never came.

"Now what?" It was Aaliyah's turn to whine.

"What happened when Hamlet disappeared from his clan?" I asked.

"I guess his family kept on living," she said, an empty little bitch soda in her hand.

I texted Liv: *Is Brittany off the phone now?*

Yeah she's shotgunning a beer in tge shower lol.

Drunk ass, I said.

"I would murder Arnie if he texted me this much," said Aaliyah.

She picked up a Ping-Pong ball and paddle and served the ball to no one. I texted Katrina to tell her to bring us some Pringles when she came back down. Maybe a little pressure would do it.

After another ten minutes, I left Aaliyah to her game and went upstairs. I didn't see Katrina anywhere, not in the foyer where we'd left her, not in the kitchen, not in the living room, not in her bedroom or the office. I checked all the closets. Even peered inside her dog's crate, which smelled like pee and rotten teeth.

Finally, I went outside to search for her. On the front step was a crushed Four Loko. She was sitting on the curb chugging what I assumed was another one. I watched her from the door to see what she would do, though I could barely make her out in the dark. She was a faint shadow doing high knees in the middle of the road. Then she stopped at some imaginary line, turned around, and switched to walking quad stretches. Now butt kickers back the other way. I was mesmerized.

She stopped to type on her phone, probably a text to Brittany, then snapped it shut, shoved it into her hoodie pocket, and took off running down the street, toward the main road. An awkward, lumbering, drunken run. I chased after her, through the ripples of light cast by the streetlights, afraid she'd get herself killed. Luckily, I was faster than her. I caught up to her a few houses down and grabbed the sleeve of her hoodie.

"Katrina, what the fuck are you doing?" I asked. I was clutching my phone in my fist.

She stopped running and looked everywhere but at me. We were both panting.

"This is why I didn't tell you where I was going," she said. "I knew you'd try to stop me."

"You left us at your house," I said.

She looked drunk out of her mind. "It's practically your house, too," she said.

"Where are you going?"

"Patrick's, duh," she said, hand on her hip now, full sass mode.

"Doesn't he live in Whitehall?" I said, knowing he lived in Whitehall, two towns over.

"No," she said.

"He does."

"No, he doesn't."

Then it clicked. Brittany only lived a couple of miles from Katrina.

"Well, at least let me walk you there," I said.

"No," she said quickly. "Just leave me alone. I'll text you when I get there."

"You don't really think I'm going to let you do that, do you?"

"You know, I wasn't going to tell you this but fuck it," she said, her voice cracking a bit. "Haven't you ever wondered why Liv's so secretive about her dad?"

"What do you know about it?" I said, my face growing numb. The world spun around me; the pavement rolled in impossible waves. I wasn't sure what was happening to me, why my body was suddenly rebelling. All I knew was that I couldn't bear the idea of Katrina knowing more about Liv than I did. But it wasn't just that, was it? There was a chilling realization underneath that knowing: there really were no secrets around here, and if there were no secrets, then mine would be spray-painted all over town in no time. Hell, they probably already were.

"I know that people love to talk," she said.

My face must have shown the extent of my panic because she seemed to soften, the whites of her eyes larger, quieter.

"Listen, maybe you should ask her about it."

"You don't know shit," I said.

"Now," she said, "if you'll excuse me."

She raised her hands, making like she was going to fix her hair, which was in a high ponytail, then ripped my phone out of my hand and chucked it into a stranger's yard. Before I knew it, she'd taken off running again. I had a split second to choose between Katrina and my phone, between Katrina and Liv. I flopped down onto the black grass and started feeling around for my phone, nearly in tears. When I finally found it, I had two texts from Liv.

You didn't ark me what my world kooked like, she said.

It looks imcomplete, she said.

Just once, I wished she'd say what she really meant, that she wanted me there, with her. On the court, our communication was perfect: a chorus of *I got you, help help help, screen on your right, watch the back door, I'm here, help weakside, step up step up step up.* But it was like the better we played together on the court, the worse we had it off the court.

I sat down for a few minutes and let my spinning head settle. Tried to think of something to say that wasn't foolish and naïve and miscalculated. Typed a winky face, deleted it. If this were a game, I'd have looked at the ref for guidance. I had no idea whose possession it was, whose turn it was to make something both beautiful and wretched. I found myself thinking about beauty, what it was, all the things we got wrong about it, all the ways we misunderstood it. I thought whatever beauty was, its opposite wasn't ugliness, but sanity, sense. Liv was so beautiful I felt insane.

I went back to Katrina's and locked the door behind me. Aaliyah was asleep on the couch, her arms splayed over her head, mouth hanging open. I cleaned up the empty bottles and cups, washed out the shot glasses, took the empties directly out to the recycling. Sleep that night was harsh and splintered; I didn't get more than thirty minutes at a time before jerking awake, little yips escaping my throat.

In the morning, Katrina called me at 6 A.M. to let her in before her parents woke up. She apparently didn't remember a damn thing from the night before. Except how to lie.

"Patrick said he picked me up once you two fell asleep," she said. "Isn't he so sweet?"

I watched her grab the Pringles can from the pantry and make her paw disappear.

11

THE WHITE-HOT HEAT
OF A FAST BREAK

The E must have been kicking in because the neon lights no longer looked like the cheap bowling alley lights that they were, but rather like a brilliant light show at the end of the earth. I was wearing boyfriend jeans and a baggy Ekron hoodie.

It was hip-hop night at Ray's, the only bowling alley in town. "Yeah!" was blasting over the loudspeaker and people, teens and adults alike, were getting handsy. At 7 P.M. it transformed from a friendly, if a bit grimy, family environment to a straight-up grindfest. It was worse than a school dance because there were no chaperones to walk around and move boys' hands up—there was just Frankie, the twentysomething redhead who worked the rental desk and always had her nose buried in a fantasy book. It wasn't super busy yet, but it was a Friday night and would fill up soon.

Grayson stood up from behind the score table and wiggled his hips off rhythm while he waited for the pinsetter to spit his ball back out, a dark-pink twelve-pounder. Ball in hand, he waited for

Ludacris to say *Then bend over to the front and touch your toes,* so he could do as the song instructed, backing his big six-foot, four-inch ass up.

"Don't tempt me," I laughed, trying not to grind my teeth, but they hurt. I wanted to bite straight through my skull. He kept going, peering over his shoulder to check if I was tempted, so I jumped up and smacked his ass a few times. This wasn't like the last time I did E, having to navigate all that tension, and confusion, and misplaced desire. Being with Grayson was easy, as natural as the gravity that made it possible for Liv and me to rain threes come game time.

I was still spanking Grayson when I heard someone say "You make a cute couple" in between giggles. I stopped and looked around and found a tween girl with braces and blond braids smiling at us one lane over. She held both hands over her heart like it was the most touching shit she'd ever seen while a bored, acned girl punched their names into the system.

"We aren't a couple," I said, glancing at Grayson. He followed the lights with his eyes, the ball still cradled between his palm and inner elbow. I nudged him and he returned his gaze to me.

"What, are you embarrassed about me now, sweetie?" he said, throwing an arm over my shoulder. I could smell his boy scent, a combination of too much sweat and too much deodorant. "We've been going nine months strong but to be honest, I'm not sure if we're going to make it. This one"—he pointed a thumb in my direction—"she's a bit squeamish. Won't even let me slip a pinky in, if you know what I mean."

"Oh my god."

"No, I don't know what you mean," the girl said.

"Have a good game," I said.

"So, you are a couple, then?"

"Nah, she couldn't handle me," said Grayson.

"Whatever you say," said the girl, returning to her sister or whoever. But she kept sneaking peeks at us when she thought we weren't looking.

I sat down and Grayson rolled a gutter ball, then immediately grabbed a smaller, lighter ball and missed all the pins again.

He turned around to face me. "He is beauty, and he is grace."

"Keep your pinkies to yourself," I said, happy to feel happy in his presence. With him, I didn't feel like I was onstage, forgetting my lines.

A lavender light danced across his face; his thick beard looked like cotton candy pasted to his cheeks. His pupils were bowling balls in his head. He dug around in his pocket, producing two gourmet lollipops, one root beer float and the other bubblegum. I grabbed the root beer and fumbled unwrapping it, my hands shaky. Finally, I stuck it in my mouth. Sweet relief. Grayson popped the bubblegum one into his mouth, moving to the right side, and I swear I could hear his teeth crack as they came down on the hard candy.

I grabbed my ball, a turquoise seven-pounder, which I liked because I could really whip it, and chucked it down the lane, not caring much whether it hit any pins or not. I managed to knock down six. That was the great thing about drugs for me—they helped tame my competitive side so I could enjoy things. On this night, I wanted to enjoy bowling because of my dad. He'd been in a bowling league all my life, forever hanging his scores on the fridge like a kid coming home with an A on a quiz. Once, he bowled a 252 and he never let us forget it. At the time, I didn't understand the appeal of a sport that didn't involve contact. Now, throwing my second ball down the lane, I understood there was a violence to it all the same. The explosion of the ball colliding with the pins, wanting to crush them all. I could see how you could get addicted to that thundercrack.

"How was practice?" I asked Grayson, without taking my lollipop out of my mouth.

He shrugged. "Same as always, man. Feels pointless. You know Coach is never gonna fucking play me."

I couldn't even work up the energy to argue with him because he was right. Even at his height, the coach couldn't find much use for him, which people seemed to view as some sort of moral failing on

Grayson's part. I don't know. Maybe that was just me projecting, but kids at school really seemed to value the stars, the athletes who could win championships and make fans forget their lives for a hot second.

"Yeah, well, Puck chucked his boot at the ceiling and got it stuck in one of the rafters," I said. "He legit went home wearing one boot."

"In the snow?" He grabbed his ball to take his turn and I followed him so we could keep talking.

"In the snow."

What I didn't say was that Katrina had been extra nice to me, fetching my water bottle, rebounding for me even when I bricked it and the ball went under the bleachers. It was, I guessed, her way of asking me to keep her secret to myself. She never would have dared approach me about it, because naming it a secret would be acknowledging an innate truth about what I'd witnessed a week ago. An innate truth that was not compatible with the future she'd already hand-selected for herself: marry a handsome, rich guy with a boring job no one understands; buy a big house by the beach; procreate as many times as humanly possible. Gobble down Xannies with breakfast. Okay, maybe I added that last one. I could picture it all so perfectly, though, the image crisp and bright while they took family photos on the beach, everyone dressed in white button-downs and khaki shorts, smiling terrifying empty smiles into the camera. How many years would I receive a holiday card before she finally forgot about me? Or rather, before she grew convinced I'd forgotten about the silly experimentation of her youth.

"Your practice sounds infinitely better," said Grayson. Another gutter ball.

"We weren't even sucking. I think he just did it to feel something."

Grayson shook his head, grinning. "He's the best."

"I know."

"I want him to be my dad."

"Me, too," I said.

All around us, balls clapped against pins, the thundercracks so close together you knew the storm was on top of you. The song changed to "In da Club." We looked at each other, both realizing what I'd just said.

"Shit, I'm sorry, man."

I waved him off. "It's fine, it's fine." I hated people tiptoeing around me. People died, it was a thing they did, were forever hell-bent on doing.

My face tingled as I tried to blink my words away, the tears bubbling in the corners of my eyes. Did I really wish Coach Puck was my dad or did I just wish I had a living dad? The thing is, the second I said it, I knew it was true, at least partially. I didn't necessarily wish he'd replaced my dad, but I guess I wished I had more than one dad, especially now that the first one had dipped out on me. I'd never once imagined I'd have to go to college fatherless, with no one to call after my games and dissect every play. Fuck calling, he would have been at every damn game, taking me for drinks after so we could reenact my highlights and explain away my errors. He would have been calling me his son again. His prodigal son.

I took my turn and knocked down four pins on the right-hand side, the last one wobbling before finally falling. When I turned around, I was assaulted by the existential anxiety on Grayson's face. I knew the reminder about my dad's death would inevitably make him consider his own death, who would give a shit enough to show up and what he'd leave behind, if anything. Determined to save us both from a spiral, I initiated one of our favorite games.

"Alright, alright, how about those two?" I nodded toward two guys, maybe seniors, who were just getting started a few lanes away.

"Oh, definitely orange shirt," he said, raising his voice over the bass of "In da Club." "What? He's wearing a Harold & Kumar shirt. Man's got good taste."

"Maybe you should make a move," I said. I hoped teasing him would mask my envy. Grayson was comfortable enough with his sexuality to play along and hypothetically fuck a dude. I mean, it helped that he'd had a beard since eighth grade, the chest hair to match. No one ever questioned who he liked. It made it easy for him to joke.

"Mack, I swear, I would, but I much prefer the gender that ignores me."

"Come on, you know that's not true."

"Fuck you, I know what people say about me," he said. I tried to interrupt but he cut me off. "I'm serious. I know they all think I'm some druggie who's bound to live in his mom's basement forever. A life of pizza delivery and my right hand."

"At least it's not your left hand," I teased.

"I'm fucking serious. They think they've got me all figured out."

"Who is they?"

"You know," he said, gesturing around the bowling alley. "They. And the worst part is, they count on me to have the best weed and pills, but when they take drugs, it's cool, it's partying, but when I take drugs, I'm a druggie. That right there," he said, pointing at me, "is the difference."

I nodded. He was ruining my high with his self-pity, but I was prepared to let him. Maybe that was what love was, sacrificing your high for your best friend. Plus, there was something in his voice that felt like it was reaching out for me, feeling around in the dark for another person who doesn't belong.

"Anyway," he said, "would it really be so bad if that was my future?"

"You act like it's inevitable."

"What if it is? We can't all be superstars."

I was used to bitter teammates talking this way, but never Grayson. I could tell that deep, core-of-the-earth pain he carried around with him was tunneling its way to the surface. The trouble was, I needed to be a superstar. I needed a future that was all basketball all the time because it was the only future I could imagine for myself. Basketball, I knew, was the only thing keeping me alive. As long as I had the game, I would be okay, there would be a place for me that existed outside of human curses like attraction and desire. On the court, in front of all the screaming, heckling, throat-raw fans, I could hide. And how irresistible it was to be celebrated without being seen.

"Maybe look again," I said. "You're allowed to dream, you know."

"No," he said. "No, I'm not."

"Then just come with me."

"Where?"

"Wherever I go."

He laughed, unimpressed. "Fuck am I gonna do? Sleep between you and Liv?"

I paused. That was the first time he'd ever acknowledged there was something going on between Liv and me, or rather, that there was a something for him to possibly get between. My cheeks grew hot with embarrassment.

"Why is it that drugs always make you act like Eeyore?" I asked.

"Not coke," he said, raising his pointer finger. "Coke makes me fun."

"I'm serious, Gray."

He stuck his tongue out at me and then went to bowl his turn. Another gutter ball, then, miraculously, a strike.

"Like you're such great company over here moping about Liv."

"Excuse me?"

"She's with James, yeah?"

"I'm not moping," I said. Then, "They're out to dinner with their moms."

"See."

"It feels like he's asking for her hand in marriage or something."

"Like he would ever."

For some stupid reason, I started thinking about what their wedding would be like. There's Liv, beautiful but awkward in a fluffy dress she doesn't belong in. But on her feet are a pair of Jordan 4s, pristine, fresh out of the box. She's standing somewhere, in a room, preparing for the ceremony, and her mom is at her feet, begging her to take off her kicks. Liv relents, lifting one foot, which her mother grabs tenderly, slipping the Jordan off like some sort of reverse Cinderella. She does the second foot. Then it's her high socks, and she's barefoot, exiting the room to greet the rest of her life at the altar. I try to insert a horse into the scene, an escape route for my runaway bride, but my brain won't allow it—it keeps deleting the horse as if it were a virus on a computer.

"Fuck them, they can enjoy their dumb, boring life," said Grayson. Then he continued our game, urging me to pick between two women in their fifties returning their shoes to Frankie, who looked annoyed that she had to set down her book. I examined the women. Both had mom haircuts, short for convenience, not for style. That was a real mom, I thought, someone who placed their kids ahead of themselves.

"Wow, thanks," I said. "Neither."

"Not an option."

I growled at him.

"Seriously? Remember that time you made me pick between a bag of sour-cream-and-onion chips and a Pepsi bottle? By the way," he said, raising his eyebrows. "I chose the chips because it wouldn't fit in a soda bottle."

"Gross."

He shrugged. "Whatever."

I could tell he was annoyed at me, so I appeased him, telling him that I'd choose both at once.

"Oh, a threesome MILF fantasy, my favorite," he said, nodding his approval.

After that, we bowled for a couple of hours, dancing to the music and talking shit. At one point, Grayson pulled out two more pills and we downed them, wanting to keep our roll going.

Midway through our last game, I noticed the bowling alley had gotten considerably louder. A rowdy group of teen guys had just rolled in. They were trying on shoes and picking out the heaviest balls possible. One of the guys was leaning on the counter, blatantly hitting on Frankie, who looked amused and skeptical. Another guy returned a pair of shoes, asking for another size. When he turned around, I realized it was James. I scanned the group for Trevor but didn't see him. I pointed him out to Grayson.

"That's him? Jeez."

"What?"

"He looks like a Roman statue."

"I hate you."

"But I love you."

I didn't say anything.

"Hey, I'm sure he, like, sucks his thumb or something."

I wasn't sure what to do, whether I should acknowledge him or not. We weren't exactly friends, were we? And what would I say anyway? *I can't stop thinking about you and Trevor kissing?* It was the truth, though. Ever since that night, I couldn't stop picturing how they held their lips together without moving, as if trying to imprint the memory on each other. The slowed time. Their quivering breathlessness. The way Liv gripped my neck like I was hers. It was maybe the only honest moment of the night. And I felt, to some extent, that as long as we had that shared night together, then nothing James did could ever hurt me. Not really. Like with Katrina, I was to be his secret keeper. I was expected to hold a second world for him, a safe distance away from everything he knew and protected.

"Yeah, yeah," I said, digging around in my pocket to check my phone.

I had a text from Liv: *What you up to?*

I told her I was bowling with Grayson. He appeared behind me, reading over my shoulder. He was probably the only person in the world I let read my messages unscreened.

Oh, Liv responded.

James just showed up. Why aren't you with him?

Liv: *I thought I'd see what you were doing . . .*

Grayson cleared his throat before raising his arms in the air and booming, "She shoots, and she scores!"

He said it so loudly that he drew the attention of the guys, including James, whose eyes snapped in the direction of Grayson's color commentary.

"For fuck's sake," I said.

Stressed and confused, I did a sort of air high five and James looked side to side before lifting his chin in the slightest of nods.

"What the hell was that?" said Grayson, laughing at the absurdity of it all.

Liv texted me again: *Fuck it, I'll just come meet you.*

No, I texted back.

"Why not?" asked Grayson.

I sat down and ripped my bowling shoes off, stepping into my J's, which were dirty and worn from my wearing them out in the snow all winter.

"We're going," I said, holding the shoes in one hand and dragging Grayson by the arm with the other. I knew that we had to pass by James in order to return our shoes to Frankie. I'm not sure what I wanted from him, but I was clearly in the mood for some type of collision. Or at the very least, to feel stimulated, to buzz with the nerves of not knowing whether he was friend or foe. As we neared, I watched James's face change from indifference to anxiety to vexation. I don't think he knew what to think or how to feel about my presence, and maybe I got off on having even the smallest bit of power. Either way, once we arrived at the table, he started laughing an obnoxious, sarcastic laugh.

"Trevor's gonna love this," he said, nodding in Grayson's direction.

"He's just a friend."

"Trev should have listened to me when I told him you were a butterface."

I didn't know what to say. I hadn't expected James to come at me this aggressively. Especially since he'd just come off a nice dinner with Liv, a reminder that she was his, all his.

Grayson jumped in, "You do realize you're calling her body hot, right?"

I didn't feel hot, I felt ugly and deformed, the type of vegetable that's on sale for a third of the price because you can hardly stand to look at it while you cut it.

"Who asked you?" said James, moving closer to Grayson.

Soon, they were chest to chest, staring each other down. Grayson raised his hand and I thought he was going to sock James and I was going to have to explain to Liv why she had to come get her fallen boyfriend whose eye had split open from the impact. But he reached over toward the counter and grabbed a stray soda, ripped the cap off, and dumped the thing on James's head like he was a contestant getting Slimed on Nickelodeon. We didn't wait to see his reaction, we took off running out the front door, waving goodbye as we raced to our cars through old, dirty snow. I peered over my shoulder one last time to see Grayson scurrying to his car, bowling shoes in hand, before I climbed into the driver's seat of my dad's junker. Only when I sat down did I realize I was still holding my bowling shoes. I set them on the passenger seat, my whole body shaking from the E and adrenaline. I leaned my head against the seat and closed my eyes, gathering myself, half hoping James would come after me so I could show Liv just what a piece of shit he was. I thought about what Katrina had said about me, how I was Liv's pet. She'd said it with such derision, such contempt, but what was so bad about being someone's pet? You had food and treats and water, toys that made you wag your tail and run around the house. Endless cuddles and pats, butt scratches, scraps from the dinner table. All your owner asked in return was loyalty. Loyalty I could give.

A rap on the window made me jump so high in my seat, I nearly hit my head on the ceiling. I opened my eyes to find Frankie peering in my window, scowling. I rolled down my window.

"Yeah?" I said.

"Who steals bowling shoes?"

I looked at the passenger seat. "Oh yeah, my bad. I didn't mean to."

She folded her arms over her chest, shifting her weight to one leg, hip popping out in annoyance. "Come with me."

I rolled the window up and did as she said, trailing her, tail between my legs. Grayson's car was nowhere to be found. Inside, she told me to take a seat. Her book was open, face down on the counter where she'd left off to chase me out the door. I felt like a little kid again. She picked up the bowling alley's phone, holding the handset to her ear, and told me to dial my parents' phone number—my punishment was the embarrassment of having them come pick me up and scold me in front of everyone. Without thinking, I dialed the first number that came to mind: Coach Puck's. I'd rather see him than my mom these days, especially if Lars would be accompanying her.

"Hello?" Coach barked into the phone. Wanting to smile, I tried to force my mouth into a neutral position.

"Hey, uh, Dad, it's me. I'm at the bowling alley."

"Now what drugs are you on?"

"I need you to come pick me up."

He coughed then cleared his throat. In the background, I heard his kids playing or fighting or both.

"Alright, alright. I'll be there in a few."

He hung up and I told Frankie that he was on his way.

"Don't move from that spot," she said. Then, more to herself than me, "These fucking kids, I swear."

She did a quick scan of the alley. James and his friends had begun their game at the lane farthest from us, so thankfully, he didn't see my return. She returned to her book, periodically peeking at me over the pages. I sat in my seat and checked my phone. Liv had texted me back: *What do you mean no? You don't want to see me?*

Hey, sorry, something happened, I texted her.

I have to head home.

See you at practice tomorrow.

A few minutes later, Coach threw open the door to Ray's and walked in, stomping the snow off his Reebok sneakers, looking a whole mess. When he got to the counter, he looked at me and then at Frankie. "What's this all about?"

"She belong to you?" said Frankie.

Coach gave me the once-over, perhaps looking for evidence of relation or family. He didn't have to look very hard to find our commonality; we were grumps, we were misfits, we were miserable, though we didn't want to be. We rejected others so it wouldn't hurt so bad when they rejected us. I saw the way parents looked at him at games, heard the way they spoke about him like he was lucky he hadn't been hanged in the town square, and though people didn't treat me that way, at least not yet, I'd always had the sneaking suspicion that their acceptance or whatever version of acceptance I was granted was conditional, was only because I could play. I hoped he could sense the orphanness in me.

"Yeah, that's my kid," he barked. "What you doing calling me down here so late?"

Frankie told him about me and my friend getting into an altercation with a kid and then leaving with my bowling shoes. He scratched his beard while he listened, pretending to be deeply interested in the goings-on of teenagers. Once she was done telling the story, he thanked her for her help.

"I'll take it from here," he said.

"No shit, I'm not a babysitter," said Frankie.

"All right, no need to get snippy," he said. "We'll be outta your hair."

We left the bowling alley and climbed into his truck, which was still running out front. We put our seatbelts on, and he began driving, not toward my house, but toward his. I understood this was because he didn't want to return me to my mother like this. He also realized what it looked like for a middle-aged man to be dropping a teen girl off at home. When we got to his house, he pulled into the driveway instead of parking on the lawn—a luxury. The lights were on in his living room. I could see his wife, or someone who I presumed was his wife, on the couch, smiling at something I couldn't see. There was something sitting on her shoulder—a bird? No, it looked too small. Either way, she didn't exactly look like the villainess I had always imagined. She was watching something, movement in the corner of the window. Mesmerized, I began to walk toward the front door. The floodlights went on, coloring us a dark blue.

I looked at Coach. "Now that you've claimed me, you can't ever leave," I said.

For some reason, in that moment, I thought of Allen Iverson's 1999 interview in *Slam*. The interviewer was asking him about his legacy and desire for success, and he said something about how he's starving for success, how he loves looking at his mom and saying, "You made somethin'. You made somethin' outta me." That's how I felt about Coach even if he didn't know it.

"Morris, I will die in this goddamn house."

"Don't talk like that."

"What are you so worried about? You're gonna die before me at the rate you're going," he said. Though I didn't ask him to elaborate, I wanted him to. I wanted to know more about my impending death. Could he see the future? What would I accomplish? Fail to accomplish? Would I get a chance to kiss Liv again before I died? Please, tell me about me, I wanted to say. Tell me who I am so I don't have to tell myself.

"I'm not even high."

"You asshole, you're fucking lucky."

"I didn't mean to steal the shoes."

"Nah, of course not," he said. It felt like he was staring into my brain where he might be able to dig up the source of my behavior. "You remind me too much of me. It's disturbing."

"What's wrong with that?"

"You think I'm playing with you? I never had a tenth of the skills you do."

"So?"

"So, ride that shit out. See how far it'll take you."

The E was doing things to me. Maybe Liv had been right, I was an exposed nerve, and all it took was a surge of chemicals for me to admit what I'd been avoiding for months.

"What if I'm afraid?"

What I meant was, what if I'm afraid to find out that it won't take me very far at all? That my talent is anything but limitless, that once I get out there in the world, I'll discover just how small I am?

"Who the fuck isn't?"

"What if this is the highest I go? What if I've peaked here? What if I get to college and I can't hang?"

We'd been standing on the front porch, and the front door opened, and out came Bryan, Codi, and the wife. Bryan was dressed in a princess dress and crown and Codi looked like a cross between a jester and a horse, a saddle strapped to her back. The wife was smaller than I expected, a tiny thing with stringy blond hair and a troll doll taped to her shoulder.

"Back to clean again, I see," said Bryan.

"What are you still doing up?"

"We were putting on a play," said Codi.

I looked at Coach to see if he was going to introduce his wife. When he didn't, I waved at her and told her my name. She said she had heard a lot about me, asked if I enjoyed watching plays. I shrugged and said I'd never seen one before.

"Well, this one you won't want to miss," she said, waving me inside.

I followed her and the kids into their house, Coach following close behind and pulling the door shut. There were toys everywhere, muddy footprints in the foyer. The wife and I sat on the couch, which had no cushions, while he disappeared into the kitchen and returned with a big bowl of popcorn for us to share. Bryan and Codi fussed with their set, a fort made of couch cushions and blankets. Coach wiggled his way between his wife and me on the hard couch, the bowl on his lap, and we both dove in, our hands touching then retreating, touching then retreating. The play began, and we were taken to a land far away in which boys could be princesses and girls could be whatever they wanted to be. It was a love story full of vengeance and revenge that ended not with a kiss or wedding but with a metamorphosis. Soon, the siblings had transformed into pterodactyls, soaring above all the madness down below, dangerous and free, dangerous because they're free. They circled us on the couch several times while we clapped and hooted and hollered and made a big stink about it.

I watched Coach Puck plant a big, gross, exaggerated kiss on his wife's cheek, the troll still sitting on her shoulder. She pretended to wipe the kiss off with her hand, but I noticed she didn't touch it, left the shiny residue there.

12

FLAGRANT FOUL

We were on track for a perfect season. Our game against Cathedral Catholic was a total blowout: 65 to 34, and Liv showed out for the Richmond scout, who was taking notes on her little clipboard. She ended up with thirty-two points, twelve boards, and six assists. I had a decent game, too, shutting down Dani, their sharpshooting point guard. I was grateful that Katrina and them hadn't talked more shit about her since the party.

Now, like always, Liv and I were the only two to shower after the game, both in our black Nike slides to avoid some nasty foot shit, everyone else too insecure or prude to strip down in front of one another and step into an open shower. Or was it that they were too suspicious of what it might mean for several girls to be naked in front of one another without the presence of boys? In a college communications class, I learned about the Bechdel Test and thought this might be the nude equivalent. Could at least two girls show their tits and vaginas to each other without a male witness? And would the two girls have names? Names people knew without their jerseys? What if one of the girls wasn't really a girl at all, but something she had no language for?

Backs to each other, we washed off the evidence of our game in delicious silence. Nothing but the squeeze of the bodywash bottle. The sweet rush of water. A soft *oh* when the water first hit skin. I washed my face, and the salt burned my eyes. I held them shut, rubbing them until I saw blue planets spinning in the dark.

During the game, I'd searched the stands but couldn't find Liv's father, which meant her mother had gotten to him, chased him away like a filthy raccoon digging in the trash can. But I didn't like thinking of him that way: unwelcome and thievish. I don't know why, but I felt a certain unearned softness toward him. I had no reason to, really; I didn't know him, had never spoken to him, but still, when I thought of him, when I pictured him clapping for Liv in the stands or giving her a postgame hug, I felt protective over him, familial. Maybe it was the mere fact that Liv had come from him, that to care for him was to care for Liv's origin. That and the fact that he and my dad had, at the very least, known each other. I once again thought of their photo. They were likely nothing more than casual drinking or jam buddies, but I was still fascinated by the way they had entire lives before we'd even existed, lives they were satisfied or unfulfilled by, lives full of desire and hope and pleasure and pain. Two men who, for one reason or another, had grown up to take their pain and turn it outward, to pass it on to others. I thought of my mom, fed up with my dad's drinking, with his glory days talk, tucking me into bed one night—I couldn't have been older than eight—and asking what's the use in being remembered by the public for a few good songs if your family got all the bad shit in private?

I peeked over my shoulder and watched Liv scrub her scalp, head back, eyes squeezed shut, her body spectacular and terrifying, a crescent moon curling into itself. Before she could open her eyes and catch me, I turned back around and played with the water, chopping it with my hands.

I cupped my hands around my mouth like a megaphone and spoke, my voice deep and booming.

"Tracy McGrady had one hell of a night tonight, ladies and gentlemen. That number one can really play."

I risked a glance over my shoulder and caught Liv looking at me. I tried not to think about what I must look like under her gaze: ass whiter than the rest of my back side, shoulder blades poking out of my skinny back like wing attachments. I turned to face her and she gulped, taking my body in, my boobs I referred to as pecs, my smooth cunt I'd started shaving in eighth grade after a guy refused to touch me and my bush.

I continued: "I mean, Dick, the highlight reel alone is going to keep us here all night."

Liv grinned. She knew I knew she loved T-Mac. She knew I wanted her to feel special, to forget the wilting feeling inside her chest. So, I performed. I worshipped.

"First quarter, he was on fire. Finished with thirteen points, including a *how the fuck did he even do that* up and under layup. Talk about hang time."

"You're so stupid," said Liv.

"Second quarter, he was really feeling himself. Top of the key, he shakes right, then left, then right, then he's gone, leaving nothing but fractured ankles in his wake."

"Stupid," she said, shaking her head.

"How does he do it, we will never know!" Then, after a moment: "Fuck it, it's Cooper's time now," I said, switching it up. "Few players have the ball on a string like this one, Dick. I almost can't believe my eyes!"

"That's all you, Big," she said. "That's all you."

I ignored her and kept on color commentating to my best friend, Dick Vitale.

"The third quarter was all about those deep threes we all know and love. If the league isn't careful, Cooper might force them to put a four-point line on the moon."

"Your stinky ass clean yet?"

I smiled at her teasing and turned to face the wall once more, rinsing the last of the soap off of me, watching the last remnants of the game swirl down the drain.

"Let's get out of here," I said. "I know the Richmond coach is out there waiting for you."

In the hallway outside the locker room waited the Richmond assistant coach, young, with dark curly hair and black-rimmed glasses. A powerful, confident stance, despite her corny Richmond polo and khakis. She smiled and waved when she saw Liv emerge from the locker room in front of me, duffle bag slung over her shoulder. I wandered off, limping due to the ice bags wrapped around my bad knee. I pretended to be interested in the wrestlers sweating and grunting in the weight room, spotting for each other and grabbing each other's asses while assisting pull-ups. I didn't need to eavesdrop on their conversation to know the Richmond coach was saying all the usual stuff: she was really glad she got to make it to the game, Richmond would love to have Liv starting at shooting guard next season, she was their top recruit, the head coach was stoked about Liv's game, Richmond would be a great environment for Liv to thrive in, they ran a lot of plays for their three-point shooters. Who knew how much of it was true, but you had to pretend to take them at their word or else you'd drive yourself crazy. No coaches were there to watch me that night, and I was grateful for a break from the old song and dance. The UCLA assistant coach's flight had been canceled because of the weather. I liked her quite a bit. She was young and intense and had a certain charm about her, but I had already decided she wasn't worth suffering under the head coach for. Plus, Gonzaga was still lurking in every fissure of my mind. When I thought about playing there, I felt calm and like a version of myself that I might even like, a version of myself that would never fall for a mess like Liv.

I felt a hand on my shoulder and looked up to find Coach Puck's scruffy face.

"I'm proud of you, kid."

"I didn't know you were still here."

"I'm always still here."

I nodded. "I get that," I said.

"Wish you didn't."

His hand disappeared inside his coat and pulled out a pack of Newports.

"Don't get too drunk tonight, Morris." He slapped me on the back then headed out the glass double doors.

I watched him light a cigarette then take that first life-giving drag, loosening his tie with his free hand. A few moms walked by, waving their hands in front of their noses. Coach didn't seem to notice them, and if he did, he didn't give a shit. Our athletic director, Dr. Hollinger, a small man who walked like a duck, approached him, shaking his head, probably telling him to put out the cigarette on school property. Coach offered him a shrug, took one last drag, and stubbed it out with his boot. When Dr. Hollinger walked away, Coach made sure I was looking then gave him the finger before making his way to his snow-covered truck.

I pulled out my phone—Lars had gotten my mom her own—for something to do with my hands. I had a few messages from 256-010, which meant they were instant messages sent from AIM. I opened the one closest to the bottom then moved my way up. They were from James. I didn't even know he knew my screen name. His was Willball4food3289, as if he'd ever had to do anything for food besides boss his mom around. I only knew who it was because the messages were urging me to keep my mouth shut about what happened in Trevor's car a couple weeks ago, that whatever I thought had happened was not what had really happened, and I better not get it twisted. He sent a few more messages, each one more deranged than the last.

Willball4food3289: *whore*

Willball4food3289: *cunt*

Willball4food3289: *carpet munching bitch*

Willball4food3289: *you cut the drugs with something I just know it.*

Willball4food3289: *and fuck your big hairy friend at Rays*

It was obvious he was unraveling over there and had been for a while. That night in the car had existed outside space and time, and now here he was, trying to return to the dimension he once knew, only to find it had collapsed in on itself.

I messaged him back and said not to worry, I wasn't going to say anything, I wasn't like that, and he could trust me—anything to get him off my back. I even apologized for Grayson's behavior. Then I snapped my phone shut and stuffed it into my pocket. I didn't see Dani, hair pulled back in a bun, sweaty, curly wisps tucked behind her ears, until she was already standing next to me, smiling in a sort of shy, self-aware way, her shoulders shrugged up to her ears.

"Nice game," she said.

"Hey," I said.

"I think you're supposed to say thanks."

"Okay, yeah, thanks."

I risked a glance at Liv. She was listening to the coach talk, both of them wearing these dumb, frantic smiles.

"I wanted to give you something," said Dani. "But you have to promise to use it."

"How do I know I want to?"

"Oh, I think you may want to," she said, her face flushing.

She reached into her jacket pocket and pulled out a piece of paper, which she folded into my sweaty palm, then walked out the door and onto the team bus. I didn't dare examine the paper out in the open, but I wanted to. Pieces of me, warring, at war.

Once I recovered, I caught the tail end of Liv's conversation with the Richmond coach.

"The signing deadline will be here before you know it," said the coach. "And we hope you'll choose Richmond when the time comes."

Outside, it had started to snow again. Flakes dappled the parking lot like thousands of freckles in thousands of Liv eyes. Liv glanced at me then took the coach's hand and forced her way through an en-

thusiastic thank-you. The coach seemed satisfied by Liv's performance and exhaled sharply before slipping her arms into her winter
jacket and heading out the glass double doors. Despite the snow, she
didn't put her hood up. I imagined a world in which those flakes
didn't melt in the heated car, and when the coach arrived at home,
weary and cold, muscles stiff from sitting, there would be someone, a
girlfriend, a wife, there waiting for her. Ready to pick each individual
flake from her head, like a gorilla grooming its mate. How nice that
would be.

"What the hell did she want?" Liv asked, her voice a punch in the
throat.

"Oh, uh"—I looked down at my hand then shoved it into my
pocket—"I guess Dani gave me her phone number." I tried not to
look pleased with myself.

"What for?" she asked.

"I think, well, to text or call her." I hated to admit it, but I was
enjoying seeing her sweat.

"What for?" she asked again.

I wasn't sure what Liv was playing at, exactly, but whatever it was,
I felt delirious, drunk on power.

"I'd imagine she wants to get to know me better," I said, smiling
at my feet.

"What about Trevor?" asked Liv. Her voice landed in that calcu-
lated space between suggestive and spiteful. I knew she knew there
wasn't anything real going on there, that the possibility had never
been there in the first place. I feigned confusion.

"Who? Oh, him. Haven't you heard? He's gay now. With your
boyfriend," I added, laughing, poking Liv in the chest, though I
didn't feel like laughing, not one bit.

"Will you chill with that?" she said. She looked around the empty
hallway, all the fans and parents having filed out long ago. "Did Dani
just assume you were, you know?"

"That I'm what?"

"All right, Mack."

"That I'm a swamp monster here to eat everyone's families?"

"Stop, you know what I'm saying."

I dropped it.

"I guess she did, yeah."

I thought about what it meant to look at someone and assume they were gay. We have all these signals available to us that indicate someone's sexuality—hair, clothes, hands, gestures, walk, talk, sit— and we always think we know what they mean, maybe better than they do. Some people think it's fucked-up to tell someone "You may not know it yet, but you're gay," but I don't. Sometimes we actually do know better. After all, it's hard to be the authority on yourself when the whole world is leading you astray. And sometimes you need someone to remind you who you are and who you want. I thought of Alex. Yeah, AAU was an hour away in Philly, but the basketball world is small and wicked. Some of the girls could have learned to talk from Katrina's School of Gossip.

"I don't know," I said. "Maybe she heard something."

Liv asked what I meant by that, what there was to hear exactly, and I bounced on my toes and looked around, searching for an out, for someone to swoop in and save me from having to explain.

"Whatever it was, I don't care," said Liv. She looked like she cared very much.

Maybe I was still high from Dani's forwardness, but I was feeling reckless and permissive, like nothing counted. So I told Liv about my ex-teammate Alex—all of it, not holding anything back—about our friendship marked by hunger and intensity, the nights spent trapped between expectation and reality, how, once we were close to collaps- ing the two, Alex dipped out, for fear of what she'd find. Liv listened, eyes wide with . . . what? Fear? Shame? Recognition? Once I was done, she said she was sorry.

"My mom won't talk to me about it," I said. "I think she'd rather me be into drugs."

"But you are into drugs," said Liv.

"Not really," I said. "I'm just fucking around, you know, trying things."

She gave me this look. "You're like a baby. You'll just indiscriminately put everything in your mouth. This drug! That drug!"

"What can I say, I'm just exploring the world."

She forced a closemouthed smile and stared at the wall behind me when she asked me if it was true, what I'd said before.

"Which part?"

"Any of it? All of it?"

"Guess it depends on who's writing the scout," I said, laughing an absurd, disembodied laugh, bringing the conversation to an end.

That night we slept over at Katrina's house, Katrina having once again enticed us with more booze and a parent-free house. Plus, there was something nice about Katrina's apparent amnesia. She never mentioned our fight the night of the Smirnoff Ices, and even though she'd instigated it and I would have loved an apology, I was happy to not have to think about it any more than I had to.

Liv and I were sitting on the couch, Katrina wedged between us, passing around a popcorn bowl and chugging then refilling then chugging rum and Cokes, the Captain Morgan bottle between my thighs, when Katrina leapt off the couch, eyes wild, a salacious grin tugging at the corners of her lips.

"You'll never guess what I found in a box in the closet," she said.

She opened the small door of the entertainment center under the TV, pulled out a black rectangle, and held it up, dangling the tape like we were hot for it.

"It's labeled 'Katrina's dance recital,'" she said.

"A unique form of torture," I said, throwing my legs across Liv's lap without thinking.

"It's not actually my dance recital, genius," said Katrina. I watched her eyes take in my legs, which made me feel self-conscious. I promptly slid them off and planted my feet on the ground. It could have been my imagination, but I think I caught Liv scowling at me before tucking her legs beneath her.

"Apparently my dad labels his dirty videos with titles he assumes no one will ever want to watch," continued Katrina, looking a little hurt.

She popped the video into the VCR and stood in front of the TV, waiting for it to come alive. I heard some awful techno music, the bass beating out of the surround sound system. Katrina backed away to reveal the screen, which had the words LESBIAN AFFAIR in bold, slanted letters, all capitals, written across it. My face grew hot, my blood beat against my cheeks like a captain banging on the lockers in pregame hype. Katrina sat on her knees on the floor, examining our faces for a reaction. I wasn't sure if it was better to look or not look at the screen—if I looked, did that make me interested? And if I didn't look, was I overcompensating for my desires? I looked at Liv—her face gave away nothing. I flipped open my phone and tried to think of someone to text. I decided to ask Dani what she was up to that night. She answered right away, talking about how she was lying in bed and watching a show I'd never heard of. When I asked what it was, she said it was this new show that just came out, basically soft-core lesbian porn. Lots of drama, lots of tits. *Oh wow,* I said, snapping my phone shut.

"You think my mom knows about this?" asked Katrina.

"Probably," said Liv.

"Really? Why do you say that?" I asked.

"She'd lose her shit," said Katrina.

"I just think people aren't as secretive as they think they are," said Liv.

In the backdrop was a normal-looking living room, all the colors dull. Sand-colored carpet, beige couch, orange and red throw pillows. Two women were stretched out on the couch. Something off-screen slurped the title up and now we were left alone with the two women.

"I'm so glad you could come over today," said the one woman, emphasis on *so* and *glad*. She had a blond bob. The other had teased black hair down to her shoulders.

"My pleasure," said the teased hair. They watched a black TV screen.

"You know," said the blond bob, scooting closer to her guest, "my husband is out of town."

"Oh, is he now?" said the teased hair. "How will we fill our time?"

"I have an idea."

The music picked up the pace, the bass even more profound than before. Now the women were leg to leg. Blond bob put a French-manicured hand on her guest's smooth, buttery thigh, working her way up to her groin, then over her lace-covered cunt. Those nails terrified me. They were good for a back scratch, not for anything this video was about to show. Teased hair was wearing a white lacy top and underwear. Blond bob wore a matching red outfit.

Blond bob slid off the couch and onto her knees. She pulled teased hair's underwear off, revealing a nice, trimmed bush. Before she even brought mouth to cunt, teased hair was moaning like she was about to orgasm.

On-screen, teased hair said, "Oh my god, Beth. Oh my god, Beth."

More moaning, and then, "My husband has never done it like this before."

Blond bob moved her head in circles, first clockwise, then counterclockwise. It didn't look like she was doing a very good job, but teased hair continued to scream and moan and make other sounds that would scare a house pet.

"Oh my, oh my. The way you use your tongue!"

More moaning.

My phone vibrated in my lap. I caught Liv glancing at the screen. I tilted it away from her as I read the message. It was from Dani.

The show is pretty good. We should watch it together sometime.

Instead of committing one way or another, I told her that I shared my phone with my mom and that if I ever said I had to go that meant I was surrendering my phone to her.

Aka don't send me any questionable texts, I said.

She replied, several texts right in a row.

Oh shit.

She really doesn't know?

Haha, has she seen you?

Shut up, I said. *Speaking of, I gotta go.*

No, you don't, she replied. *You already told me where you're at. But I get it, I made you uncomfortable.*

Liv kicked me and made a face for me to get off my phone. I smiled, happy to see her jealous. I heard a door close, although I couldn't tell where the noise had come from. The surround sound system made it sound like the door was upstairs, inside Katrina's house.

"Oh, is there about to be some threesome action?" I said, nodding at the TV, where the women had yet to stop what they were doing and look up.

"Not exactly," said Katrina. She raised her right eyebrow, then her gaze floated upward, over my head. I turned around to find James, Trevor, and Anthony, their teammate and Katrina's new boy.

"So, this is what you girls get up to when you're alone," teased Anthony.

Katrina jumped up to her feet and ran into his arms, making a big production out of kissing him all over his face. Little pecks like a chicken.

"I put it on to surprise you guys," she said. "Duh, why else?"

I risked a glance at Liv, who was tracing the heart line on her palm, or maybe it was her head line. I always forgot which was which.

"You're so sweet," said Anthony. He was this little shrimp of a man, acne everywhere. He took her ass cheeks in his tiny hands.

Once Katrina finished her performance, she looked at me and Liv and said, "See, I brought you guys a treat."

When Liv didn't get up off the couch to greet James in a similar fashion, he said, "Wow, way to make a guy feel special."

"I didn't know you were coming," said Liv.

I sat there watching this all go down, resenting James for the way he avoided eye contact with me after sending me those threatening messages. I didn't realize Trevor expected anything from me until he looked at James and told him this was a big waste of time. They both scowled at Anthony and the love he was receiving. It occurred to me that one drugged-up fuck was enough for Trevor to believe he owned me, had unlimited access to my affection and attention. But nobody owned me. Not even me.

I wondered what it meant to be worthy of someone's attention and affection. A person's worth implied the presence of another, someone to assign that value—in Liv's mom's case, her father. A precarious situation for anyone to find themself in. And a person's worth was different depending on the currency. There's sex, of course, but that was just one thing. There were also full scholarships, the phone ringing off the hook with coaches' offers. The coaches needed us, wanted us to choose their school, their offer. But now that I needed that scholarship in a practical way, it wasn't just about bragging rights, I could see that there'd always been a power imbalance involved. Someone was watching me run up and down a court and assigning me value. Sixty thousand dollars a year. Thirty thousand dollars a year. I felt like a prize hog. The trick, I knew, was to be the one to give yourself worth—then no one could take it away at a moment's notice. But who knew how to do that?

"Well, look who it is," said Trevor, biting his lip at me.

It was clear both James and Trevor were drunk off their asses. That was the new normal for them. Ever since that night in the car, they'd been drunk as often as possible. Liv told me they'd even begun sneaking drinks at school during study hall and lunch; she could tell by the way James's texts slowly made less and less sense, became garbled by clumsy thumbs and slow-firing neurons. For a moment, I felt sorry for them, but then my sympathy dissipated and in its place was resentment: we were all going through it—figure it the fuck out, I wanted to say.

James came up behind Liv, leaned over the back of the couch, and draped his arms across her chest, hands resting at her belly button. She didn't react; I hoped his touch felt repulsive. He whispered something in her ear I couldn't make out then kissed her on the cheek and stood back up, staring me down.

"Can I talk to you real quick?" he said, nodding toward the ceiling. "Privately?"

I mumbled sure and followed him up the stairs to the living room. I got this strange idea in my head that he was here to apologize. He paced back and forth for a while, not saying anything, just pressing his hands to his temples and rubbing, his eyes both deranged and absent, scanning the floor, the walls, and then me. When they landed on me, he stopped pacing and approached me.

"Now," he began, "I know you've had Trevor, but have you ever had a real man?"

I wasn't expecting him to raise two hands to my chest and shove me with enough force to send me flying backward onto the couch.

"What the fuck you do that for?" I said. I planted my hands at my sides to help me sit up.

Already he was ripping off his letterman jacket and working at his zipper, stepping out of his jeans.

"What are you doing?"

"That dude doesn't know clit from asshole," he said. He was hovering over me like a hawk.

I didn't say anything. I felt oddly calm, detached from my body, like it was happening to someone else, someone I'd never even met.

"I'll fuck the dyke right out of you," he continued. "Won't that be something?"

I scooted to the edge of the couch. With one quick push he had me on my back once more. Down to his boxers, he said, "Tell me you don't want me."

"I don't want you," I said without affect.

"Okay, fine, fine," he said. He raised his hands in defeat and backed away from me as if he'd just read the room wrong. I don't know why I didn't get up and leave, instead watching him pace yet again. He slipped out of his boxers and turned to me, wagging his soft, limp dick around.

"I want you so fucking bad," he said.

I could feel something, a meanness, bubbling inside of me. I wasn't afraid of it so much as I was energized by it.

"I think you have me confused with Trevor," I said.

"What the fuck did you just say?" he growled, climbing on top of me and pinning my arms above my head with one hand. He bit at my jaw, my neck. He squeezed my boob so hard I thought it might pop. I felt a yelp bubble in my throat, but I swallowed it. On my thigh I could feel him grinding his lifeless dick against me. I was still wearing my T-shirt and sweatpants. They felt like the only thing protecting me.

What had been bubbling inside me, I realized, was not a meanness, but envy. I was envious of the kiss James and Trevor had shared. Unlike our kiss in the ice bath, which only happened because we became an older straight couple without any real problems or concerns, what had happened between James and Trevor in the car had been real. Even if just for a moment. Even if the aftermath threatened to dismantle them both. And maybe that was what I wanted—to be decimated beyond recognition so I would have no choice but to rebuild, without the influence of others.

"Stop it, James, this isn't fucking cool," I said. "I meant what I said."

"This is what I want," he growled. "A woman."

"I know," I said.

A familiar thought banged around in my head, and for the first time, I allowed it to stay, to dent the walls with its weight: that if he wanted me, then it wasn't a woman he was after, not really, anyway.

"I know," I repeated.

I turned my head to the side, away from his open mouth, his

coming-for-me mouth. The old owl clock on the wall read 10:06. It was such a horrific coincidence, I wanted to laugh. I blinked, and just like that, it was 10:07; the moment had passed. I closed my eyes and squeezed my thighs together, hoping he'd come to his senses.

After a few moments, I heard Liv's voice. She was in the living room. I opened my eyes. She was running up behind James, hand clenched in a fist. She punched him in the left eye, and he lurched backward, probably more stunned by the surprise hit than by its force. In the kitchen stood Trevor, eyes wide, mouth hanging open, and after a few moments, he snapped to attention and grabbed an empty liquor bottle by the neck. James pressed his fingers to the bone under his eye and pulled them away, examining them for blood.

"You piece of shit," said Liv. "Go home. Now." She put her body between James and me.

Trevor, swinging the empty bottle a little, said, "Come on, man, don't make me throw one, too."

James looked at his friend, then looked down at his crotch, as if to consult his cock. Time expanded and contracted, undulating with the collective breath of the room. I snapped my hair tie against my wrist. Thwack, thwack, thwack. James stumbled to his feet, grabbed the clusters of his clothing, and pushed past Trevor. We heard him stomp down the hallway and slam the front door.

"You okay?" Liv asked, turning to face me. I could have kissed her.

"Let me know if there's anything I can do," said Trevor, before leaving us alone.

I told her I was glad she was the one to find me. She squinted at me in confusion.

I said, "I didn't think you'd believe me otherwise."

"Oh, Mack," she said. She looked at the ceiling, blinking back tears. "I always believe you."

I nodded, waiting to see what I might say next. I wasn't in control of myself right now. I was floating thousands of miles away. Thwack, thwack, thwack.

"Stop," she said, reaching out to grab my wrist before recoiling, perhaps afraid to touch, afraid to break me. "You didn't do anything wrong."

"I want to take a shower."

"We can make that happen."

Liv grabbed my hand and led me upstairs to the master bedroom. I floated along behind her, staring blankly at her back. In the bathroom, I saw myself in the mirror. I was crying a passive, soundless cry. I tasted salt and blood. Liv turned on the shower and tested the water with a shaking hand. I took off my clothes, climbed in, and sat on the ground, hugging my knees to my chest, the water bleeding down my head, my neck. Liv stripped down and stepped in behind me. She grabbed a bar of soap and sat behind me, creating a lather. Slowly, tenderly, she brought her hands to my back.

I stared through the blinding white tiles into my future. I had X-ray vision. My future was coming at me so fast I needed it to slow the fuck down, maybe get distracted by some roadside attractions.

"I'm scared," I said.

"He's not going to try anything with you again, I'll be sure of that."

Liv wrote words on my back I couldn't decode. My throat felt clogged. I leaned forward and spit blood and saliva into the drain.

"What?" I said. "Oh, yeah."

I let her believe I was afraid of James, but really, I wasn't even thinking about him. Not yet, anyway. It would take years to process what happened, to understand just how powerless I was, and how much power can get away with.

But before all that, sitting there in the shower, drowning, I was thinking about life, how much it scared me to be alive. All of it. I was afraid I'd commit to the wrong college, play for the wrong team, spend my whole career regretting my decision. Within that fear was a more haunting, more disturbing fear. I worried that the game would never be the same without Liv, that I no longer loved the game for what it was but only for what it was when I was with her. I was afraid to find out.

HALFTIME

I looked up at the scoreboard, but couldn't, for the life of me, figure out who was winning and who was losing. The numbers blurred and swam before me, trying but failing to tell a story that was less about the score and more about who gets to keep it.

SECOND HALF

13

SWEEP AND GO

The sound of a creaky door opening came out of the computer speaker, and I knew that Liv had just logged onto AIM. A few seconds later, I received a message from her asking what I was up to that night, did I want to hang and watch a movie or something? A bunch of smiley faces with their tongues sticking out. I told her the first lie that came to my head.

Bballmack12: *sorry I can't tonight*
Bballmack12: *hanging with Grayson*
Coopdeloop: *oh bro night*
Coopdeloop: *no Liv allowed?*
Bballmack12: *you know I haven't seen him in forever*
Coopdeloop: *yeah I got you, Big*
Coopdeloop: *guess I'll just have to entertain myself*
Bballmack12: *I'll text you, number 1*

I put up some pining away message I expected Liv to know was directed at her. Dashboard or New Found Glory or Bright Eyes.

Something with a lot of hard-hitting lines about waiting for love and breaking your own heart ten thousand times over. I don't know what I expected after everything that went down at Katrina's house, but we never spoke of it again and nothing changed between us. In some fucked-up, twisted way, I was glad James had shown what a piece of shit he really was, even if it was at my expense—otherwise, I wasn't sure Liv would have ever left him. And having left him, I thought maybe, just maybe, Liv might notice what it was she'd been missing all along.

It was a selfish, futile hope, one I felt ashamed to admit. I wasn't entitled to Liv any more than anyone else was. But I simply wished Liv would, somehow, against all sense, against all understanding of the world and how it works, choose me.

Sometimes it felt like all I'd ever done since meeting Liv was wait, and I didn't want to wait around any longer, not while there was someone out there like Dani, who knew what she wanted and went after it with an earnest conviction. I figured, fuck it, I might as well see what she's about. I was supposed to be getting ready to meet her, but before I could get up from the computer, my phone dinged. It was Coach Harris, the assistant for Gonzaga.

Hey, Morris! Hope you're doing well. Check your email when you get a chance. My wife helped me make something just for you.

The ease with which she said *her wife* gave me vertigo. I opened my email and found a photo of this year's Gonzaga women's basketball team. In the back row, standing beside one of the forwards, was a photo of me in a Gonzaga jersey, the picture recycled from an old AAU photo I was guessing she'd found online. I looked to be about eight feet tall. The Photoshop job was janky as hell, but I appreciated the effort, felt flattered by the attention. Did she do this for all the recruits? I liked to think that I had something not everyone else had. A combination of natural talent, hard work, fortitude, and angst that kept her coming back for me. I texted her back and thanked her for the photo, said I guessed I didn't look half bad in blue and red.

Upstairs, I got ready in the bathroom, hopped up on pre-date jitters. The mirror was framed with various magazine cutouts of AI, my favorite being his *Slam* cover from 1999, him in a throwback blue jersey and Afro, next to the words ALLEN IVERSON IS SOUL ON ICE.

I opened the bottom drawer and pulled out a bottle of hair spray and sprayed it onto a hand towel then brought it to my face, inhaling deeply, indulgently. I found the hair spray was much better than the permanent markers I used to sniff when I was younger, bored and irritable in the back of class. The hair spray produced this sort of dreamy, goofy high in which I felt I was made of wet sand, the kind you use to make a drippy sandcastle like my dad and I used to make at the beach on family vacations in Sea Isle City. He'd always make a big stink about what a good dad he was, how no matter what, he always set aside enough money for us to go there on vacation. It took me years to realize that it wasn't me he was trying to convince. It was the only place I'd ever been besides our town and wherever AAU tournaments happened to take place. My world was unbelievably small and terrifyingly, unknowably big. Either way, my dad had been very serious about drippy sandcastles. Our MO was to drop the wet sand from great heights to see where it would fall. It was a surprise each time. No two drippy sandcastles were the same, not like the dry ones, limited by the shape of the buckets and laws of physics. I think he wanted me to know that something solid and good could be built from seemingly unstable elements. The wet sand dripped and sagged and made a mess of itself. Then it dried and held its place. My dad, standing by, hands on his hips, would examine our work as if it were a piece of fine art.

And just like that, my high was gone, and once again, I was made of earthly things, meat and bone and connective tissue. I did it once more: spray, spray, spray, inhale. But it wasn't the same. I couldn't get back to that beach.

If he were here with me, right now, he would have pulled away the towel. Said something like *How is this helping, kid?* Or *You've gone and lost your damn mind.* I ran into my room, grabbed my dad's Sixers hat, and threw it on backward. Returning to the bathroom, I stood in front of the mirror and puffed up my chest, pretending to be my father lecturing me.

"What you trying to do, huh? Mess up your one chance at greatness?"

I removed the hat and became me again.

"I'm not going to mess this up, don't worry so much."

The hat went back on.

"Let's better hope you can handle the pressure, kid."

"Not this again."

It went that way, back and forth, arguing with the version of my father that was hardest to love and easiest to remember.

"Just saying, you've got something special. I'd hate to see you still here in thirty years, bitching and whining about what could have been. Or even worse, holding it all in."

"You mean like you?"

A big, hearty laugh erupted from my belly. I had the hat facing forward now, the brim pulled low over my eyes.

"Yeah, exactly," I said, trying not to cry for my father, for everyone who'd ever wanted more from their life but been unable or ill-equipped to ask for it. Briefly, I allowed myself to wonder about him and Liv's dad, how well they had really known each other.

I ended my little performance in the mirror, remembering I had somewhere to be. Dani was waiting for me at her school. Her coach trusted her with a key so she could practice when the weather outside was bad. I wasn't sure if I was interested in Dani exactly, but I didn't want to question my impulse to meet up with her, didn't want to overanalyze the situation. We were just going to shoot hoops and drink some drinks. Nothing crazy. Oddly, though, or maybe not oddly at all, I felt as if I were cheating on Liv, and I hated myself for it, hated how I felt as if I were in a constant state of miscommunicating with myself. My atoms were alive with the potential of the evening. Hot, hot wires, severed and sizzling.

I headed downstairs with a backpack of vodka and Sprite, trying not to shift the bag so the bottles wouldn't clank together. In the living room, my mom was sitting on her yoga mat in front of the TV, drinking straight out of a wine bottle, which was nearly empty. At least eight salt lamps lit up orange around her like giant lightning bugs.

Before I could ask what was wrong, she took a swig of wine then said, "Lars left us, honey."

"Us," I said.

"Us," she said.

I wanted to say something mean, but I ended up saying I was sorry. I felt a strange sort of softness for my mother. My mother had lost just like I had. And now, with no anchor, she floated about the atmosphere like a rogue balloon from a children's birthday party, snagging on whatever trees she happened upon.

"Sorry doesn't do me any good." She turned away and burped into her hand.

"Okay, then I take it back."

"Why won't you just accept a damn scholarship already?" she asked. She finished off the bottle and slammed it down on the carpet. "It's not like your grades are going to do you any favors."

"I don't know, Mom."

"What exactly are you waiting for?"

"Are we done here?"

Pissed, I went into the kitchen and poured a glass of water for her, practically shoving it into her hand. She examined it for a few seconds then set it on the floor next to her.

"I need the phone tonight," she said.

"What happened to yours?"

She sighed then pulled the smashed thing out of her pocket.

I looked at her, hoping she was drunk enough to forget her words right after saying them.

"That's not going to be a problem, will it?"

"Only if I can borrow your car," I said. Dad's junker was being more cantankerous than usual.

"I'll think about it."

"No, I mean, right now. I'm going somewhere."

"And where is somewhere?"

"Please," I said. "Don't act all mom on me now."

"I don't need to act," she said. "It's what I am."

She didn't seem so sure of herself, but I wasn't looking for a fight. Just wanted to get out of there.

"Fine, I'll ride my bike," I said, handing the flip phone to my mom.

I didn't need the phone anyway; Dani was already waiting for me at the gym. And I was diligent about deleting my texts every day, not that my mom seemed to care enough to snoop. Part of me wanted to hand her a phone full of my secrets, wanted her to sit me down and tell me I was okay, I would be okay. I looked out the window. It wasn't snowing but there was frost on the trees. My mom followed my gaze then said the keys were in the kitchen drawer.

Dani was shooting foul shots when I pulled open the heavy gym doors, suctioned shut by the strong winter wind. She stopped mid-shot and turned around, smiling at me. The lights were dimmed, the air took on the cool silver of Cathedral's home court. It felt weird to be here for a reason other than a game.

We stood rooted to the ground, staring at each other for a few seconds before I made my way over to the side of the court, where I took off my street shoes and sweats, revealing shorts underneath, and put on my basketball shoes. I dug my ball out of my backpack. Dani watched me with what I hoped was a keen interest. Every day with Liv, I felt as if I were under a microscope, but this was different— I knew what would come of the observation, knew the intentions of the person hunched over it, looking through its seeing eye.

"How many in a row?" I asked.

"What?"

"I assumed you were counting," I said, nodding at the basket.

"Oh," she said, looking sheepish. "I made eighty-six out of one hundred."

"I guess that'll have to do." It felt good to do this flirting thing so openly, to do it for its feel-good sake.

My joints snap-crackle-popped as I climbed to my feet. Bone grinding bone, a young body that wouldn't slow down.

"What was that, your ankles or knees?" asked Dani.

"Yes," I said.

She laughed.

"You're different than I thought you'd be."

She didn't look away when she said it, didn't turn and take a jumper, didn't brush off the moment like a leaf fallen on her sleeve. She touched her lips thoughtfully, waiting for me to bite.

"Fine, how so?"

I shot the ball into the air to myself as I spoke, grateful for the distraction. It was too much, to look at someone and see them. I forgot all about the liquor in my backpack, the balm I thought I'd need in order to do the things I knew I wanted to do.

"I don't know. Before we met, I was intimidated by you," she said.

"And now you're not?"

She shook her head no.

"Fuck," I said, smiling.

"You're softer than I imagined."

"Softer."

I must have sounded incredulous because Dani laughed again. She showed no signs of self-consciousness now.

"Yes."

"Softer?"

It was like someone learning a new language or studying for a vocabulary quiz. The words sticky in my mouth, having lost all meaning.

"Yeah, it's nice," she said. "But."

"But what?"

"Nothing."

"No, no, that's not how this works."

She shook her head. "Fine, it's just, I can tell basketball is maybe covering something else up."

I frowned at her but quickly fixed my face, realizing Dani's comment hadn't actually perturbed me; it was quite the opposite, in fact. I thought nothing was sexier than being picked apart this way. I felt as if Dani were performing an autopsy on me while I was still alive.

"Tell me more."

"I don't know, I shouldn't have said anything, I'm sorry."

"Nah, now I'm waiting."

"All right," she said, looking at me, really meeting my eyes for the first time. "I'm sitting here wondering who you are when no one's looking. No crowd, no fans, no nothing."

Sometimes I wasn't sure how I felt until my body reacted, and in that moment, I felt my heart quicken, my pulse punch me back so I knew I was nervous, but also stimulated.

I stepped onto the court, the place where I felt most myself. Even someone else's court I could find a way to make mine.

"What happens after all this is over?"

"I'm going to play in college."

"Then what?"

"I'll play overseas and in the WNBA."

"Everyone has to retire eventually."

"What are you getting at?"

"Nothing, nothing, forget it."

"I wish I wasn't this way."

"And what way is that?"

I shrugged, shot a half-assed layup, unsure of what to say. I was used to evasions, to speaking through basketball, through drinks or a quick hit. How was I expected to explain to this stranger that the more I desired, the more those desires emptied me? That if I could be anyone else, I would.

"I see," said Dani. "How do you know you don't want it, then?"

Maybe it was the finality of Dani's question as she turned to take a layup or the disappointment in her voice that inspired me, but I grabbed Dani's arm just above the elbow and turned her around so she was facing me. I leaned in and kissed her, a chest-collapsing, nerve-stricken kiss. She tasted sweet, decadent even, a faint suggestion of strawberry. When I pulled away, Dani gave me a weird but pleased look.

"Now how do you feel?" she asked.

I turned away. My face was hot, my hands tingled with pleasure and fear. The kiss hadn't made me fall off the planet or anything, but it did make me forget the curious depths of my loneliness, how it burned and filleted me.

I kissed Dani again, a slower kiss, one without anywhere to be, anyone to answer to. Dani's hands moved from my waist up the back of my shirt and under my sports bra. Her cool, callused hands against the skin of my back made me shiver, lose all of my air. Behind my eyelids, I saw Liv watching from the corner, arms crossed over her chest. A stoic statue watching what could have been hers. I opened my eyes and once again pulled away.

"I take it you and Cooper broke up then?" said Dani, a little breathless.

"What?"

"Sorry, I just assumed," she said. "The way she was looking at you after our game." She trailed off, shaking her head. "Never mind, forget it."

I nodded slowly, not wanting to give away my feelings for Liv. I asked Dani if other people thought that, too. Everywhere I went, people talked. Just once, I wished they'd leave me alone.

"I don't think so," she said, though I could tell she was lying.

"Well, what about Kelsey, on your team?"

"What about her?"

I shrugged and spun the ball in my hands.

"I see," she said. "That was over before it ever really began."

Having gotten the kiss out of the way, and with it, some nervous anticipation, we shot around for an hour or so, me showing off with behind-the-back layups and and-one mixtape moves. Dani watched me, meditative, like a duck floating in a pond. I was enjoying myself, but I didn't feel the fierce intimacy I did when Liv and I shot around. Our balls didn't sync up in an irreplicable melody, there was nothing ethereal about our time together.

We played a casual game of one-on-one, neither of us bothering to keep score, just relishing the small moments the game yielded. Because we'd played Cathedral twice and I never forgot a player's game, I knew everything Dani liked and didn't like to do, knew she was ambidextrous, would pull up for a jumper with either hand, knew she was a pump fake extraordinaire. She was a decent player, probably D-II or low D-I caliber. I asked if she knew where she was going to college yet, and she told me she was going to Penn.

"Oh, nice. I haven't seen them play."

She looked at me blankly for a moment before it clicked.

"Oh, I'm not playing there." She passed the ball between my legs and ran around me to retrieve it on the other side.

"What? Why not?" I said. "You're definitely good enough."

Dani laughed. "Thanks, but it's not about whether I'm good enough or not. I'm going for premed. Just want to focus on academics."

I felt stupid, a bit dumbfounded. It had never occurred to me that Dani, or anyone else for that matter, might not want to play in college. I assumed every athlete's dream was to play in college and then pro, like me. If not, what was the point? Academics were an afterthought. Whenever any of the scouts asked what I wanted to study, I shrugged and said basketball, assuming an area of academic interest would eventually jump out and reveal itself to me.

"I can see you're struggling with this concept." Dani laughed. "But I play basketball for fun."

I never understood people whose hearts weren't in it, people who were playing for community or exercise or friendship or something to do after school. I mean, it was all fine and good, but it felt like we were playing two different sports. Dani didn't notice or appreciate the poetry of her pump fakes—she simply used them for their designated purpose. I guess what I mean is there was no romance.

"Fun isn't exactly the word I'd use."

"Then why play?"

"It's the only time I feel okay."

Dani placed her ball at her feet and moved in to give me a hug. Her body felt good pressed against my body. I nuzzled her shoulder, breathed in her salty musk. It was the first time I'd admitted that aloud before. The confession calmed me, loosened my tight-wound jaw. It felt good to say something that felt so bad. I wasn't sure if it was Dani's embrace or my confession, but I was feeling reckless, turned-on. Maybe the Catholics were onto something after all. Maybe they all left the confessionals with boners and soaked thighs and snuck off to go fuck in the back pew. I considered asking Dani if this happened at school after they were required to go to confession but decided against it. I was done talking, I wanted Dani under me. And she knew it, too, because she grabbed my hand and led me to the side of the court, where she sat down and began unlacing her shoes. I sat down beside her and did the same. We looked at each other as our hands worked, each daring the other. Shoes and socks off, I got on my knees and crawled in between Dani's spread legs.

"What do you think you're doing?" she whispered, snaking a hand around my neck and gripping the base of my skull. She pulled my face to hers and forced my lips open with her tongue. I leaned forward and guided Dani to her back. I grabbed my sweatshirt and put it under her head as a pillow and Dani smiled, biting my lower lip, conjuring a moan out of me. I ground my body against Dani's, feeling her push back, breath hot against my cheek. We moved this way, in a rhythmic wave, for a while, the pressure below my waist and between my thighs building and building. It had never been this way with guys. No electricity, only boredom, dissociation. I bit at Dani's neck and jaw, moved my hands up her shirt and massaged her breasts.

Dani's breathing quickened. She took my hand and stuck it down the waistband of her shorts, down her underwear, where her wetness soaked my fingers, and I felt my clit throb, my lips pressing tightly together to prevent another desperate moan. This was all so new to me, I felt at once fascinated and terrified, clumsy and unstoppable.

"Is this because of me?" I asked. She laughed.

"Who else would it be for, Mack?"

"I don't fucking know," I said.

Dani was so wet, so ready for me, that I entered her with three fingers, wanting to fill her up, take up as much space inside her as possible, and Dani said, "Oh, oh. Too many," pulling on my wrist. I mumbled sorry, embarrassed, worried that I was bad at this, then used two fingers this time, going slowly at first before picking up the pace at Dani's direction. I curled my fingers backward with every stroke like I'd do to myself when I discovered that it had never been penetration I disliked, but just how guys did it.

Dani's body flexed under me, hands pawing at my back muscles. Then she moved her hands to my chest, playing with my nipples through my sports bra and running her hands down my stomach, playing with the waistband of my shorts. She moved a finger down toward my cunt, moving in small, teasing circles. For a second, I forgot where I was and thought it was James under me, trying to have his way with me. I jerked away from her, backing my hips up, out of Dani's reach, my arms on either side of her, pressed up into a plank. When she asked me what was wrong, I shook off the terror that had sucked my air pipe closed.

I didn't want Dani to fuck me, it felt too intimate, too vulnerable, too everything. I whispered in her ear that she needed to be patient, needed to listen to me. This small, insignificant taste of domination was enough to make Dani playfully whine in protest, clearly liking being told what she could and could not do. We started to make out while I worked at her pleasure.

When I closed my eyes, Liv reappeared. She uncrossed her arms and slipped out of her shirt, her nipples showing through her navy sports bra. Then she played with the waist of her shorts, digging her thumbs into her hips. I moved from Dani's mouth to her shoulder, burying my face in it, biting at it. Liv's shorts came off, as did everything else. My clit throbbed so hard I found myself whispering "I'm so fucking hard right now," even though I knew that wasn't what girls said, and even though the arousal wasn't for Dani. I continued to bite at whatever piece of Dani I could get at—neck, shoulder, chest, while Dani thrust, tightening around my fingers, her moans escalating into these uninhibited cries that made me feel real fucking good, like some god who'd temporarily come down to earth to remind the people why life was worth living.

She placed two hands on my cheeks and pushed me back so she could look into my eyes.

"Look at me," she said, moaning beautiful, wanting moans. She came hard and long, her body quaking under me, and as her body calmed, I felt a deep, suffocating dread overcome me.

I slowly pulled out and tried to smile despite the vertigo of truth blurring my vision: I'd never felt more alone than I did right then. I had thought that accepting myself would be the end of suffering, that everything would be good after I gave in to the call of my hunger. That after I did that, I could really start living. What I didn't know: that at the end of suffering was just more and different suffering.

"Was that your first time with a girl?" Dani asked. I rolled off of her onto the cold, hard gym floor.

"Oh my god," I said, covering my face with my hands.

"No, no, I didn't mean it like that," she said. Her voice was gentle, as if holding me with two hands. "I just mean, I don't know how someone else hasn't gotten to you yet."

I nodded, avoiding eye contact, plotting the best way to get out of there.

"Oh. Oh no," she said.

I looked at her, waiting.

"It's all making sense to me now."

"What is?"

"You know there's a big bad world out there, right?" said Dani. "Cooper's just one person." Suddenly her voice had an edge to it, as if embittered by her recent revelation about me and my lack of emotional availability.

"Thanks," I said. I dug the vodka bottle out of my backpack, unscrewed the top, and dumped the liquor down my throat, smiling as I swallowed, welcoming the burn.

"You're mad, I can see that. So, what, you're going to drink about it? Real cool, real cool."

Suddenly, I felt hostile—not toward Dani, not toward our sex, not toward Liv, but toward myself. Was this the way I was going to continue to live for all of my years? Behaving as if hovering close to what I wanted was the same as having what I wanted?

I told her I wasn't mad at her, I just needed some breathing room, needed to get out of that gym. We said our goodbyes—a quick, awkward peck on the lips that had me running for the door so fast I accidentally left my ball behind. I wasn't ready to go home, so I drove around, unsure of where I was going, feeling sorry for myself. I wanted to keep drinking but didn't want to prove Dani right. I didn't want anyone but Liv, and there wasn't a damn thing I could do about it. Sometimes I wasn't sure if I knew how to function without her. Like if I was away from her for too long our connection would sever and I'd float away like an astronaut, high and alone in the blackness of the universe. I didn't know what the fuck to do. There I was, wedged between two worlds, or rather, falling off the face of both of them.

I drove and drove until I ended up at the entrance of Sycamore Beach, where Liv and I had first played together. All those red cedars staring down on me, questioning. I thought of Gonzaga and wondered if Spokane, Washington, had real sycamores, what kind of secrets their roots might hold. I could picture myself climbing one and hanging out there all day, just watching all the students on campus live their lives, unaware that someone was bearing witness. Down the dirt path I drove, hitting pothole after pothole, guided by nothing but the light of the full moon and its big, swollen head.

I parked on the grass and cursed myself for forgetting my ball at Cathedral. Then, in a fleeting moment of hope, I turned around to grab a ball out of the back seat before remembering I was driving my mom's Saturn and didn't keep a ball in there. The court was calling to me anyway, so I followed its coaxing voice, all stiff-limbed and zombie-like, entranced by the night's quietude. I could just barely make out the new graffiti on the backboards:

> THE RULES ARE SIMPLE
> DOWN TO DIE

Since I had no ball, I began to mime instead, taking some warm-up dribbles before pulling up for a jumper. Free of physical limitations, I swished half-court shots, made left-handed threes, sunk impossible floaters—every shot buttery on its way down. I was a ballet dancer on the world's stage, I was the maker of thousands of miniature creation stories, I was what happened when art and beauty collided.

I tried to channel what it felt like when I was young and I played for the pure love and joy of the game, unaware yet that there were other reasons to play. For some reason, I thought of this one AAU tournament from when I was ten. My dad was coaching our team that year. Most of my teammates were awful skill-wise, but we were quick and scrappy. We ran teams into the ground, chasing them all over the court and trapping them in every corner. We, or rather my dad, found a way to turn impossible games into close games, though we usually lost in the end. I remember he'd just taught me the in-and-out move and I'd been perfecting that shit for months. Finally, I used it in a game and damn near made my defender fall. Afterward, a grown man stopped me and complimented my in-and-out, told me it was a man's move, that I was a real baller, he could tell. I wasn't even mad he acted like only men had handles like that, and maybe I should have been, women's rights and all that. I just remember feeling satisfied knowing that someone noticed me, that they could corroborate my skills. Suddenly, playing wasn't just playing anymore; it was performing.

An hour or so later, I drove home, lonely, reeling from the evening. In the driveway, I gave in to my cravings and chugged half the bottle, forcing it down, down, down in that desperate, can't-drink-it-fast-enough way. When I walked in the door, a wad of mint gum in my mouth, my mom was where I'd left her, drinking a new bottle of wine and staring at a black TV screen, practically catatonic, her hair wild. I felt a perverse desire to pull the vodka from my backpack and clink it against my mom's wine bottle: Look at us, would you just look at us now? Absolutely fucking killing it at life.

Without looking at me, she said, "You're late, you know," even though she hadn't given me a curfew.

"I used the moon to guide me."

It took what felt like hours for her to answer.

"You did what?"

"Nothing," I said.

"Oh," she said, nodding.

"Mom, can I ask you something?"

"Yeah, of course, come over here and ask me while I lie down."

She fell onto her back and ran her fingers through the knots in her hair. Our cellphone was flipped open beside her. I could see she'd been going through her phone book and had landed on Lars's number.

"What do you know about Liv's dad?"

"Who?" She found a particularly unruly knot and ripped and tore at it.

"Liv?" I said. "The person I spend, like, all my time with?"

"Oh, yeah," she said. "Her, of course."

"Did you know Dad and her dad were friends?"

"That was before we met. Back when he was still a man whore."

"What about after?"

She sighed, slow-blinking. I felt like I was asking too much of her. Like it put her in physical pain just to answer my questions.

"Mom," I said.

"Mackenzie," she said.

I felt like a little kid, in need of reassurance, a story to defy all stories.

"Can you tell me the story of how you and Dad met again?"

The liquor had hit me like a bulldozer of a screen nobody bothered calling out for me. I realized I was probably slurring my words, but I didn't care, a part of me wanted my mom to catch me drunk, to have to confront what she'd been avoiding for years: the incongruence of her child being a stud athlete with a hungry, hungry penchant for escape.

"Oh, I don't know, honey. It's late," she said.

"Do you even miss him?"

"Why are you talking crazy? What is this? It's complicated, okay?" She paused to gather the fragments of her thoughts. "I miss wanting to miss him."

I didn't know why I'd asked. Regardless of what she said, I knew that on Wednesday nights she went to his work basketball league and sat in the stands with a flask. A space where the men didn't remember him for anything other than his monster screens, his celebration dance after a blocked shot. Maybe, at first, they approached her after the game, wiping their foreheads and arms with towels, but after a while, they probably dashed to the door the second they got their sneakers off. In reminding myself of this, I began to feel tender toward my mother, the private disaster of her. I wanted to bend down and kiss her eyelids. But I didn't.

"Sure," I said. "Night, then."

I swiped my phone off the ground and went upstairs to bed. There were no new message notifications on the phone, which I thought was weird, but when I went to my inbox, I saw there were a bunch I hadn't seen before, received in the hours I was out. They'd all been opened.

Grayson: *Got some good-ass coke, can't wait for you to try some.*
Grayson: *Like, I had no face for a while there.*
Grayson: *You good?*
Grayson: *Alright, hit me up then when you're around.*
Liv: *Hey Big*
Liv: *What are you up to?*
Liv: *Getting high without me?*
Liv: *What would you say if I said I missed you rn?*
Liv: *I'm wearing your hoodie, it smells just like you*

My mom had read my messages, had been faced with the reality of my self-destruction and sexuality, the interconnectedness of the two, and made the decision to say nothing, to leave it alone. All of it. It felt worse than a blowout, than a punched-in wall; it felt worse than a million missed buzzer-beaters. If I couldn't have a dad, I thought I at least deserved a mom. I was dying for a mother, to be mothered.

There was one last text.

Coach Harris: *You'll fit right in with the bulldogs* ☺

Maybe Coach Harris at Gonzaga would become the overbearing, overinvolved parent I'd always pretended to hate. And maybe she would always leave her office door open so I could stop in whenever I struggled to handle the mess of my life. Maybe I'd break in a seat on her couch from spending so much time in there just coexisting in comfortable silence. And maybe after I graduated, Coach Harris and I would be lifelong friends. I'd go over to her house, have dinner and drinks with her and her wife. Maybe I'd tell them about all the trouble I got into at the local lesbian bar. Maybe they'd laugh, tease me about how young I was, how much time I still had to enjoy that trouble. It sounded nice.

I checked the time; it was only 7 P.M. on the West Coast, a perfectly acceptable time to call. I flipped open our cellphone and scrolled through the address book until I got to the C's. So many names. Coach this and Coach that, some with the names of the schools next to them so I could keep them straight. My heart palpitated as I hovered over Coach Harris's name. I pressed call and held the phone up to my left ear. It felt like I was about to walk down the aisle and I'd forgotten how to move my feet. She answered on the third or fourth ring, and it took everything in me not to hang up on her.

"Hey there, Mack. I was just thinking about you."

"You were?"

My voice was tightrope-walking over a canyon; my chest quivered with every breath. I was so easily flattered, so easily moved to sentiment.

"Yeah, I saw you dropped a triple-double last game," she said.

In the background, I could hear game film running. Referee whistles, commentators filling the silence with fun facts about the players on the court.

"Oh, yeah," I said.

"So, what's going on, kid?"

I putzed around for a bit before I finally just came out and said it, that I wanted to come to Gonzaga. She turned off the game film, I could hear her smiling into the phone. I got this idea in my head that I wasn't just a number, that she really did care about me. We talked logistics. This was just a verbal commitment, which wasn't technically binding—I'd sign my letter of intent in a few months. Then I would move into my dorm in the summer to get my feet wet, take a class or two, start going to workouts and playing pickup. I'd be getting the fuck out of Ekron even earlier than I'd thought. When we hung up, I texted Keisha, the player who had hosted me during my Gonzaga visit, and she replied with a million exclamation points.

As I drifted off to sleep that night, I tried to imagine a beautiful, want-for-nothing world. I couldn't picture it. Could only hear waterfalls roaring all around me. Crowds doing the same. Whistles tweeting. Sneakers squeaking. My name in the mouth of the announcer. I couldn't see any of it behind my eyes.

14

STEP-BACK JUMPER

I had mentioned to Liv that I wanted to visit Cornell. In reality, I had no interest in checking out their program, even before I had decided I would accept Gonzaga. Cornell didn't offer athletic scholarships—something about being an academic school first. I imagined everyone draping ivy around their necks before class. Weaving ivy through their hair at sober sleepovers. Chopping up ivy and throwing it in the blender with kale and mango. Their basketball teams probably sucked a fat one.

Anyway, I was glad I hadn't said the last part out loud because Liv said she had a friend on the team we could crash with, and the next thing I knew, I was sleeping over at Liv's before heading to Cornell the next morning, sitting at the top of the stairs listening to her and her mom fight about James. I missed the start of the fight, but I could infer that Liv had just broken the news to her mom. I knew she'd been putting it off for reasons so obvious we didn't bother talking about them.

"You're making the biggest mistake of your life," said her mom. "You'll regret it when you see how slimy college guys are. James is a real catch, how can you not see that?"

"You don't understand," said Liv.

"Why did you do this to me?"

"To you, Mom?"

"Now what do I have?" she said.

Her mom was crying by then and by the sound of it, she was digging around in her purse for a tissue to wipe away the streaks of mascara I knew would be there. Pretty sure she wore makeup to the mailbox at the end of the driveway. Her selfishness enraged me—she hadn't even asked how Liv was feeling, if she was okay, if she needed anything. I didn't understand why people like that had children. If I ever had children, I'd lift them up so high sky watchers would mistake them for stars.

"Thanks, I guess I know where I stand now," said Liv. Her voice was shaking. I crept down the stairs, pausing on the bottom one to peer around the corner and into the kitchen. Her mom was standing at the kitchen table, Liv behind the island.

"Don't be so dramatic, Olivia. I just don't know what I'm going to tell my friends."

"What, my many scholarship offers and 3.9 GPA not exciting enough for the Bloody Marys?"

"You know I hate when you call them that," she said. She opened a compact mirror and reapplied her lipstick. Smooth, practiced swipes that reminded me of an eraser on a whiteboard.

She continued, "Don't act like I don't love you."

When Liv told her mom we'd be heading up to Cornell in the morning for a college visit, her mom's demeanor went from reconciling to challenging. Her whole body stiffened.

"I don't like you running around with that Mack person," she said. "I see everything. I hope you know that."

That last bit stole the breath from my chest—I didn't want to imagine what might go down if she knew what we got up to. But then again: there wasn't anything for her mother to know, was there?

She squinted at Liv as if she were doing the seeing right then and there. I got the sense the argument was coming to an end, and I didn't want to get caught, so I turned around and crept up the stairs, back to Liv's room, where I sat on her bed and wrote down a play I'd come up with. In it, Liv set three different screens before finally running off a baseline screen herself, setting her up for that baseline jumper she liked so much. The only act of love I knew how to reliably give: basketball.

Liv didn't come upstairs for a long while. And when she finally did, she looked like a husk of herself. She sat down next to me and studied the play, which I'd left on her pillow for her to find. She smiled weakly at me then grabbed a Sharpie from her desk and named the play *Impossible*.

I didn't know how Liv did it. It must have been exhausting living under her mother's searing spotlight. I wanted her to want out, to want to escape the stranglehold her mother had on her. I knew she loved her, but I thought maybe that love might have room to breathe from three thousand miles away.

The next morning, we tossed our duffle bags into the trunk of Liv's Jeep Wrangler and took off for Ithaca. Liv drove how she did that first day we met at my dad's party: her right arm draped across the back of my seat so that if I leaned back, her fingers would tickle my shoulder. I was feeling just as confused as I had been then—only now that confusion was laced with secrecy. I was hiding things from her. Besides committing to Gonzaga and sleeping with Dani, I was also withholding the fact that I really wanted to visit because my dad went to Cornell as a freshman before transferring home to be closer to my pregnant mom.

He hadn't told me for years, and when he finally did, he tried to play it off as if I'd always known this about him. When I pressed him, he said dropping out wasn't exactly something you bragged about.

"Transferring," I'd corrected him.

"Same shit," he said.

Liv didn't say much at the start of the drive except for "Hope the drive isn't too boring." And it was, just endless two-lane highways that seemed to drive straight into the bottom of the sky. Dead trees, lots of browns and yellows emerging from the whispers of snow. Some farmland and cows dappling the grass.

"Look, cows," said Liv, whenever we saw cows.

I didn't know why I hadn't told Liv about Gonzaga yet. I guessed it was just one of those things. And Dani, well, I was in the process of tricking my brain into believing she was someone I'd dreamt up. But it wasn't going so well. My brain was rebelling, it wouldn't shut the fuck up.

"Did you know Tracy McGrady and AI have played against each other a total of twenty-three times so far?" I asked.

"And who's won more games?"

I raised my eyebrows to communicate that she already knew the answer. "AI, of course."

"That'll change," said Liv. "Just give them a few more years."

"Iverson shook Jordan, he can do anything."

Whenever there was silence for even a few seconds, I started to itch all over, worried I'd broken out in hives. So, I kept talking some dumb shit.

"Did you know tornadoes are usually invisible until they pick up dust and debris?"

She looked at me, readjusting her two hands on the wheel.

"Wow, cool," she said.

"Yeah, so like, in a way, the things they destroy are what give them an identity."

"Mm-hmm."

She smiled at me and stuck the tip of her tongue out between her teeth. I could tell she was teasing me, but that was okay, that was better than the alternative. Once I thought about it hard enough, I realized Dani was what I was most concerned about. The other shit was whatever, but I didn't want Liv to know about Dani, to misinterpret its meaning. It didn't mean shit, not really, not in that spooky, world-rearranging way. I loved Liv, but I didn't trust her, not fully; and how cruel it was to not trust her, to take away the chance to live up to that trust.

"What? It's interesting, right?" I said. I felt my heart palpitate. "Right?"

"What the fuck is going on?" said Liv.

"Just think about it. You don't see this huge death tunnel until it's already slurped up your Jordan collection. And your mom's rosaries."

"How'd my mom get involved in this?"

"Rosaries aren't immune to natural disaster."

"Mack, why are you acting like your brains have been replaced with birds?"

"I'm not," I said. "I'm just trying to connect with you."

Liv peered at the gas gauge then back at me.

"Remind me why we are driving my gas guzzler again?"

"My mom."

"Oh, that's right," she said. "You missed curfew last week."

"I famously don't have a curfew."

I didn't know what was going on; I'd never used the word *famously* before. I felt like someone in an old-timey movie puffing on a cigar.

"You didn't tell me how your night with Grayson was."

"Huh?"

"You said you were meeting up with him?"

"Oh, yeah, yeah, it was cool, great to catch up," I said.

She eyed me suspiciously. I've never been good at lying. Or even withholding information. I was, still am, the type of person who is compelled to give someone their birthday present weeks before their actual birthday.

"Hey, get off at the next exit," I said, changing the subject.

"You have such a baby bladder," said Liv.

"No, there's a roadside attraction I want to see," I said.

"Oh?"

"The grave of Exterminator."

"Don't make me ask."

"He's a famous horse," I said.

Liv did as she was told and got off at the next exit, following the signs to the Whispering Pines Pet Cemetery. An American flag hung at the entrance next to a sign welcoming us. We parked and got out. I told her I'd looked up the attraction online, and that Exterminator, also known as "Old Bones," had been a Kentucky Derby winner. She said she didn't like horse racing, thought it was cruel and unnecessary. I agreed, but still, I wanted to see him.

Nearby, a stout man was digging a grave. He had no hair except for a patch directly on top of his head, like the world's tiniest hat. We watched him dig for a bit, his rhythm strong and persistent. He seemed to never tire. I thought of Coach Puck's children playing in the hole he'd dug, how Bryan had pretended it was a grave, the eerie morbidity of childhood, how you either could not imagine dying or imagined dying all the time; there was never any in-between. It was Liv who disrupted the man's work to ask where Exterminator's grave was. He planted his shovel into the ground and leaned on it, pointing toward the back of the cemetery, where a huge willow tree loomed. We followed his finger, winding between graves of dogs, cats, birds, pigs, you name it.

We found his grave easily enough: Exterminator, 1915–1945. Two other horses' names were on the tombstone: Sun Briar and Suntica.

"Who are they?" Liv asked.

"I don't know," I said.

"Less famous horses, I guess."

"I wouldn't want to be the less famous horses."

"I don't know," said Liv. "Maybe they had good lives."

It hadn't occurred to me. We both admired the tombstone for a bit, paying our respects.

"Maybe they got to do whatever they wanted," said Liv, rubbing her hands together in the frigid air.

"Yeah," I said. "Maybe they were together."

"Maybe," said Liv.

We stood a while looking at Exterminator's grave, not saying much of anything, taking in the strangeness of a famous horse no one's ever heard of, in the middle of Bumblefuck, New York, a great distance away from Kentucky. I hoped the horse had had a nice retirement, got some peace and quiet, finally got to rest.

It started to snow. Big, heavy flakes touching Liv wherever they pleased. Hair, cheek, nose, shoulders. I thought I hadn't seen such arrogant flakes in all my life. Liv stuck her tongue out and licked a flake from the tip of her nose, said we should get back on the road if we didn't want to join Exterminator.

When we arrived at the basketball house, we were greeted by Liv's AAU friend, Simone, a thin, dark-skinned stud with short locs and from what I could tell, an extensive and vibrant sock collection, and her housemates, a few other underclassmen on the team. They handed us shots of 99 Bananas and asked if we were ready for college life. Simone introduced everyone: Eva, a six-foot, four-inch Swede who apparently loved strip clubs and hook shots, Tiff, a light-skinned center who moved like a guard and was clearly the life of the party, and Jada, a dark-skinned femme who was redshirting due to a torn Achilles tendon.

"Oh, and she's my boo," said Simone, throwing an arm around Jada's shoulders and kissing her cheek.

Jada made a big show of being annoyed but was obviously enjoying the attention. I smiled nervously at them. Liv looked like a constipated dog.

"Aw, lookit, my buddy is in culture shock," she said, grinning at Liv.

Eva laughed then grabbed Tiff, wrapping her arms around her and pretending to lock lips. I knew they were joking about being together but couldn't tell if they were joking about being gay, too.

"Don't listen to her," said Liv, trying to steady her voice. But I could tell it was too much for her, she had to look away, help herself to another shot.

"This isn't high school anymore, Coop," said Simone.

"Yeah, everybody's gay," said Tiff. "And if they're not gay, then they're still gay." She laughed.

Then Liv said what I was thinking: "I'm not sure I've ever heard someone say that word so casually before. Like it's a good thing."

"Well, now you have," said Simone.

"It's good to be gay!" Eva cheered, raising a spilling shot glass then throwing it back.

Tiff poured a few more shots and passed them around, chanting "Why are we waiting? We could be masturbating! Drink motherfucker, drink motherfucker, drink!"

We all clinked our shot glasses and downed the banana-flavored vodka, strong, stoic faces all around. Simone said it was almost time to go, we'd better hurry and change. We both looked down at our sweats then blushed at each other. Simone herded us into her room, duffle bags in tow, and shut the door behind us.

We began to change into something a little more appropriate for a college party. Some bootcut jeans and tops from Forever 21, laid out on Simone's bed. I pulled off my sports bra and turned away from Liv to face the full-length mirror. I was wearing burgundy boxer briefs that I thought accentuated my ass and hamstrings. It was only my third time wearing boxer briefs, but I felt powerful in them. Glass-slipper-type fit. It had been worth the weirdness of having to check out with the older female cashier who said, "How nice of you to go shopping for your brother." I watched Liv watch me in the mirror when she thought I wasn't looking. Her eyes peeled my boxer briefs off. Her mouth formed a tight O. I pretended not to notice her gaze and crossed my arms over my chest, hands tucked under my armpits so my small boobs, my pecs, were completely covered, compressed. The way my arms were crossed made my biceps look bigger, my shoulders more defined. I tilted my head to the side, chin up, and examined myself in the mirror. Everything about me right then screamed masculine. I felt like a heartthrob posing for a magazine cover. How could Liv not want me now?

"What do you think?" I said, meeting Liv's eyes in the mirror. Liv choked on her spit before answering.

"About what, exactly?" She rubbed the back of her neck.

"How do I look? Do I look like a boy?"

"Do you want to look like a boy?"

"I don't know," I said, tilting my head to the other side, readjusting my hands under my armpits. "I think I just want to look like a not-girl."

I could tell the words were on her lips, she was so close to giving me what I wanted—an indulgence, a fantasy, a made-up world where we could be something—then she pulled on her jeans and her little femmy top and she was out the door, back into the common area.

Out in the living room, Eva distributed beers to everyone, forgoing one for herself since she was driving and her New Year's resolution was to stop drinking *while* driving. And oh, don't look at her that way, the party was just down the road, an infant could drive us there safely.

"You two, snyggingar!" she said, patting first me then Liv on the head like little kids, her little kids. Weirdly, and maybe it was because Eva was so tall, I felt this was the most normal thing in the world for her to do. Everywhere, mothers who weren't my mother.

"What does that mean?" I asked.

"Bitch is telling you you're a couple of hotties," shouted Simone from across the room.

She was hugging Jada from behind and nuzzling her face in her neck. I looked at Eva for confirmation, and Eva nodded.

With a little pushing and shoving, Simone was able to herd our group out the front door. Six of us were expected to fit in a Jetta. When I mentioned that this might be a challenge, Tiff suggested I lie across everyone's laps in the back seat, so I did, climbing in awkwardly, careful not to stab anyone with my sharp elbows. I lay down on my back, head in Simone's lap and ass in Liv's, but I was only peripherally aware of whose body was whose and how they were arranged in space—I tried to distance myself from the meaning of touch and reminded myself, repeatedly, that right now these bodies were mere cushions for my body, no more, no less, and to think of them in any other way was venturing into dangerous territory. I tilted my head back and looked out the window. A blur of campus lights and headlights, groups of students, drinks in hand, moving like amoebas through campus. Their mouths were moving; I knew they were loud, but I couldn't hear them. All I could hear was the ringing in my ears, the thrashing blood that betrayed me with every breath. A hand, there was a hand touching the bottom of my thigh, stroking it playfully. I looked at the hand, immediately knew that hand, would know that hand anywhere, then I glanced at Liv, who was staring straight ahead out the front windshield.

"Eva, why are you stopping?" asked Tiff, guzzling down her beer. She'd been stuck with my lower legs and feet, which were curled up toward my chest.

"Ethan's memorial on the left."

Eva rolled down her window even though it was snowing and stuck her head out of the car, looking at the bench with his name on it. A spray-painted skateboard lying next to a photo of him, all bright-eyed and curly-headed.

"Here," said Jada, passing Eva a half-full beer. Eva took it and poured some out in front of the bench.

Simone petted my hair and said, "We're not called the suicide school for no reason."

I couldn't see Liv's face very well, but she must have been frowning because Simone said, "You see, we've got no shortage of bridges for people to hurl themselves off of."

"Just because they're there—" Liv started to say, but I cut her off.

"All it takes is the suggestion," I whispered, and everything and everyone stilled.

I wondered about my dad's relationship to those bridges, if he found them tempting when my mom called him up and said yes, she was sure, she'd taken three tests. I imagined him walking around campus at night, a spiked coffee in one hand, a cigarette in the other, staring down at those pretty, roaring gorges. I wondered if he was still friends with Liv's dad back then. Maybe he was the type of guy my dad could have confided in. The A-word might have been uttered between them. Then I wouldn't be here, half seduced by the idea of nothingness.

When Eva started driving again, Simone got to asking us about college, where we planned to go. Liv said she didn't know, the whole thing was making her feel immobilized, like no matter where she chose, she would be making the wrong choice. I stayed quiet, reveling in Liv's hand still exploring my thigh.

"I mean, how the hell are you supposed to know what's good for you when you're seventeen?" said Liv.

"Just remember," said Tiff. "They're always going to treat you nice when they're trying to get you to commit. And then bam"—she punched her hand for emphasis—"you get there and it's a whole different story."

"Yeah, you can't trust what they say," Jada said over her shoulder.

That got my attention. Logically, I knew everything they were saying was true, but something about Coach Harris made me want to believe her. Made me want to believe I was too special to lie to. The compliments, the future-painting, the fawning. I guess I figured eighty thousand dollars was a pretty expensive price tag for a kid you didn't intend to play. Or treat right.

"How are you supposed to tell the difference?" Liv asked.

"Easy," said Simone. "You don't. Only thing you can do is pick a school you'd be happy at even without basketball."

"Now, that's crazy."

"Maybe," said Simone. "But that doesn't mean it isn't smart."

"Seriously," said Tiff. "Wait until you're freshmen again and back to being nothing. Your ego has to be able to handle it."

Liv didn't respond but I could feel her body stiffen with argument beneath me. I knew what she was thinking because it was the same thing I was thinking: I'm different, I'm irreplaceable. We didn't have the guts to consider the alternative.

"Sounds like you guys really hate your coaches," I said.

"Oh, nah," said Eva. "They're all like this."

When we got to the party, it was already packed, charged with the potential of the night. A butch field hockey player greeted us at the door and passed around blue Solo cups, told us the keg was in the basement, liquor and soda on the kitchen table. Kanye vibrated through the speakers. On the living room walls hung a huge rainbow flag and a black-and-white poster of two girls kissing in bed, wearing just their underwear and tank tops. A pale, freckled girl with curly red hair sunk a beer pong shot then celebrated by kissing her partner, an Indian girl in a field hockey pinny. Two girls switched off giving each other a lap dance over by the couch. Neither was very good but they seemed to be having fun.

I grabbed Liv's cup and headed into the kitchen to make her a rum and Coke. When I got back, I had to shoo away a guy that was circling her like a shark. Besides him, there were only two other guys in the whole place. I shoved the drink in her face, smiling and taking it all in.

"This is what it's going to be like for us soon enough," I said.

"This drink tastes like lighter fluid."

"Just a few short months then we're out," I said.

Across the room, a drunk waited on all fours while another girl climbed onto her back. When her rider was settled, she neighed then crawled around the room while her rider said, "I wouldn't put my money on this one, folks!"

I laughed, expecting Liv to join in, but she didn't. She chewed on her fingernails and looked at the floor, the ceiling. I didn't come all the way to Ithaca to spend the night observing a party from the corner, so I slowly inched my way toward the center, away from Liv. No matter what I did, who I talked to, I felt Liv watching me. I felt her watching me when I did a line of coke with a pretty blonde. I felt her watching me join a game of Never Have I Ever, felt her watching when I admitted I'd kissed a girl, hoping she assumed I was counting ours. I wondered what she thought about what she saw, if she thought, *This is Mack with the brakes removed, foot on the pedal, going, going, gone*—because that's what I thought. There I was, in my element; why look back?

Eventually, I no longer felt the heat of her gaze and turned to find that she'd gone outside onto the balcony. I could see her through the glass doors, leaning on the railing and looking at the sky, smoking a Black & Mild. A few minutes later, I followed her out there. I leaned on the railing and looked out at the world.

"I hear you get a better buzz if you shotgun," I said.

Of course, I was teasing. I had no interest in shotgunning a Black & Mild. But I felt a certain lightness, an ease I hadn't felt on the trip up there, as if I were already speeding by Liv, leaving her in the dust. As if I were already looking back on our relationship with a lighthearted wisdom, having moved on to more serious things.

Liv stubbed the small cigar out.

"Or that," I said. I sipped my drink.

"I take it you're having fun."

Her voice sounded bitter, accusatory. I didn't respond right away, that lightness now replaced by anchors in my gut, my jaw wound tight like a spring. Words clawing their way out. I needed to stop delaying the inevitable. I needed her to know where she'd be able to find me, if that was something she was interested in.

Finally, I turned to Liv and said, "I'm going to Gonzaga."

"What?"

I repeated myself.

"I mean, I heard you. I just—" She faltered. "When did this happen?"

"Damn, I thought you'd be happy for me."

"How long have you known?"

"A few days. I have a good feeling about Gonzaga. I love the coaches and style of play. They like to run and gun. They even fast-break on made buckets. It's a fucking dream."

"I know they like to run and gun," said Liv, reminding me that I wasn't the only one being recruited by them. "And so do I," she mumbled.

"Well?" I said, asking without asking.

She didn't have shit to say to that.

"You know, the whole drive up here I kept thinking, 'What's Liv going to say when I tell her? What's Liv going to say?' And never once did I consider it would be nothing."

"Look, I don't want to fight with you, Big. We all know—"

"Don't call me that," I said, interrupting her.

"Why? I thought you liked it."

"Save it for someone else you plan to jerk around," I said. "You know, your next pet."

She closed her eyes and tilted her head back, frozen like that for a few seconds. Her body looked like it was wilting, held up by nothing but the railing.

"I can't stop thinking about Suntica," said Liv.

"Who?" I said, exasperated.

"The horse."

"Oh, yeah," I said. "The horse, of course, the horse." I nodded.

I wanted to ask why she couldn't stop thinking about Suntica, what it meant for three horses to be buried side by side, why the unknown horse was the one snagging on the corners of her mind, but I didn't bother. In my mind, I was already in a packed Gonzaga stadium, fans chanting *Go Bulldogs, go Bulldogs,* one of the cheerleaders giving me a wink as I inbounded the ball. Taking the team to the playoffs—not just to the big dance, but to the Sweet Sixteen, the Elite Eight, maybe even further. Shaking hands with all the coaching greats, them pulling me aside to tell me I had that unnamable quality you know when you see it because it infects the entire game. All of this and more. If Liv didn't want to be by my side for it, then that was on her.

"You know what I think about those damn horses?" I said.

Liv raised her eyebrows, swallowing hard.

"I think, if given the chance, they wouldn't have thought twice about trampling us dead," I said. "That's what I think."

She looked as if I'd uncovered some secret past life of hers, one in which she'd already been trampled dead by stampeding horses, throwing their heads back and stomping their feet.

15

TIME-OUT #3

We spent all thirty seconds bent over, hands on our knees, catching our breath.

16

A HIGH-SOARING REBOUND

We wanted a perfect season for the same reason anyone wanted a perfect anything. We wanted to become small gods, to be invincible, transcendent; we would outlive the record books, the thousand-point banners, all the imperfect technology tasked with remembering us. We knew how this whole thing worked. Perfection meant freedom; it meant bursting into flames under the spotlight and liking the burn.

It was the last game of the regular season, and we needed to beat Jericho again, this time at their place. Liv and I were sitting side by side on the locker room bench while a few teammates banged on orange lockers, the skull-rattling song that meant we were coming for them. Katrina made a headband out of pre-wrap and carefully secured it in place. Aaliyah ripped med tape with her teeth and taped up her wrist. Sam adjusted her sweatband on her forearm, nervously running her hand over it. Bree turned on some shitty rap and dropped it low in the middle of the locker room, an act that was more disturbing than sexual or appealing. We waited for Coach Puck to enter and deliver his pregame speech.

A thing I always loved about basketball—and maybe this is why I still struggle with communication off the court—is that as soon as we switched into competition mode, it was like all of our problems, disagreements, and resentments fell away. I didn't resent Katrina; I felt kinship with her. I didn't feel bitter toward Sam and Bree; I felt bonded to them, so close that I was them. It was magic; it was also sad. But Liv, she'd disrupted that sick, sad magic.

For once, I didn't need to move my body to pump myself up, didn't need to punch the wall or shove Liv. I was weirdly calm and unrattled. I sat quietly and reached a space so meditative it was almost violent, a space where nobody knew what to do with my hypnotic silence. I leaned forward, elbows on my knees, with my hands folded, and stared at the whiteboard, faded whispers of marker still visible from teams come and gone. Liv reached for my hands, extracted the one closest to her, and placed it on the bench between us, leaving her hand on top of mine. I was pissed at her and she knew it, which is why she was taking uncalculated risks with our bodies on that bench.

The night before, I'd dug out my parents' wedding album from our overflowing hallway closet and spent some time flipping through its pages, trying to understand how time just kept on going. Underneath a photo of them standing facing each other at the altar, hands tied together, it said *Handfasting, now we're stuck with each other!* When I looked it up, I learned that it was an ancient Celtic ritual symbolizing people's devotion to each other. Normally, I would have thought it was obnoxious or performative, but when I imagined Liv's hands tied to mine, I got hot all over and unsteady on my feet.

"Don't do that," I growled, taking my hand back. She nodded at the floor and rubbed her hands together. They always needed to be doing something.

"Listen," she said. "I'm sorry about the way I reacted the other night. It was shitty of me."

I cracked my knuckles and watched Katrina do high knees, her blond ponytail whipping back and forth like a horse's tail.

"I just, I don't know," she faltered. "I felt left behind or something. And I guess I just thought you'd tell me before you committed."

"Why apologize right now?" I asked. "When you've had so many other chances?"

She rubbed the back of her neck, eyes examining the floor. I decided I wouldn't tell her that Coach Harris was going to be at the game to support me, that she'd been bugging me about Liv, asking what her deal was, wanting to know if I could persuade her to commit, too. I was too proud to try to persuade Liv to do shit. She was going to do what she was going to do. We both were.

"I realized I didn't want to step out there without you on my team."

"Impossible," I said, my anger already a distant, fruitless thing. I couldn't stay mad at her when she said shit like that. Or maybe it was that I couldn't commit to caring about my anger.

I paused, considering whether to continue with my runaway thoughts, then decided fuck it, what's it matter anymore. "Out there," I said, nodding toward the door, "we're together."

She smiled and leaned her shoulder into mine, a small gesture of reunion.

"Fuck the Great Barrier Reef," she whispered into my ear, her breath warm and life-giving against my neck. It took me a second and then I remembered the tub, her role-playing. This was, in a way, maybe the most romantic thing Liv had ever said to me—no more pretending, let's be us and no one else.

Then she reached for my hand again, only instead of holding it, she ran her fingers over the hair tie on my wrist, the weapon I used on myself time and time again, then slowly, tenderly, peeled it off, as if handling a tiny, injured bird. I interrogated my naked wrist; there was a tan line from years of what I'd convinced myself was discipline.

"There," she whispered. She was close enough to me that I could smell the sweetness of Gatorade on her breath, the musk of nervous sweat radiating off of her in an intoxicating rush. I took a deep breath and thanked her with my eyes because I knew that's what she wanted. I tried to let go of the idea that I needed that hair tie to achieve perfection, but it wasn't that easy. Maybe she knew that, maybe she didn't. But if I couldn't give myself the gift of freedom, I figured I might as well give her the satisfaction of believing she could heal me, however twisted that was.

We heard Coach Puck's familiar knock on the locker room door, and I yelled that people were engaging in a naked pregame ritual, he better come back later.

"You idiot," he yelled through the door.

"You're good," called Aaliyah.

He barged into the locker room, followed by his kids, who were shoving each other and passing insults back and forth. He told them to sit down and be quiet, and Bryan flopped down right where he'd been standing in front of the whiteboard, sitting cross-legged, his face in his hands. Codi sat down beside him and poked his cheek with her pointer finger, mouthing something that looked suspiciously like *fuckhead*. Without looking at her, Coach gave her a little smack over the head and she made this fake-affronted face, like we all couldn't tell she loved the attention. Everyone settled into a spot on the bench or floor, prepared for Coach's pregame speech. I was curious how this would go. He gave some really good speeches over the years, but he also gave some god-awful ones. It really depended on how sour his life was at the moment, on whether he thought we deserved the effort it took to inspire.

"Forget Jericho, forget the refs, forget the fans," began Coach. "Forget your stats, what they'll say about you in the paper, what their coach is telling them about you right this very second. All of that nonsense is out of your control."

He looked around at us. Some people nodded, some people looked at him with big, dumb eyes. We wanted guidance. Tell us what to do, said our faces.

"You know what you can control? I mean, shit." He laughed, shaking his head. "Almost nothing. You can control almost nothing."

I glanced at Liv. She was stretching out my hair tie and smiling at her feet.

Coach told us to close our eyes. To imagine tip-off. Where are we standing, how do we feel, who do we sense beside us? How bad do we want it? Sort of bad? Really bad? So bad it makes us want to rip our skulls off? The ref tosses the ball into the air.

"Imagine you chase down the tap," he said. "Turn toward your basket and drive as hard as you fucking can to the hoop. I don't care who you run over to do it. Bulldoze their whole team if you have to. Just get there. If you can decide to get there, you can decide to do anything."

He covered his mouth with his hand and cleared his throat. He looked around the room then settled his gaze on me, his eyes small, dark tunnels. I gave him the nod I knew he was looking for, our language of understanding. Coaches and point guards have this special relationship. They do if the coach is worth a damn, anyway. And not just because we point guards are extensions of our coaches on the floor, though that's part of it. Mostly, it's about the way we look at the game, like it's the only thing in the world powerful enough to break our hearts. And it does, it does ten, twenty, a million times over. And each time, we come back for more.

Coach broke our eye contact and turned toward the whiteboard, where he picked up a blue marker and started writing in his quick, slanted writing, all capitals. Then he moved away from the whiteboard so we could see what he'd written.

His message to us: *How you play is how you're going to live.*

If that was true, in life would I always be fierce and self-punishing, chasing a perfection, a high, that didn't exist? Maybe, but it didn't do any good to think about that then.

"Hell yeah," said Bree, throwing her fist in the air.

"Hell fucking yeah," said Sam, grinning at her twin.

We jumped to our feet and started chanting Hornets, Hornets,

Hornets, moving together as one, my fingertips tingling with our collective electricity. I glanced at the kids; they were chanting, too, but their words were different from ours.

"Life," said Codi.

"Monster," said Bryan.

"Life," said Codi.

"Monster," said Bryan.

He held his hands up like bear claws and roared in Codi's face, and she gave it right back to him, and Coach smiled at his cubs like he couldn't believe they'd soon be grown and gone.

Slowly, we made our way to the door, where we counted down three, two, one, and then we were gone, into the unknowable future.

During warm-ups, Liv asked me if I could take a look at her foul shot; something felt off but she wasn't sure what. I nodded, gesturing for her to take a free throw. She walked the ball to the foul line, tucked it under her arm, and wiped her hands on the sides of her shorts several times, giving in to the temptation to scan the stands. I couldn't tell if she'd spotted the Gonzaga assistant or not. She was sitting up in the corner, away from the obnoxious Ekron student section, rabid fans moshing like they were at a punk concert.

Selfishly, I didn't want to tell Liv how Coach Harris had been bugging me about her. I didn't want her to choose Gonzaga because of the coach's pressure or flattery, but because basketball and I had become so irrevocably intertwined in Liv's mind that she couldn't differentiate the two—she needed to follow me to keep the basketball high going.

Liv's eyes returned to the basket. I watched her line her left foot up with the center of the hoop. A slow, precise act. Then she dribbled the ball three times and spun it back to herself. This was the way that I liked it, like no one else was in the gym but us and our desire to conquer the unconquerable. I was free to observe Liv down to the smallest of details, and it was a pleasure to study her every micromovement without insecurity, without judgment, and understand how it all added up to the person I saw before me. She bounced a little with the ball at her waist then brought it to shooting position, locked and loaded. Her elbow forming a ninety-degree angle, her wrist bent back so it was nearly parallel with her bicep. The ball rested on the pads of her hand, a small window where the ball didn't touch her palm. Her right hand placed on the side of the ball as a guide hand. Everything looked perfect. She bent her knees slightly then shot. The ball just clanked off the back of the rim and straight down through the net. Nothing pretty about it, but a point was a point.

"Something still doesn't feel right," said Liv, shaking her head.

I laughed. "You took three dribbles."

"What?"

"Your routine is normally two dribbles and a spin. Not three," I said, thinking how wonderful it was to know someone so well. For me to witness that knowing on the move.

"Oh, fuck, you're right."

In that moment, I could tell we both felt it, that we were collaborating on something, making a discovery, although we hadn't gotten there yet, hadn't yet made the discovery. It was the process we were after.

When it came time, our team stood in a line and held hands while a student sang the national anthem. I hated the song but loved the ritual: the stillness, the anticipation leading up to the start of the game. The oneness of team, the embarrassment of sweaty palm against sweaty palm, the sexiness of such vulnerability. The song ended, and we huddled up. Coach nodded at me and said, "Captain, you got any words of wisdom to share with the team?" I said the truest thing I knew at the time: This moment is never going to happen ever again so we might as well do it right. Something only a dumb-fuck seventeen-year-old would say or think, though that didn't make it any less true. We brought our hands in, fastened by a hunger that couldn't be satiated by anything but winning and staking our claim on Ekron's athletic history.

Come tip-off, Jericho was all snarl and hiss, body hitting body, but it didn't matter, it was Liv's game and no one else's. Not mine, not Katrina's, not Jericho's. Bucket after bucket, she was absolutely unconscious, operated by some higher power. It was like proof nobody owned this game, not the gatekeeping college scouts, not the coaches that subbed us in and out, not even us. All we could do was devote ourselves, worship the game, day in and day out, and hope our loyalty would one day be rewarded. And today was Liv's day. Of course, I was there to do our little tricks, our *now you see us now you don't*s, our magic made manifest, our *Houdini doesn't have shit on us.*

In the beginning of the second quarter, after it became apparent that man-to-man defense wasn't going to cut it, Jericho switched to a diamond-and-one, with their best defender face-guarding Liv. But that wasn't going to stop her. I turned it on and found creative ways to get her the ball. I called for her to set me a screen and gave her a nod, and she slipped to the basket before she could set the pick. I jumped into the air and gave her a bullet of a pass. She caught it, took one power dribble, and finished in the lane before help side defense could get there. She was so sexy, so irresistible; *I do, I do, I do,* I thought. Another time down the floor, her defender still face-guarding her, I motioned for her to post up, pushing the defender to the high side so all I had to do was lob it over her outstretched hands, and that was another bucket for Liv. I snuck a peek into the stands and saw her mom cheering her ass off, all flustered and flushed, no longer a buttoned-up Catholic mom. For once, she was just a mother who was excited for her daughter.

Near the end of the first half, Liv drove to the basket and jump stopped before going in hard for a layup, absorbing contact—no foul call—finishing at the rim. The defender bounced off of her and landed on her tailbone. Liv looked down at her then stepped right over her like she invented this form of humiliation, like Allen Iverson stepping over Tyronn Lue didn't have shit on her. And the refs just ignored her, no tech, no nothing. That's when I knew she'd reached this untouchable state. The basketball gods were betting on her. I checked on Coach Harris and she had her fist over her mouth, rocking back and forth, laughing that sort of incredulous laughter that comes with witnessing greatness.

The second half was the same story. Liv was lights-out, Jericho never had a chance. Even Katrina, who was prone to envy, quick to whine for more touches, was cheering Liv on. Toward the end of the game, only two minutes left and up fifteen, all the starters had been subbed out except for Liv. Coach wanted to let her ride out this high of a lifetime. One of our freshmen, Angela, shook free of her defender and launched a long-range three. It hit the back of the rim and bounced high; players banged around underneath, working for position. Elbows flew, heads bucked, asses pinned bodies in place.

When Liv jumped into the air for that rebound, it looked like she might never come down. She was metaphysical up there, she was unearthly, ethereal, transcending the physical limitations of body and muscles and gravity; she was a meteor flying through space. A celestial body, a myth, swirling, almost levitating. She outleapt everyone in the gym, her hand snatched the ball out of the air like a frog catching a fly with its tongue. All human noise had been sucked out of the gym, leaving nothing but a hollow, whistling wind in its place.

But then she landed and her ankle crumpled beneath her. The sound came back in one huge, crushing, excruciating, stomach-turning snap. Liv's guttural scream, her face twisted in pain. I looked on in horror, tears burning my eyes. There is little in the world worse than watching someone you love get injured. I could feel the pain in my own ankle, shooting up my leg, tearing at my hips, my chest, which slowly separated at the sternum, wanting to pull Liv inside where she would be safe.

I hopped off the bench and ran to her, crouching beside her writhing body. The athletic trainer and Coach Puck followed.

"Give her some space," said the trainer.

"Is Gonzaga watching?" Liv said, jaw clenched, making a conscious effort to slow her breathing. So, she had clocked Coach Harris up there in the stands after all. What Liv meant was, there are thousands of recruits out there that aren't injured, that coaches have dropped recruits for less. And for the first time, I realized that Liv might actually want to go to Gonzaga with me, that maybe it had taken getting hurt for her to access that part of herself.

We needed to pretend that Liv was not hurt so we wouldn't worry Coach Harris. I told her to walk it off, that this was no big deal, she'd be fine, and the trainer scoffed at me, recommended that I back off and let her evaluate Liv.

"I'm good, I'm fine, I'm fine," Liv told her.

"I got you," I said.

I grabbed Liv's hands and pulled her to her feet. If we were going to pretend she didn't just fuck her ankle up big-time, then Liv was going to need to walk on her own. And Liv knew this. So she stood still for a moment, perhaps waiting to see how her ankle would respond to her weight. Fans murmured in the stands; a few people started to clap, slow, hesitant claps at first, then more joined in, and soon Liv was walking to the bench, brow furrowed in concentration as she tried not to favor her good leg. Heel to toe, heel to toe, relearning how to walk.

After the tainted win, I stood up from my seat at the front of the bus and made my way to the back, slinking past Katrina, her gold KATRINA necklace glinting in the moonlight, to where Liv sat with her headphones on, forehead pressed against the cold window. Liv slipped her headphones off, leaving them dangling around her neck, and patted the space beside her. Ice wrapped around her ankle, a puddle at her feet. I sat down and laid my head on Liv's shoulder, tracing the cracks in the fabric of the seat in front of us.

"Why?" whispered Liv. "Why did this have to happen?"

I continued tracing the small tears that resembled streaks from a jet in the sky, my pointer finger occasionally pushing on the foam, both to feel its bounce and to see if it would push back.

"It's weird seeing what's on the inside," I said.

Liv messed with her hands in the front pocket of her sweatshirt. I could smell the sweet, salty stink of the game on her body. I resisted burying my nose in it, the aftermath of our last game together, although I didn't know that yet—I thought we had league playoffs and districts left. I only knew that I was feeling unsettled, agitated by an unspecified anxiety that pecked at my skin. It occurred to me that I wouldn't mind if the bus driver decided to drive the bus straight off a cliff, just to put a stop to the nameless terror. What would I have done differently if I'd known this was our last game together? Would I have made sure to use all of our time-outs, just to stretch the game out longer? To delay the inevitable?

"I can't miss districts, I just can't," said Liv, sucking in her breath, eyes on the headlights speeding toward us, her breath fogging up the window. Through the glass, the round rim of the moon followed our bus.

"You need an X-ray." I said it just to get it out of the way. We both knew Liv wouldn't be getting an X-ray, but I felt less like a piece of shit if I dished out a perfunctory instruction.

"What would you do if you were in this situation?"

I sighed, flexed my jaw against Liv's shoulder. I knew what I would do if the roles were reversed, so I'm not sure why I pretended to think on it. I would do whatever it took. If it hadn't been for my dad, who had forced me into an MRI and surgery sophomore year, I would have played on a torn ACL if it meant not sitting out a minute. The five months I missed out on AAU two summers prior nearly killed me, just like missing districts would kill Liv. In sports, there was an unspoken agreement between the players who couldn't live without playing: there is no higher honor than sacrificing your body for your team.

"I know a guy," I said.

That night, Liv slept at my house. I propped her foot up on the couch and made a new ice bag, twenty minutes on, twenty minutes off, all night into the early morning quiet, even when Liv had fallen asleep, her mouth hung open in a deep, dreamless sleep. To an outsider, it might have looked like I was taking care of Liv because I needed her for playoffs, but I didn't need Liv to win, and it was precisely that lack of need that was the point.

The next morning, Liv woke up suddenly, with a jerk, and I made us some eggs, which we chased with gallons of coffee. Once we felt alive enough, we left to meet up with Grayson in the CVS parking lot. He gave me a hug and said, "It's been a minute." My heart picked up, the cacophony of my blood nearly drowning out Liv's questioning words: hadn't we just seen each other the other night? I changed the subject and asked Grayson if he had a hard time getting the drugs. He opened the back door of his mom's van and laughed as we climbed in. We sat in the very back row, watching him plop down in one of the middle seats and lay his leg across the aisle, foot up on the other.

He opened his backpack and pulled out a small clear bottle of human growth hormone and a syringe. I'd never tried it before, but I knew HGH could help speed up healing. Still, it wasn't exactly safe, especially because I had no way of knowing if this stuff was legit or not. Some perv could have cooked it up in his basement for all we knew.

"Heart disease," I said to Liv. "Cancer. Liver damage. Want me to keep going?"

I watched her eye the syringe, could hear her breathing quicken beside me, but she didn't answer, made no indication whatsoever that she'd heard me. Grayson made a face at me.

"Olympians drink this shit for breakfast," he said. He turned to Liv. "You'll be fine."

It was the second time we were in the back seat of a car together, only this time I wouldn't be doing the drug with her. Guilt was starting to nip at me. I was used to sabotaging myself—that was old news—but now I felt responsible for what happened to her.

Grayson demonstrated for us, on the meat of his thigh, how to inject it intramuscularly.

"Just grab a little fat and push it in," he said, smiling. "You'll be feeling great in no time. I swear, it's like a magic elixir."

Now that I thought about it, he did look in good spirits, less in need of mind-altering substances.

Liv fucked with a scab on her knee. I waited for her to ask more about the potential risks but the question didn't come. She said she didn't think she'd be able to stomach injecting it herself, that she'd need some help. She looked up from her knee and met my eyes, asking without asking. Now that we'd made it this far, I wasn't sure if I could go through with it, if I could be the reason she might never be the same again. She was putting all of her trust in me, in the people I trusted. And that trust felt big and ugly and severe. I knew injecting her would be the point of no return. It would bond us in that trust, and in fear, and in stubborn ambition.

"Please," she said.

I nodded, trying not to think about all the things that could go wrong, and Grayson got out of the car and stood guard while Liv pulled down her sweatpants so I could get at her quad. She was wearing a pair of turquoise lacy underwear that I pretended not to notice.

"Go on then," she said, closing her eyes and turning her head away, waiting for me to heal her.

17

VIDEO REVIEW

If the visit to Cornell had driven a wedge between us, then the devastation of Liv's injury had brought us back together again. But her ankle seemed to be feeling somewhat tolerable, thanks to the HGH regimen. I went over there every night to stick her in the thigh and tell her it would be okay, she'd feel better in no time. And the fact that she'd made first-team all-area helped a bit, too. Me, I was all-area player of the year, and we were supposed to do a photo shoot with eight other honorees that afternoon. Before we showered and prepped, I asked if she was sure about HGH—it was some sketchy shit for a reason.

"Don't let me fuck you up," I said.

"You aren't," said Liv. She rolled up her shorts and looked away, her fear of needles still just as intense as the first time. I watched her grip the bed frame, her knuckles bulging under pink-and-white skin. "I'm fucking me up."

We got ready in a warm, glowing silence, towels around our waists like boys, sharing combs and wringing our wet hair out on each other. We slathered our bodies in cocoa butter, we posed in the bathroom mirror, made like we were some hot shit draft picks; we were ready for our big debut.

Once we had our jerseys on, I watched Liv lean closely in to the mirror and put on eyeliner, her eyes watering each time she accidentally poked herself in the eye.

"I was almost in a beauty contest once," she said. She dabbed cover-up on her nonexistent chin pimples while I busied myself with adjusting my forearm sweatband, swapping it between arms. "When I was a kid. I couldn't have been older than eight."

"Why almost?" I was standing behind her, so we spoke into the mirror at each other.

"The night before, I took a pair of scissors to my hair." She laughed a small, terrible laugh. "You should have seen my mom in the morning. She was shaking so hard she broke two plates and a mug."

I made this sort of debutante motion with my hand and put on my best mid-Atlantic accent. "I hope it wasn't the good china."

"Sadly, it was," she said. "The plates are buried out back."

I smiled at her, charmed by the ease with which we played. She looked at the sweatband on my right forearm.

"Wear it on your left," she said, meeting my eyes in the mirror.

"Why?"

She shrugged. "I like your right forearm."

I yanked it off my right and slipped it over my left hand and situated it just below my elbow. My dad had always hated my sweatband, said he'd never once seen me actually use it, that basketball wasn't supposed to be a fashion show. All that matters is the game, he'd lecture. He didn't get it; it was that look-good, feel-good, play-good mentality. It was about feeling powerful in your own body, so disgustingly confident you knew there was nothing you couldn't do.

"You know you look good without all that makeup, right?"

"Knowing you'll be there with me makes me hate pictures less," she said.

She'd moved on to foundation and powder then seemed to re-member something and dug in the drawer for mascara. Downstairs, I could hear her mom watching *Dr. Phil*, the volume turned up so loud it sounded like the devil child was in their living room.

She finished her makeup and turned toward me, still beautiful, just a different type of beautiful, like she belonged in a storefront window. I imagined us living together, every day getting ready side by side in the mirror, brushing our teeth and trying to talk through our minty, foamy mouths.

"It could always be like this," I said. "You realize that, right?"

"Like what?"

"Come on, Liv."

"Come on, what?"

"Nothing," I said. "We should hurry up."

"I'm here," she said. "I'm right here."

The photo shoot was at Parkland, a public school that had so much money it looked like a college campus. They had one main gym and two practice gyms. When we entered the stadium, we got a taste of what the next four years of our lives might look like, how the smaller we looked out there, the larger we'd feel.

We were the first ones there besides the photographer, a young squirrelly-looking guy with eyes that never stopped moving. Back and forth they went, scrambling like rats in a cage. We grabbed a few balls off a rack at center court and messed around with them a bit, spinning them on our fingers and whatnot, but nothing so crazy that we'd break out in a sweat or fuck up Liv's ankle even more. I warmed up my grip so I'd be able to palm the ball when the time came. After a little while, the rest of the all-area team started rolling in. First, Courtney Parker from Coatesville, who could get real sassy on the court, Alyssa Watkins from Parkland, a tall, skinny chick who was going to Harvard, then Reilly McNulty, who thought making a bunch of threes meant she could ball. We nodded at them, made small talk, tried to act like this was an everyday occurrence for us. Just a small-town paper that nobody reads, who cares, yada yada

yada. A few more rolled in, same deal. By then we were all congregated in a loose circle, some people messing with their uniforms, making sure their shorts lay right, others flipping their hair around and checking each other's teeth for stray food bits.

I looked around at these other players. Out of every player in the area, I was the best. Decided by a unanimous vote. Everything I'd worked for, sacrificed for, suffered for, had come to a head. This was just the beginning. I'd have a stellar college career, then graduate and play overseas in the winter and with the WNBA in the summer. Little girls would wear my jersey. NBA players would sit sideline at my games. Iverson would ask me to teach him a thing or two.

But what if none of those dreams were realized? What would I do then? Run away to the desert and become one of those people who make art out of mannequins and recycled car parts? If I could see into the future and witness my failure, would I call the whole thing off? Maybe, but also maybe not. Maybe knowing better would only strengthen my desire, would make me all the more hungry to close the distance between who I thought I was and who I really was. I don't know why the fuck this all occurred to me right then and there when I should have been basking in my success, taking it all in. I was proud of myself, yeah, but that pride messed with my head. I was terrified to lose that feeling. To fold under the pressure.

How could I have forgotten that Dani might be on the all-area team? She was the last person to walk in the door, looking all bronzed, like she'd just gotten out of a tanning bed, her mouth fighting for its neutral position. A chill swept over me, raised goosebumps on my arms. Whatever was about to happen, I knew it wouldn't be good. I turned my back to her and put my foot up on a seat to untie and retie my shoe. Liv kneed me in the ass and asked if I was going to greet my girlfriend.

"What? She's not my girlfriend."

"I'm just fucking around," she said. "I mean, she did give you her number, after all."

When I didn't respond, she laughed and said she guessed I threw it straight into the trash and forgot all about it, though I got the sense she wasn't so sure about that. After I'd taken eons to tie my shoe, I turned to find Dani making the rounds. She hugged a few friends, gave everyone else daps. When she got to me, she stopped a few feet away and looked me up and down, shaking her head as if she were disappointed in me, as if she didn't want to catch whatever disease I had. I said what's up and she shot me the scariest smile I'd ever seen.

"Surprised you didn't get drunk for this," she said.

When I didn't respond, she laughed cruelly and joined Courtney, who was fixing her face in a pocket mirror. I had half a mind to grab Liv and run out the door, claiming that I'd had a premonition the building was about to collapse on us.

"What did she mean by that?" asked Liv.

"I don't know," I said. "She must not like me or something."

"What? Why wouldn't she like you?"

I shrugged and Liv squinted at me out of the corner of her eye. The photographer cleared his throat and asked if Mack Morris was here. I raised my hand and he told me to come with him while everyone else hung out. Even though I didn't ask her to, Liv followed us and smiled from behind the photographer while he directed me to stand this way and that way, to cross my arms over my chest, to put one leg up against the wall, to palm the ball and act like I was playing keep-away. He told me to do some crossovers and between the legs and spins on my finger, to do whatever moves I had in my bag of tricks. In the background, across the court, I caught Dani looking up from her conversation to watch me.

"Bet I could beat you in one-on-one," said the photographer, snapping away.

"Real original," I said.

"You must get that a lot, huh."

"I'm going D-I," I said, thinking of my dad telling everyone who would listen at the Sixers game, those little kids who were starstruck by my celebrity. Wherever he was, he was probably taking bets right now on how many points I'd score my first collegiate game. A cigar between his teeth.

"Fancy-pants." He stopped shooting and glanced at the screen for a few seconds before raising it to his eye again. "When do you want to play?"

"She's seventeen," interrupted Liv. He turned to look at her.

"You don't need to be here."

"Yes, I do."

"Okay, well, you might as well pose with fancy-pants over here. People love a dynamic duo."

Liv did as she was told and then it was the two of us, arms thrown carelessly around each other, passing the ball between our legs, playing faux defense, goofing off, and this fucking guy loving it, egging us on like it was a runway, saying shit like "Work it, ladies," and "The camera digs you."

"How long have you known each other? I'm guessing your whole lives by the looks of it?"

"Just this season," I said.

The photographer raised his eyebrows. "Huh," he said.

"We aren't going to fuck you, man," said Liv.

He rolled his eyes then said we were done here, let's return to the group. So we did, and soon the ten of us were pretending to like each other. No matter how the photographer arranged us, I did my best to stay at least a person away from Dani. My heart was beating something terrible. I didn't want to upset Liv, even though she didn't exactly claim me, even though I was getting sick of trotting at her heels like a needy pup. I wanted to find the idea of her getting pissed about Dani unreasonable. But people are never anything but unreasonable. If you don't love them for it, you'll go crazy.

"Almost done," said the photographer. "Let me get just a few more."

He climbed on top of the announcer's table, peering down on us through his lens, and instructed us all to huddle real close together. Everyone sort of shuffled around, and somehow, I ended up shoulder to shoulder with Dani. Liv was on the end, a few girls away from us. We smiled up at the photographer, mouths taut, jaws hurting, toward the rafters, like if we just thought about our all-area honors hard enough, we'd be able to fly up there like a bunch of Peter Pans. I crouched down and pretended to fix my laces. As I stood back up, I inconspicuously inched to the left. Coincidental, nothing to see here.

"What, now you're too scared to even touch me?" mumbled Dani out of the side of her mouth, still grinning at the camera. Courtney, who was standing behind us, cleared her throat.

"Can you just chill? Please?" I begged.

"I don't want to chill."

A few of the girls around us stirred. It didn't take much to disquiet the herd, which slowly dismantled and expanded into a circle around Dani and me. All eyes on us. Someone swore that nothing good ever happens when you get a bunch of rivals together. The photographer said he was done anyway, we'd all started to look like unblinking plastic psychos. I stood very still, trying to think my way out of this, but my thoughts were gummy and slow-moving. It was just me and the dread that slithered up my midsection.

Then Liv stepped into the circle, demanding Dani tell her what her issue with me was. My protector.

"Why don't you ask her yourself?"

Liv looked at me, and I shrugged.

"I don't know any more than you do," I said.

Alyssa, the Parkland nerd, spoke up and said she thought everyone should just take a breather, but no one took her advice, they were all riled up, almost as if they'd been primed for an explosion and had only been waiting for someone to light a match.

"What's going on?"

"Will you two shut up?"

"My money's on Dani."

"Fuck Cathedral Catholic."

"Fuck Ekron."

"Fuck you all."

"Cooper's got that long reach, though."

I don't know who threw the first punch, but suddenly Liv and Dani were rolling around on the ground and then Courtney jumped in, followed by Reilly and a few others.

"Oh, what the hell," said Alyssa, who got thrown into the mix when she tried to pull Reilly out.

Instead of joining in, I stood with the photographer, admiring the brutal ballet before us. He took photo after photo. I knew there must be sound, of pain and fury, of repressed emotions and desires, but I couldn't hear anything. Legs kicked, arms swung, hands clenched and grabbed and swatted, mouths closed around flesh. It was beautiful and merciless, and I wanted it to last forever; I wanted violence to always make that much sense.

After some time, the photographer nudged me and my hearing returned.

"Have you ever seen anything like this?" he asked. I said no, I hadn't.

"Courtney let the men's team run a train on her."

"Margo's dad steals from the collection bin at church."

"Alyssa cheated on the SATs."

"Liv's dad's a total fudge packer."

"Dani got her period all over Anna's bed."

"Reilly's mom has two husbands."

"Mack's dad was a gambling addict."

"Liv dumped James because he doesn't have a cunt."

All of the town's secrets were being thrown in the air like dollar bills, and I started to laugh. Eventually, everyone stopped beating on each other to look at me.

"What's wrong with her?" Courtney asked Alyssa.

They both had huge bumps in their hair that made them look like roosters. Courtney's mascara had turned to eye black under her eyes. When I didn't stop laughing, Liv joined in, and then it was just the two of us, emptying ourselves, releasing anything we'd ever held on to, honking, choking on our laughter, eyes bleeding tears, holding on to each other for support.

It went that way until we finally sat down and made ourselves calm down for fear that we might throw up. Liv sat panting next to me, a half smile smeared across her face. I was waiting for her to recover from our laughter and realize that she was pissed at me. For her to call me out for lying to her, for fucking a girl who wasn't her, for being a fraud. The smile had that type of nasty undertone to it. But she didn't.

She turned to me, still wearing that dopey half smile, and said, "I won."

I wondered if all prizes felt this way: afraid their owner would put them up on a shelf and never play with them again.

After everyone settled, Liv and I had to talk the photographer down a bit, convince him not to sell those damning pictures to a journalist who would inevitably run some crazy story about the dark side of high school girls' basketball. We didn't even need to threaten to expose his penchant for underage girls. He let me monitor him while he deleted every picture from his camera. Hate to say it but I think he was just happy to see a bunch of teen girls roll around on the floor together. What was left behind, after he deleted the evidence, was just a memory card full of boring pictures of a bunch of made-up, hairstyled girls who wanted everyone to know you could be pretty *and* put a ball in a hoop. Just what we, or at least everyone around us, wanted.

Every morning at school for the next week, we found each other in the hallway and said, "Not today?"

"Nope, not today."

"They're probably busy trying to find a way to crop your big-ass head," said Liv.

"Yeah, and those gangly arms of yours broke the printer," I said.

"Better to strangle you with." She threw her arm around my neck and put me in a headlock, my cheek pressed to her chest.

Finally, it arrived. It was Saturday, and I had slept at Liv's and woke up to a bunch of texts congratulating me on the beautiful article. Liv was still asleep, her body pressed against my back, arm wrapped around me. Her hand was inside my T-shirt, resting on my sternum. I loved her that way, just waking. I peeled her arm off and rolled over to face her, gently shaking her awake and whispering that today was the day.

We threw on hoodies and headed downstairs, eyes still groggy with sleep, feet shuffling across the floor. Liv's mom was already out running errands, according to a note she'd left us, but she'd laid the front page of the sports section on the kitchen table next to some pancakes, eggs, bacon, and orange juice.

"What got into your mom?" I laughed, examining the breakfast spread.

She wasn't one for hospitality, at least not when it came to me. Whenever I slept over, I felt like a gnat she was shooing out the door, only to pat herself on the back for giving me a second chance at life.

"Fuck if I know," said Liv.

Didn't matter, though, because there, on the table, was a blown-up photo of me against the gym wall, one leg bent, my foot pressed against the wall in a casual lean, arms crossed over my chest. An unsmiling mouth, jaw clenched, eyes forming a threat. I smiled at this version of me that had refused to smile for the photographer, who'd insisted people would prefer a friendly, nonthreatening Mack to an assassin Mack.

"Holy shit, look at you," whispered Liv. "This really is something."

I don't know why, but it felt right that she was whispering, like there was some spirit present we needed to respect, or rather, didn't want to disturb.

Standing behind me, she rested her chin on my shoulder and wrapped her arms around my waist, reading the headline aloud.

"Star Point Guard and All-Area Player of the Year, Mack Morris, Has Verbally Accepted a Full Scholarship to Gonzaga."

I flipped the pages. Throughout were more photos of me: me facing the camera, ball tucked lazily under one arm, another of me palming the ball, stretching my arm toward the camera like I was going to stuff the ball in the reader's face, a few of me bent over at the waist, doing a crossover.

"All right, enough about me."

I opened the paper up to the list of the all-area team. There was a small action photo of Liv dribbling the ball down the court, eyes up, looking for someone to pass to.

"Looking for you, I bet," she whispered.

I felt her jaw spread into a smile against my trap muscle. It was divine, a privilege to exist with her this way.

I tried to ignore her cellphone on the table, vibrating with messages from "Dad," one after another. Me and him, two gnats buzzing around their family. I tried to shake off my resentment at the fact that she had a living father, one who wanted to be present, who was desperate for her forgiveness, to come bursting back into her life.

"Wait," she said, lifting her head and moving around me to grab the paper. "What the fuck is this?"

A photo from the crime section was cut out neatly and taped beneath Liv's photo. The headline read "POLICE: Pair used sex insults in beating outside gay club: Two men charged with aggravated assault."

Liv looked up at me with pale, bloodless cheeks and sorry howling eyes. I didn't want to know any more details, but I watched her scan the article, her pointer finger following each line, making sure she didn't miss a word. Something someone had yelled during the all-area brawl rattled loose in my head, something about Liv's dad that I hadn't registered at the time. It occurred to me that she was searching for his name.

"They broke a beer bottle over his head," she said, still reading. I waited for more, for her to tell me it wasn't her father, for her to tell me just how bad it was. I needed to know it wasn't that bad, needed to know it for my own future.

"He lost a lot of blood, but he's okay," she said. "At least, physically."

Finally, she released this great, painful sigh when she realized the victim was a younger man in his twenties who'd been followed out of the club. How strange, to be grateful for someone else's suffering.

I don't know how I didn't notice it before, but in the white space above the headline, someone had written *What a preventable tragedy* in black pen.

"Your mom," I breathed.

What was this? A threat? A warning? Was she trying to remind us, or rather, Liv, of what her life could end up like if she didn't find James 2.0?

"No, no, no." Liv balled her hands into fists, not taking her eyes off the article. "She wouldn't."

"I'm so sorry," I said.

I gestured to the breakfast spread, to the towering stack of pancakes neither of us had touched, the pitcher of orange juice that suddenly seemed sinister in the face of what we both knew but Liv refused to accept. It had the eeriness of a last meal.

I leaned in to give her a hug, but she wriggled out of my arms, leaning on the kitchen table with both hands. I got woozy how I did whenever she moved away from me. I got this idea in my head that desire was really about distance and all the small and big moves we make to close and expand that distance. What moves had Liv's dad made in the name of desire? Moving closer toward someone almost always means moving further from someone else.

"You're going to go away now, aren't you?"

I didn't mean to sound so pathetic, but it was how I pictured it: her going away as if to disappear behind a veil.

She wouldn't look at me. I wondered what was worse: an impossible or possible desire. Did the possibility make it hurt worse or just differently? Once you closed that space, once you held that person in your hungry palms, the desire melted away into a reaction, or maybe more accurately, a judgment: What would it be like to finally, after all this time, know satisfaction? Would it be disappointing? Hollow? Ugly? Would it be world-ending? Wondrous? The possibilities dizzied me. Maybe an impossible desire was what I was after. Wasn't there something clean and easy about wanting but never being able to attain?

I thought of Coach Puck's obsession with the power of visualization. Standing there, waiting for Liv to respond, I closed my eyes so I wouldn't have to see her avoid me any longer. Instead, I pictured a day at the beach, white sand, pristine water, dolphins jumping, all that. Her dad with us, splashing and playing in the water with a devastatingly handsome man. I pulled her dad out of the water and handed him my camera, asking him to take a picture of us. I threw my arm around Liv, whose hair was wild with sand and salt water. Her face was a golden pink, freckled under her eyes and on the bridge of her nose. Her dad didn't have to instruct me to smile for the picture because I was already smiling. At the last second, Liv turned and kissed me on the cheek and that's when I heard it: a splintering note of glass breaking. I opened my eyes to find scrambled eggs everywhere, light-blue shards covering the white marble floor. Liv examined the mess then looked at me, accusing me with her eyes.

"Thought so," I said, swiping a pancake on my way out the door.

18

TECHNICAL FOUL

The ref blew her whistle and made a T with her hands. The crowd was too stunned to react; they were used to a certain violence, but still, this was intense, remorseless.

Coach signaled for me to take the two free throws. I bounced the ball, took a few deep breaths, but couldn't swallow enough air. I knew Liv was standing behind me at the three-point line, but I couldn't feel her presence, knew not to reach back for a low five after I sunk the first shot.

19

ALLEY-OOP

Liv had missed the past three practices. League playoffs started in two days. She wasn't answering my texts. I didn't know if she was keeping up with the HGH or not. If she had spoken to her dad or gone to visit him. Had she confronted her mom? I doubted it. All these unanswered questions kept me up at night; I couldn't sleep worth a damn, so I took to the driveway like I had so many nights before.

My mom was out of town at her friend's wedding, somewhere in Ohio. Under the garage light, I took a mid-range jumper then warmed up my handles, the sound of the dribbling ball echoing. I focused on nothing but the ball and the hoop. Shooting around in the dark under the garage light was always a different experience than shooting during the day. My shadow danced with the shadow of my ball, crickets played their music, and I always felt an intoxicating selfishness in knowing that I might wake the neighbors, but oh well, the ball was calling to me. It was the only thing that could quell my restlessness, time and time again. The threat of waking the neighbors gave every dribble, every shot a forbidden feel.

I heard a small noise, someone clearing their throat. I looked up and at the end of the driveway stood Liv, water bottle in hand. Neither of us moved. Liv watched me, ball tucked under one arm, her other arm dangling loosely at her side. I didn't move.

Liv approached me, slowly, as if approaching a wild animal.

"You're here," she said.

"Where else would I be?"

"I don't know. Thought you might be with Katrina or something."

"I'm here," I said. "Where've you been? Coach is ready to kill you."

Liv took a drink from the water bottle and made a face, then handed it to me. I set my ball down on the grass behind the hoop then raised the bottle to my lips expecting it to be Gatorade and vodka, but a sour taste hit the back of my tongue.

"Is this—"

"Skippys? Yeah," she said, smiling.

Something in me broke, and suddenly I felt the urge to sit down right where I was and stick my thumb in my mouth. If I'd still had my childhood blankie, I would have clutched it tight, wound it around my neck like a boa constrictor. But I didn't want to seem like a baby, so I took a few more disgusting sips and focused on how bad my dad's taste had been. I imagined Liv's dad teasing him about it, the same way I might give Liv shit for adding extra pickles to her Big Mac or leaving a tough-guy away message on AIM. I wondered if her dad ever thought about mine, maybe when he heard a certain guitar riff or happened to walk into a grungy bar and a band was playing their hearts out, basically fucking their instruments. I knew I would never know who they were to each other or how my dad felt about him, but I hoped he was at least kind to him.

"Let's go," she said.

She wore a navy zip-up and gray sweats, the sweats tucked into the tongues of her Jordan 6s.

There was something severe about her in that moment, as if she were reprimanding me. I wanted to dislike that tone, the smallness it made of me, but I didn't, knew I never would.

I took her ball and dribbled between my legs while we walked down the middle of the street, past the overgrown lawns and broken windows and American flags, past the sugar maple and white oak trees, past the locked doors and lights-out bedrooms. The sound of the bouncing ball carried. It's one of my favorite things about basketball—dribbling has a rhythm that crawls inside of you and continues to live its life elsewhere. It's everywhere music. I feel most sexy when I'm handling the ball.

"My mom wasn't always like this, you know," said Liv. She took another drink then poured my father's favorite drink into my mouth, some of it running down my chin. I wiped it away with the back of my hand.

"Unbelievable," I said.

"What?"

"You're actually defending her."

"You aren't listening."

"If I'm not listening, it's because you're not fucking saying anything."

She inhaled sharply and held the air in her lungs for so long I thought she'd stay that way forever, the air swirling, searching for an escape route. When she looked at me, I knew I'd become that air if I could.

"I wish she were dead, I really do."

"Nah, you don't mean that."

"I do, I really, really do."

Discreetly, beneath her sweatshirt sleeve, she snapped a hair tie, my hair tie, against her wrist, wincing. She wasn't used to the sharp thwack, thwack, thwack, the concentrated pain on one spot over and over.

"Okay." I wasn't sure what else to say, what I was and was not allowed to ask about.

"Mackenzie," said Liv. I started—she never used my full name.

"That's not my name, Olivia."

Liv swiped the ball from me and shot it to herself while walking, the ball spinning back to her each time.

"Mack," she said.

"Liv."

We walked like that, saying each other's names back and forth, the darkness enveloping us. Walking down the street like that, repeating each other's names, it was easy to imagine we were inventing a prayer. No matter how many times Liv said my name, my heart still jumper-cabled every time.

"Where are we going?" I asked.

Without answering, Liv turned to me and began to shuffle sideways, wincing through her ankle pain, the ball clutched to her chest, prepared to pass to me. Liv nodded for me to copy her positioning, but I continued to face forward, eyes on the silhouetted trees and houses ahead, on the cracked-open sky, where a waning crescent moon was just rising behind some puffs of blue-black clouds.

"Look, turn to me," said Liv, grabbing me by the shoulders and maneuvering my body. She was just a few inches from my face. I could smell the Skippys on her, the sour sweet laced with bite. I felt a rush of wetness between my thighs and closed my legs instinctually.

"Open up," laughed Liv, wedging a foot between my knees. "That's not how the state's number-one point guard plays defense."

"Unfair," I said, meaning she was unfair, her very existence, entering my life and shaking it until it exploded.

Liv agreed, it was unfair how my game was levels above everyone else's.

"We're going to our spot, where else?" she said.

"Our spot," I repeated, stealing the water bottle from Liv's sweatshirt pocket. I took a few big gulps then handed it back. Liv did the same. We were throwing kerosene on a fire.

"Now, pass with me, Big."

I rolled my eyes but obliged, and we shuffled sideways down the street, passing the ball back and forth between us. It was an easy drill, one you learned in elementary school. Disciplined, I passed the ball to the same spot every time—Liv's left breast, just below her shoulder—and maybe it was the way our bodies so effortlessly coordinated, even in the dark, even tipsy, but the wetness continued its pulsating rhythm down there.

"Signing day is in six weeks," I said, a question lingering under my statement.

"What does it mean to be the best?" said Liv, stopping sliding. I stopped with her.

"I don't know," I said, because I didn't.

I wanted to believe I was the best point guard in the country, but I knew it wasn't true; UConn didn't want me, Tennessee didn't want me, Notre Dame didn't want me. But I was also convinced anyone who didn't want me was an imbecile. They only looked at stats and prestige, an elementary understanding of the game at best. If basketball was a book, then stats were no better than the table of contents. You had to really dig in to unveil how someone could put no points on the board and be the most effective player on the court. And usually, it was only when a team lost that player that everyone began to understand how they changed everything. Nobody wanted to be appreciated in subtraction, in the negative space around a game.

"And even then," she said. "Knowing you're the best. What will that do for you?"

"Are you asking me personally?"

"No matter what, there's always going to be someone better."

"No one was better than Jordan."

"But people still beat him," she said. "I don't know, Big. Strip away basketball and what do we have?"

I didn't answer. Although it was phrased as a question, I knew Liv already knew the answer: we didn't have shit.

"Come to Gonzaga with me." I hadn't planned on saying it, but there it was. What did I have to lose? What was one new way to hurt myself? Liv had been avoiding this conversation for months. What was it going to be?

Liv took another drink. We resumed walking, enough space between us to fit our team's entire bench.

"I'm going to miss you," she said.

"Guess that's a no," I said. I looked down at the ball. It was the one she'd gotten signed by Tracy McGrady the previous year. A normal person would have locked this ball up in a glass case, but not Liv. I liked that she loved it enough to ruin it. It's how I wanted Liv to feel about me.

"It's not anything more than what it is."

"I'm sure you'll find a new point guard in no time," I said.

I tried to make my voice sound light, like I was someone else, someone who knew how to share Liv, but my voice betrayed me; the gravity of our potential anchored my unease to the ground.

"I could fucking punch you," said Liv. "I really could."

I looked up to find that Liv had stopped walking. She was crying. I wrapped my free arm around her shoulders, rubbing the side of her bicep. I told her I didn't mean anything by what I said, that I was just being a dick like usual.

"I'm fine, I'm fine, everything's fine," said Liv.

She shoved me off of her and wiped her eyes on the sleeve of her sweatshirt. She took another drink and handed the bottle to me. I finished it greedily. It was the only thing I was certain of in that moment, my desire to get good and drunk so I could forget the snarling animal of my body, its simultaneous bark and whimper.

I handed the empty bottle to Liv, who tucked it into her backpack. We arrived at our spot, Sycamore Beach. The court was dark, the lights having been turned off hours ago. It was the most peaceful place on earth. Instead of meeting me on the court, Liv flopped down on the grass, sitting with her hands planted on either side of her. I took a few jumpers, missing them all, too distracted to focus on anything but Liv.

"That's why you're a pass-first, shoot-second point guard," Liv teased, waving me over. She patted the grass next to her and I sat down, acutely aware of my body in time and space. I leaned back, my hand not an inch away from Liv's. For the first time, I noticed Liv's arms were shaking, though her face gave away nothing.

"Fine," she said. "Say we do it. What will it be like?"

I raised my eyebrows at her, urging her to say more.

"Going to college together, I mean."

I thought about it for a minute. I only had one chance to get it right. I thought of our first evening shooting around together, the Lionshead cans we'd passed between us.

"You know the sound of a beer can opening?" I said.

"Yeah," she said, cocking her head in amused confusion.

"It'll be like that. It'll be as satisfying as that first sip after you hear someone crack one open."

Liv laughed, smiling and shaking her head as if she could already feel the satisfaction.

"Okay, tomorrow then. I'll call Coach Harris and commit," said Liv.

"Don't fuck with me."

"I'm not," she said.

"We can learn to like hiking or camping or some shit."

"I'll get bird-watching binoculars."

"What about your mom?" I asked. "What will she say?"

"She lost her right to say anything," said Liv.

"Not sure you mean that, but okay."

"I need you."

"I know," I said. "But you can need other people, too."

"Say it back."

"But what if I don't need you?" I said, swallowing hard.

Anyone else would have leaned into the intimacy, but I knew Liv, knew if you pushed her far enough, she might just pull you in with her.

"You don't believe me that I'll do it, do you?" said Liv.

She took out her phone and said fuck it, she'll call right now if that's what it takes to prove that she's her own person, that she's serious about following me to Washington. I told her I'm not sure it's such a good idea, it's late and she's drunk, but she was already holding the phone up to her ear, grinning like some dumbass who just went all in on a sixteen seed in the NCAA tournament. I could have grabbed the phone and hung up, but I didn't; I let Liv leave a message declaring that she was committing to Gonzaga and she couldn't be more excited to become a Bulldog. This Liv, this uninhibited, impulsive Liv, she was my favorite Liv. And in letting me witness this version of her, in letting her guard down, well, I thought it was like watching her masturbate under the stars.

When Liv hung up, she inched closer to me, our outer thighs now touching. Her thumb grazed my knuckle. My heart forgot its rhythm. I craned my neck back and looked at the sky. I could feel Liv studying me, taking in every moment of me.

"How honest would you be?" I asked the sky.

"What?"

"On your scout on yourself."

"Oh," she said. She didn't move, though I could hear her consciously breathing, manipulating the ins and outs. I focused on the stars, the way they bled light in all directions.

When she didn't elaborate, I finally allowed myself to face Liv, who looked brand-new, pulsing with decision. I could barely breathe. My blood broke through long-built dams. Liv placed her hand on my cheek, and I placed my hand over Liv's as if to say, *Don't move.*

"Say it," whispered Liv.

"Nope, I won't do it."

"Say it."

"No."

"Fucking say it," growled Liv.

"Make me," I said, daring Liv to make a move.

I worried I might have pushed her too hard, pushed her to retreat into coolness, into that textured nonchalance I constantly wanted to reach out and move aside, but she didn't retreat; she gave in to the trample of impulse. She leaned in and kissed me, hard, like nobody, no boy, not Dani, had ever kissed me before. It was the kiss of a thousand fears and a thousand slaps in the face, a kiss full of nights spent withholding, a brutal, hot-tempered kiss, a rabid, hunted-down thing.

I kissed Liv's lips, her neck, the flex of her jaw. And then Liv was peeling off my sweatshirt, which got stuck at my neck, and she had to tug a few times to get it off. I would have laughed if all my muscles hadn't already gone weak. And then Liv pulled off her own, never breaking eye contact. She'd never looked calmer, more sane, than she did right then. She must have fantasized about us before, right? I wanted to know every detail, wanted access to her secret world, to the way she touched herself when she let herself want me. I licked my lips, savoring her salty, candied taste. She pulled my shorts down, and I worried that she might hate my boxer briefs, might think they looked stupid on me. Also, I hadn't shaved recently; would she think I was gross? When she got to my boxers, she smiled then bit at the waistband, pulling it back from my skin then releasing it in a quick, sweet snap. It stung a little, but I liked it. It was Liv asking, not telling me to pay attention. She tongued and bit at my waistband a few more times, each snap more satisfying than the last. My pussy throbbed, and I felt a rush of wetness between my thighs—I wanted to take her hand and show her what she did to me, wanted her to plunge her hand inside me, to fill me up until I was more her than me. At one point, she lost her balance and fell on top of me, laughing before she pushed herself up on her forearms again.

Finally, she pulled off my underwear, which was soaked, and she looked at me for permission. The look wasn't sexy; it was honest, and sort of sad. I nodded, and then she positioned herself between my thighs, her mouth on my throbbing, begging clit, her hands gripping my thighs like they were her last anchor to this world. I couldn't help it, I gasped, the desire for pleasure and the fulfillment of that pleasure finally colliding. I thrust my hips upward, wanting more, more,

more. Greedy, insatiable, could think of nothing else. Tingles, inspired by Liv's small, beautiful moans, shot through my spine, pelvis, and swollen lips, lingered on my lips. I couldn't believe this was happening. I wanted to trap the feeling in amber and keep it with me for all of time. She worked slowly at first, as if to savor the moment, savor me. I watched the bob of her head, and when I moaned, Liv moaned in response, into my body, still licking and sucking, working away at my pleasure. This was better than hitting the game-winner, better than having a gym full of fans chanting my name. It was private, and it was exposed, and it was all mine.

Liv ran her hands down my stomach, digging her nails into my flesh, leaving behind white-pink streaks. Already, I was so close—no one had ever touched me and wanted it to be about me before. I was so fucking close that I finally ripped my eyes from Liv's face and tilted my head back, the bruised sky unfurling above me. I closed my eyes tight, blue and white waves dancing in my vision. And then, cool air between my thighs, the pressure of Liv's upper body gone.

I opened my eyes to find Liv pulling her hoodie over her head, a shadow retreating into the night. There she went, with all the important pieces of me stuck to her.

20

BREAKAWAY TURNOVER

I don't remember much about what happened next, but I remember running home and grabbing the keys to my dad's car and texting Grayson that his ass better be awake, and I remember putting on one of Dad's Warren Zevon tapes, the one with the song about not letting us get sick or old or stupid, and I remember packing a bowl at a stoplight on a quiet street, my hands shaking so hard I had to hold one still with the other, the ice before me a stage for the neon lights to perform, and I remember thinking it was only because I loved Liv so much that I had the capacity to hate her, and I remember taking a hit as the light turned green, and the smoke burning my throat and chest, and my eyelids suddenly feeling very heavy, and I remember flooring it, anything to put more and more distance between Liv and me, anything to get out ahead of the abandonment, and I remember how claustrophobic I felt, in this body, in this town, in this stupid heart that wouldn't stop splintering, and I remember driving by James and Trevor, who were juggling flaming tennis balls in a Sunoco parking lot and peacocking for some girls, and I remember watching them get smaller and smaller as I drove away, the world screaming past, and the snowman in someone's front yard, how it had a cigar in its mouth and a Phillies hat on its head, and how one second I had control of the car, and the next second I was spinning out on the ice, the world a dizzying snow globe around me, and when I went off the road toward the ditch, and when the car left the ground, was in the air for a second or two, the basketball in the back seat floated beside me, twirling on its axis, like there was zero gravity, like I didn't need it where I was going, where my dad was waiting for me, where we could fly, we could really fly, we could dunk like all of our heroes, we could hang from the rim and let our feet swing beneath us, animals of the jungle, father and son, father and prodigal son, reunited: I've finally returned, Dad, it's okay, it's okay, you can stop worrying, we'll be together again, and the music won't ever stop.

A sharp, otherworldly pain shot through my hip, my lower back, and immediately, I blacked out, all the world softening into absence. There, in that quiet, merciful space, I saw Liv. My disturbing, beautiful Liv. She was standing in my driveway, sweaty hair matted to her face and a white cutoff Ekron T-shirt on, leaning against a rack of basketballs. It was dark out, but the garage light spotlit her. One by one, she began to swallow the balls whole, like a snake engulfing a rabbit family. I'd never seen her look so calm. I wanted that calm for myself. Slowly, I floated over to her—it was clear she couldn't see me—and instead of passing through her like a ghost, I moved inside of her. Liv and I as one.

There was only one ball left. It was worn, it'd seen some things. We spun it in our hands, getting to know its texture, its story. Then we took a lazy jumper and missed it short, the ball barely grazing the front of the rim.

"If this is love then we don't want it," we said to no one.

Then we wailed so loud, we couldn't hear ourselves think, not even when we allowed our thoughts to coalesce into: If this is love then we want it. We really do.

21

CARRIED OFF THE COURT

I woke up to whiteness, everywhere. White walls, a white ceiling, cheap fluorescent lighting. White sheets, a white blanket pulled up around my chest. My mom sat beside me, quiet at first, not realizing I was awake.

"Mom," I croaked, my throat dry.

"Oh, honey." She placed her hand over my hand, reassuring me that everything was okay, I was in the hospital, I'd broken my pelvis and three vertebrae, but the doctor said I'd heal just fine, would be able to walk in a few weeks.

"What about basketball?" I asked.

She cleared her throat and looked out the window. Outside, the inky light was ominous. The snow on the ground looked like ash from a volcanic explosion, all gray and desperate. The reality of what had happened was slowly settling in, as was a frigid ache behind my eyes. My mom had driven straight to the hospital from her friend's wedding reception a state away, and despite the half-moons under her eyes, she looked unbearably pretty in her green dress, which had long sleeves made of lace. I'd never really looked at my mom before, not like that, not in that curious, unarmed way that allows you to look at people as a stranger might, if only for as long as it takes to say *Who are you really?*

"Mom," I said, sternly. "What about basketball?"

She didn't say anything, just tapped my hand and smiled sadly at me. I noticed she was wearing her wedding ring again. It was modest, just a few tiny diamonds set in the band. Bought back when my dad was honest about what kind of money he did and didn't have. I waited for her to speak, waited for her to tell me what would happen next. I needed to believe in all her new age shit, that she was, in fact, an oracle, capable of channeling the universe and all its messages. I needed her to tell me that I'd step on the court again; I needed to believe her when she said it.

"Let's just take it day by day. You've been through a lot."

I nodded, pushing the tears down. I was still having trouble processing what had happened. Everything was murky, I felt I couldn't trust my brain. But my hands were stuck in permanent fists, like I might turn them on Liv, on myself. My mom cleared her throat. I braced myself for a lecture on positive thinking.

"You know, when your father and I met, he used to say *Baby, I'm betting on us.*" She chuckled to herself, her eyes transporting her through the years to that rosy past. "I thought it was sweet at the time."

Having realized that she wasn't talking to me so much as she was talking to herself, I didn't reply. I didn't want to disturb her reverie.

"Guess I still do," she admitted. "I remember seeing him from across the bar and thinking *That's the most wonderful man I've ever seen.*" I could tell she was forcing herself not to cry. "He wasn't doing anything but standing there."

"I feel like that's how it goes, right?" I said, thinking of Liv in her ugly sweaterdress at Dad's deathday party. "We love people when they're at their least remarkable."

She tilted her head, considering this sentiment, then smiled in agreement, perhaps wondering what I knew about love.

"I don't know what's going on with you, Mack, and that scares me," she said. "It scares me not to know."

"But you do know," I said. "You do."

She shook her head but didn't respond. I wondered what I'd say if my dad were here. What would I ask him? I'd probably lose all my words and squeeze him so tight his heart would have no choice but to jump-start again, my arms a silent question: If you could do it all over again, would you still choose me and Mom? Fuck the fame and fortune, fuck the touring life, fuck the groupies hooked on each arm. Lying in that hospital bed in a back brace, unsure if I'd ever play again, I wanted, no, I needed, to hear him say that no amount of fame and glory could have ever lived up to drinking bad beer in the nosebleed seats with me.

I was so tired I could barely keep my eyes open. Mom whispered for me to rest, and I quickly fell into a heavy, heart-tired sleep. I didn't want to think about what my accident might mean for the future I'd built. What had at first been blurry around the edges and amorphous, a drippy sandcastle, had over time become solid and well-defined, a stronghold built by longing, by an ache so deep it felt a part of me, of my DNA, of my history. Now it was a fortress with a sinking foundation.

When I opened my eyes, Coach Puck was sitting where my mom had been, reading a Stephen King paperback. It was bright outside.

He smiled at me and said, "You dumb fuck."

I smiled weakly. This was Coach Puck's way of saying he loved me and he was sorry this happened.

"I know," I said. "I know."

I blinked back tears and Coach leaned over my bed for an awkward hug, his hulking body cocooning me, my face wetting the front of his flannel, which smelled like cigarettes and dog, with a whisper of something sweetly bitter, like dark chocolate.

"What now?" I asked once he sat his ass back down.

"Let's focus on getting you better, kid."

"What if I can't ever play again?"

He scratched his beard, pretending to consider my question, but I knew he wasn't considering so much as avoiding. Nobody wanted this question, to ask or receive it.

He ran his hands through his hair a few times. This strange, soft man who'd claimed me. This man who always, from the beginning, could see me, even when I wasn't wearing a jersey.

"There's always coaching," he offered, though I could tell he knew it was a concession, that coaching could never give me—had never given him—the same rush as playing. I must have had a disappointed look about me because he shook his head and said, "Nah, fuck that. You'll do something great, way greater than telling some punk-ass kids how to put a ball through a hoop."

Who was I without basketball? I was about to find out.

Just then, I heard the hospital room door open. I figured it was a nurse, but then standing before us was a red-eyed Liv with her big eyes and her perfect lips and her bitable jaw and her storm of a birthmark. It was then that I realized she hadn't had the birthmark in my dream after the crash. I wasn't sure what that meant. All I know is, I didn't say anything, not at first, but I wanted to say, *I dreamt of you.* I wanted to say, *Tell me everything's going to be okay, tell me I'll make it to the league, tell me I won't be alone when I get there.* Something stirred in the air. I wondered if she remembered me stepping inside her body last night, if she could still feel the remnants of me, the whispers of sameness I'd left behind.

"Oh god," I groaned. "Why is she here?"

"Not getting in the middle of it," said Coach. "Gotta pick the kids up at gymnastics anyway."

Coach gave us a nod goodbye then slipped on his jacket before leaving, his hands already reaching in his pocket for a cigarette.

Liv sat down beside me.

"Hey," she said.

"What's up," she said.

"I don't want to see you."

"Yes, you do."

She always seemed so sure about everything. That's what gave away that she knew nothing at all. Then she said something about the Sixers game that was to be on that night. Or maybe it was the night after, or maybe she didn't mention the Sixers at all. Truthfully, I didn't know what she was saying. All I know is, she didn't mention my accident, didn't mention committing to Gonzaga, didn't mention her face between my thighs. In fact, she was behaving as if nothing out of the ordinary had happened between us. I, on the other hand, could hardly look her in the eyes after last night, after I'd witnessed an unrestrained Liv, a Liv with the brakes cut, a Liv who devoured me in a feverish, primal blur of surrender. Our bodies, fluent, sincere, wild, our bodies sublime. And then she had run. The more I thought about it, the more sense it made that in the event of a collision, it would always be Liv who extracted herself from the wreckage first. When you're running from something, onlookers are always going to assume you're being chased. And as much as Liv hated to admit it, it mattered very much to her what onlookers thought. But just as I was grateful for my dad's deathday party because it brought Liv into my life, I was, at least temporarily, grateful for my accident because it brought us back together, if only for a short time. We could focus our attention on this one large thing looming outside of either of us, a hostile force we both knew how to hate appropriately and fiercely.

I reached for her hand and squeezed it tight. I asked her, without words, to tell me what it was she'd refused to tell me since we first met. She lifted her other hand and I thought, for a second, that she was going to wrap it around my shoulders and pull me close, probably destroying my back and pelvis, but instead, with her pointer finger, she began to write something on my forearm, and even when I closed my eyes to focus on her touch, I could make out everything, the *I* and the *L* and all the letters that made up the words that I'd always wanted to hear.

When she finished, she underlined the words then brought her finger, like the barrel of a gun, to her mouth and softly blew.

"My sniper," I said, waving my free hand in front of our faces as if to get rid of the smoke.

She smiled all cocky at that but didn't say anything.

"Your mom must be wondering where you are," I said.

She cleared her throat and studied the ceiling, her forehead vein a highway down her face, then cleared her throat again. "Actually, my dad is," she said, trying not to smile though I could tell she'd been dying to tell me. "I'm sleeping at his place tonight."

We kept holding hands, despite our slippery sweat. Liv raised our enveloped hands to her chest, pressing the back of my hand to her sweatshirt. Her heart did its heart things. I imagined her chest cut open, our collective fist wedged between her ribs, and I told her as much—there was no use in hiding anymore. She paused, then asked me if I thought I could do it, if I could manage to hold her open, just a little while longer.

I didn't respond—what was there to say but everything? I thought about kissing her, thought about giving her my life, my future, my everything, thought about showing her that all the pain wasn't for nothing, but for once, I wanted to keep myself for myself; I would need me wherever I was going.

THE FINAL SCORE

It's been years now, and we still want legacy. Now, though, we also want wisdom, we want quietude, we want the sweet decadence of boredom. We want to strip away the glory, if only to see what's underneath. No records, no banners, no headlines, none of that shit. We want to make history of our bodies.

We want private legacy, intimate legacy. We want a fondness for who we are long after the final buzzer has sounded and the fans have headed home and it's just us, the hoop, and a ball, bouncing into eternity.

Fuck it, I no longer know what Liv wants, maybe I never did. But me? I'm as full of wanting as ever.

I want to love long and hard; I want that long, hard love to be my legacy.

I want zero regrets. No, I want to marry my regrets. To find a way to adore them for their sharp endless need.

I want to live forever, but now, in the future I didn't know if I would ever touch, I want my forever full of shameless love. Full of big, big love, of *I'll keep on trying always* love. I want, with the flick of a hand, to make miracles out of nothing. I want Iverson and McGrady to quiver before me. I want every ballplayer who found a way to walk away from the art before it killed them, before it drove them mad, to reach through time and shake my hand.

I want a mind that doesn't wander to the game, to the adrenaline, to the knee-torn, bone-broken sacrifice.

I want someone who didn't know me before, who can't supply the *remember when*s, who knows me not as a basketball player, not as a cocky punk, but as a new animal entirely.

And hell, if I can't live forever, I want acceptance. I want to find a way to sit with my grief, to let it coexist with all the goodness.

I want the game to be an important thing, but not *the* most important thing. I want the time I spent playing to matter; I want it to matter far less.

Some nights, I fall into dreams of competition, of the bright lights, the crowds that infected my every cell. I have nightmares, too, of sloppy handles, of turnover after turnover, of body disconnected from mind. I dream of walking on endless treks in the desert searching for a court. When I find one, it is surrounded by a cage with no door, and people are playing a game without me.

How do I get in? I ask, but no one answers.

In my waking life, I want the knowledge that I can lose myself in something other than the game. Fruit trees. The sky. The softness of a child. When I shoot around at the park, I may miss four, five, six shots in a row. I may get a little huffy, but I shake it off; I will have more beautiful things to love and lose in this life.

More than anything, I want to pass by a game of pickup and want to keep on walking, to feel happy when a kid crosses somebody or throws down a dunk, to feel uncomplicated about that happiness.

I no longer want to be treated like a god; I only want to be human enough to admit my fear.

At night when I crawl into bed, my body warming under a blanket sewn together from old tournament T-shirts, I sometimes wonder what it would have been like if we'd met later in life, maybe in a coffee shop or a wine bar, maybe in line for the movies or waiting to send a package. But in my imagination, we don't ever greet each other. We don't say, Hey, we don't say, What's up?

Instead, we look and we look and we look at each other, unabashedly, for all the times we looked away. And then the moment is over, and we continue on, back out onto the court for another heartbreak.

ACKNOWLEDGMENTS

Endless gratitude to my wonderful agent, Maggie Cooper, and all-star editor, Katy Nishimoto—you two are the dream team. To JP for your support and guidance throughout the process. Thank you to everyone at The Dial Press who made this book possible—I'm grateful to have such lovely and caring people in my court.

Big thanks and hugs to my workshop pals who read early chapters at the Bread Loaf Writers' Conference and Lighthouse Writers Workshop. And thanks to my brilliant workshop faculty, Laura van den Berg and Bryan Washington.

My writer pals, I owe you everything. You know who you are. And a special shout-out to my Sewanee people, my new family. I'm grateful for the ways my circle keeps on growing.

My teammates far and wide, I love you.

Sweatpants and blue Gatorade, I love you, too.

A special shout-out to Hanif Abdurraqib, whose work, especially about basketball, continues to inspire me.

My parents and siblings for cheering me on since my Fisher-Price hoop days.

My family, my family, my family—I couldn't love you more. Every day you enchant me. Let's go shoot hoops at the park.

ABOUT THE AUTHOR

MARISA CRANE is a former college basketball player and the author of *I Keep My Exoskeletons to Myself,* a *New York Times* Editors' Choice, an Indie Next Pick, and a Lambda Literary Award winner. They have received fellowships from the Sewanee Writers' Conference, American Short Fiction, and Vermont Studio Center, and their short work has appeared in *Literary Hub, The Sun, TriQuarterly, Prairie Schooner, Joyland,* and elsewhere. Originally from Allentown, Pennsylvania, they currently live in San Diego with their family.

marisacrane.org
X: @mcrane_12
Instagram: @marisa_crane
TikTok: @marisacranewrites

Books Driven by the Heart

Sign up for our newsletter
and find more you'll love:

thedialpress.com

@THEDIALPRESS

@THEDIALPRESS